Bring Me Home

Safe Harbor
Book 1

Annabeth Albert

To Rae Marks.
My tireless sprint buddy, virtual officemate, and friend. You embody found family for me.
Thank you for being there.

Author's Note and Content Advisory

Safe Harbor is a made-up town somewhere between Astoria and Portland, Oregon. Any resemblance to real towns, persons, places, businesses, and situations is entirely coincidental. The series does center around a town secret, but the criminal case takes a big backseat to the stand-alone love stories in each book. No gruesome details and happy endings are absolutely guaranteed! BRING ME HOME lightly touches on Don't Ask, Don't Tell military service, realities of modern military service, and absent parenting.

Chapter One

Monroe

One summer. I could make it one last summer in Safe Harbor. And if I gave myself that pep talk frequently enough, maybe I'd actually start believing it.

"Monroe! Hold up!" Rob's voice sounded behind me as I reached for the door of the Blessed Bean coffee shop. My lower back tingled a warning, but when the chief of police called my name, I generally listened. Also, he was my good friend, so I slowed long enough for him to huff up beside me. "I have the solution for your problem."

"Which one?" I groaned. I doubted Rob's ability to help with anything on my lengthy to-do list.

"Wait. What do you have on?" Rob turned on his cop voice as he cast a skeptical eye to my black T-shirt. I had decades of law enforcement experience, yet his stare made me squirm like a naughty teen. I had to make a concerted effort to resist the impulse to cross my arms over my black T-shirt proudly proclaiming *I DO CREW*, with colorful stick figures of two grooms. Rob's expression turned comical. "Something you want to share?"

Lord, save me from small-town gossip. It wasn't just Rob. Rob would talk to his wife, who would talk to Rob's parents, who would, in turn, talk to the rest of Safe Harbor. They'd have me married off by sundown. I should have known better than to give into my cold-brew craving. It had only taken a few weeks of being back in Safe Harbor to get me mentally packing. Bring on some good urban anonymity.

"I'm going to an old NCIS friend's bachelor party tonight in Portland. The organizers mailed out shirts to everyone."

"Oh, that's right. You mentioned your trip to the city at the station the other day. Number three for this friend, right?" Rob seemed in no hurry to enter the coffee shop. I was doing a favor for him and the woefully understaffed police department by reviewing old cold-case files while I was in town. Thanks to advances in forensic science over the last few decades, some previously shelved cases had new possibilities for being solved, and my work was to sort out which cases most warranted a fresh look. Rob wasn't exactly my boss, and we'd known each other enough years that I could give a loud snort.

"Jorge says this one is true love." I added an eye roll before stretching my triceps out, getting ready for my drive into the city. "Hope springs eternal and all that. And I wasn't stateside for the other two weddings, so I don't mind that Jorge and his new love, Tyreece, are going all out."

"I mind that shirt." Rob cackled. He looked all official in uniform, his closely cropped brown hair starting to show some silver.

"Says the guy who wears the same thing every day." I

still struggled to reconcile this particular version of Rob with the skinny freckled teen who'd befriended me in high school.

"Says the guy who did his twenty in navy blues and should have better fashion sense now that he's out." Rob shook his head at me like he knew anything about fashion himself. He was such a dad now. "Anyway, back to my great idea."

"That sounds ominous. Last great idea of yours in high school led to a cracked collarbone and food poisoning." Chuckling, I risked a discreet glance at my watch. Portland was only an hour or so away, but the navy had made sure I hated tardiness of any kind.

"This is a way better plan. Promise." Rob grinned, a hint of that teen prankster still there behind his wire-rimmed glasses and rounded more fatherly face. "And you're cranky because you're only in town to get your aunt's big old house on the market, and you want to be in the Bay Area by fall."

"Ideally." An image of the condo I had toured in the Castro flickered in my brain. Urban. Anonymous. No one to tease me about my attire, and plenty of options to keep busy beyond DIY lists for my aunt's old house. I was grateful, if a little befuddled, as to why she'd picked me to leave it to.

"If you want to meet that goal, then you, my friend, need a roommate." Rob beamed like he was the first to make this suggestion.

"I tried telling him that idea." Our mutual high-school friend, Holden, wheeled up the short sidewalk to the coffeehouse, not even pretending to give Rob and me privacy. "I said he should put up an ad. Offer a room in exchange for someone who can actually use a drill."

"I am not entirely helpless." I gave them both my best, hardest officer glare. I'd scared plenty of new recruits, but my old friends weren't having it. "So what if home repair isn't my usual skill set? I'm learning. I don't need some random person responding to an ad."

"Well, I have something better. Knox is coming home for the summer."

I blinked, taking a moment to remember who Knox was. "Your kid?"

While I'd left for the navy and the rest of our high-school crowd had scattered, Rob had stayed local and had a kid with his high-school girlfriend mere days after graduation. I had the vaguest memories of a red-faced bawling infant before heading to the academy. But, by the time I'd returned for one of my very sporadic visits, Rob and Petra had split. Last I'd heard, the kid mainly lived with Petra in Seattle and summered with Rob and his new wife.

"Knox just turned twenty-three. He's not exactly a kid now. Graduated last weekend from college. But his lease is up, and the landlord is selling the building. His other room-mates are heading for jobs in various cities, but Knox doesn't leave for grad school until the fall."

"Has he told you yet that his boy got into an Ivy League architecture program?" Holden laughed.

"Hey, I'm a proud dad. What can I say?"

"Say he can stay with you?" I tilted my head, still trying to figure out what Rob wanted from me.

"That's what he usually does every summer. He comes and works for Measure Twice remodeling, same as he has since high school. But this year, my wife's sister is here from Australia to spend the summer until the new baby comes. She's got a six-month visa and is already in Knox's old room."

"Ouch," Holden and I said simultaneously.

"And the old guest room will be the nursery." Rob swallowed, skin going slightly green like he'd just realized he was about to have four under four in the house.

"And you have triplets," Holden helpfully pointed out.

"Them too. Luckily, they're still young enough to share one big room. And Knox is all, 'I can take the basement.' But that's little more than an unfinished laundry room and storage area. And apparently, he's now bringing a cat."

"A cat?" Not that I was remotely considering this roommate suggestion that was already closer to a babysitting gig. Add in a cat, plus this Knox kid, and the drinks at the bachelor party better be extra strong.

"You like animals." Rob remembering that would be sweet if he didn't clearly have an ulterior motive. "Jessica is allergic, her sister's allergic, and probably the triplets too. I know Knox and the cat are a big ask, buddy, but he's amazing with home repairs. Watches all the shows. He's strong like an ox. Good endurance. Takes direction well."

"Are you selling me on a roommate or a racehorse?"

"You need someone like him. Admit it." Rob clearly wasn't going to let this drop.

"A college kid who's watched a lot of DIY TV with a tendency to collect pets?" I shook my head. Nope. I knew perfectly well what I needed, and it wasn't that.

"Free labor?" Rob's smile turned beseeching. "How many favors have I asked you for over the years?"

"Not many." I could admit he'd been a good long-distance friend, never trying to get me to use my naval connections on a case or asking for money, even though there were undoubtedly years he could have used it. "Can I think about it over the weekend?"

"Sure. Come by Sunday night after you're back in town. We're having some folks over for a barbeque."

"Maybe you can wear your awful shirt to that too." Grinning, Holden leaned back in his chair. "Are you seriously hoping to get lucky in something that cheesy?"

"I'm hoping to help friends celebrate. Not out for a hookup." And if I was going to entertain Rob's ridiculous plan, I better get used to a summer of no sex in a hurry. Babysitting some college kid along with working on the house wasn't going to leave me time for any hookups, not that those exactly grew on trees in this tiny town anyway.

I'd planned on dreaming up an appropriate excuse during the drive to Portland. However, the trip passed with no brilliant reason why I couldn't let Knox and his cat have one of the many bedrooms in the old Victorian my Great-Aunt Henri had left me. I had to set aside my dilemma over Knox once I arrived in downtown Portland because I was swept up in a flurry of old friends, new introductions, and wedding festivities.

By the time we headed out for Jorge's bachelor fun, I'd almost forgotten Rob's request and our ridiculous attire until Jorge had to go and demand a selfie of the group in our matching shirts.

"Good lord, do not tag me in any of those." I groaned as Jorge attached his phone to a stick-like thing to take a good half-dozen snaps.

"You have social media?" Jorge's cousin, whom I'd met a handful of times, had stuck way too close to me all evening. "I was under the impression the navy frowned upon personnel doing social."

"They do. I'm out now." I glanced around the packed bar. It wasn't Pride weekend yet, but early June in Portland was tourist central with the Rose Festival, fleet week, and more. The crowd was decidedly younger than most of us, a bunch of twenty-and-thirty-somethings who'd probably never heard of Don't Ask, Don't Tell. I was out now, on multiple levels, and it wasn't something I took for granted.

"Cheers to that!" Jorge raised an invisible glass to me. Like me, he'd served through various rules and regulations before retiring, and he sure had enthusiastically embraced same-sex marriage rights. For his sake, I hoped the third time was the charm. Across from us, a younger group of friends was clustered near one of the go-go dancers. The dancer's wrestling singlet was hot, but my eyes kept drifting to one of the guys in the group who had a muscled back and shoulders and possibly the most perfect ass I'd ever seen.

"You're still fit as fuck." Jorge's cousin had corn chip-scented breath and sweaty hands with a tendency to roam. Leering, he gave me another admiring glance. "Who wants drinks?"

"You go ahead. Line's too long for me." I gestured at the crowd around the bar area. I didn't need a cocktail badly enough to spend a half-hour waiting to give my order. And I was counting on the others being thirstier than me to get a little break. I loved Jorge, who had been a young chief on my first assignment, and it was nice to see a few friends from other duty stations, but I was due a break from the hours of socializing. "Never know. I might dance."

"Oh fine. Make me feel old." Jorge rolled his eyes at me as he followed his cousin and the others to join the line at the bar.

Speaking of feeling old, the hot guy turned, and he was younger than I'd thought. Short beard, long hair pulled up in a ponytail bun thing, the sort of signature northwest look that could be anywhere from twenty to thirty-five.

This guy was probably around twenty-five or twenty-eight, but there was something irresistible about him. And it wasn't only the young and fresh factor. Military towns always seemed to skew super young, and while I was careful to never screw an enlisted subordinate, I could admit to a hookup or two where I'd felt rather ancient.

I should have looked away. But I didn't. Couldn't. And the more I looked, the more I admired. His energy, the way he kept making his friends laugh, how he bounced on his feet, never staying still, showing off that ass with every wiggle. I especially liked the way his eyes sparkled when he smiled. I was a sucker for a great smile.

And then he headed my way, smile shifting to a predatory gleam.

"Hey there." He nodded at me. "We're twins."

"Pardon?" I squinted at him, trying to follow. Even our hair was different shades of brown, mine sandy and his dark chestnut. He was tanned and had maybe an inch on my six-foot frame. I'd sure as heck remember being related to this buff Greek god.

"I mean, you're wearing my shirt." He pointed at my chest. I narrowed my gaze as my eyes finally left his compelling face. Yup. Same silly *I Do Crew* shirt. "See? Twins."

"Oh." I laughed, but there was absolutely nothing familial about the surge of heat in my stomach, the way warmth licked at my ribs and spine before heading south. It had been a long damn time since someone revved my engine this hard. Maybe it was my lucky night after all.

Chapter Two

Knox

As far as pickup lines went, declaring myself and the hottest dude I'd seen in quite some time twins wasn't my best work. But I'd spotted this guy and his friends when they'd walked in. And he didn't belong in that shirt. Or with that crew. He was younger and fitter than the rest of his friends. Older than me, but I dug the air of maturity and self-assuredness around him. He looked military and was probably in town for fleet week. His military vibe was enhanced by his lean muscles, great posture, and alert eyes. And he seemed uncomfortable in that T-shirt, like he'd rather be in uniform. Or maybe a dress shirt. Yeah, I could see him in something with buttons...

Sure, he was older and probably out of my league, but why not shoot my shot? Our matching shirts were as good an in as anything.

"Oh, so we are." The guy looked down, clearly not overly impressed at my powers of observation. "You're not here with Jorge though?"

"Nope. Popular shirts, apparently. 'Tis the season for weddings. Our I Do Crew is here for Tony and Ross. They're making out on the dance floor." I gestured vaguely toward the dance area behind the bar. My friend group had an unspoken agreement whenever we went out that we were free to socialize with others. It wasn't like I was abandoning the party to chat up this dude, and indeed, a quick glance over at my friends yielded a host of thumbs-ups and way-too-obvious cheerleading.

And that was another reason the older guy was intriguing—I was so over the immaturity of the college scene, even my own friends.

"Jorge and Tyreece are doing separate bachelor parties." The guy half-smiled as he shared, and I seriously dug the way his eyes crinkled and his shoulders lifted. "Tyreece's friends and family are doing a movie night and slumber party for him. Not sure which I'd rather be at, honestly."

"I know." I laughed. "Sign me up for movie night. I'd even find cute jammies for the occasion. Wouldn't want to scandalize the relatives with my usual sleeping attire..."

"I learned the hard way not to sleep naked." He shook his head, sandy hair brushing his ears in a way that made me want to lick his neck. Or maybe it was how he said *naked* that made electricity zoom to all my interested parts. "All it took was one ill-timed fire drill in the barracks, and I bought a whole stack of flannel pants."

"Oof. That sounds cold." And yup, I'd been right on with the military. My dad had an endless assortment of first responder and military-type friends and contacts, so I'd pegged his bearing as soon as I'd spotted the guy. "Frosty naked is not the fun kind of naked."

"It was definitely chilly. But you make pajamas sound fun, not practical." His gaze roamed over me like he was mentally dressing me. Or undressing. That would be even better. "Yeah, maybe I should have gone with the movie-night group. But I didn't used to be the type to turn down a night out."

"I totally am. I own my homebody status. I got more than enough of going out in college. Tonight I'm just here for Tony and Ross." My airy tone made college sound further away, which was intentional. No sense in emphasizing our age difference. And besides, I wasn't lying. I'd always been more of a stay-at-home type, happy to hang with friends or family. I'd much rather lend someone a hand than take them out for a beer.

"Rebound!" X-ray bounded over. He was the human equivalent of a sheepdog puppy, but after two years as roommates, I found him more endearing than annoying. Usually. Right then, I could do without the interruption. "We're getting drinks. You want anything?"

"Nah. Thanks. You go on." I waved him away without trying to introduce him to my new friend. Loved X-ray, but the guy tended to be a walking disaster, not the sort of distraction I needed. Also, I wanted the stranger all to myself a little longer.

"Rebound?" His head tilted as he considered me.

"It's a nickname." I shrugged, not one to get embarrassed easily.

"I've heard all sorts of crazy nicknames in the navy, but not that one. How'd you earn Rebound?"

"I like pickup basketball." I smiled when his gaze turned more pointed and expectant, like he knew perfectly well there was more to the story. "And okay, I have a little bit of a rep from college. I didn't really date, but somehow I was always people's rebound guy. Get over a bad guy..."

"By getting under a good one?"

11

"Yep. You get the picture. I didn't intend it that way, but the nickname stuck, especially when my basketball friends started using it too, so I was doubly screwed."

"I bet." The corners of his mouth lifted. I hadn't meant screwed as innuendo, but if he took it that way, I was okay with it. The nickname made me sound like far more of a player and stud than I actually was. A couple of sympathetic flings freshman year, and boom, a stupid nickname that made it sound like I'd banged half the campus.

"What do they call you in the navy?" I asked.

"I'm newly out of the service now, but sir. Lieutenant. Or if they didn't have to salute, my friends called me Butter."

"Butter?" I loved this already. And lieutenant made him sound older than I might have assumed, but there was no reason the sexy officer and I couldn't have a little fun together.

"Hey, you asked." He laughed, showing off more of those sexy eye crinkles I loved. "Word was I was gunning for butter bars—second lieutenant rank from day one at the academy. Also, I could make things happen. Grease the wheels. Like butter."

"Cute." I spied some of his friend group headed back our way, loaded down with drinks. "Wanna dance, Lieutenant Butter?"

"I..." He sounded like he was about to let me down easy, then he turned, noticing his approaching friends. "Sure. Why not?"

"That's the spirit." I steered him toward the dance floor. "Come on, let's hide from our friends together."

"You're on." He smiled again, wider this time, and yeah, I had a serious thing for the softness in his eyes, a depth of emotion there that was almost hypnotic.

"I am." I pulled him into one of the farther corners of the dance floor. Lieutenant Butter was a surprisingly good dancer. He had a solid rhythm, and even better, he effortlessly followed my movements.

Closer, closer. Forget the lyrics of the actual song playing, my brain played a tune just for him, beckoning him ever nearer. Most tall, built dudes only wanted to lead. A tussle for the top that I wanted no part of. Instead, I loved this: an easy back-and-forth, me leading, then him, then me again.

Sway, sway. My internal music turned even more seductive. I always loved dancing, but this was sublime. No rigid rule structure where he took control simply because he was older or I seized it because I was slightly bigger. Instead, we danced as equals, the age difference fading into the background along with the rest of the bar, only him and me and the music—a pulsing, driving club mix.

At first, we danced together but barely touched, strangers feeling each other out. Then I crowded into his space, and he met me easily, crowding me right back until our bodies brushed with every beat.

Touch me, touch me. My head music shifted as need colored my every movement. The lieutenant's torso was every bit as firm as it looked, and every point of contact was muscled and strong. Our thighs rubbed and our hands tangled. His hands were big, solid as the rest of him, and I wanted them everywhere. Each new spot we touched—thighs, hands, chests—was a fresh discovery, a lightbulb flipping on until my whole being lit up like a disco ball.

As one song bled into the next, I circled him, wrapping him up from behind. And fuck, so good, he melted against me. His head tipped back, a bead of sweat running down his neck, and I chased it with my mouth. It wasn't a kiss precisely, but I dragged my scruff against his bare skin until he hissed.

"I have a great idea." I ground against him, letting him feel how hard he made me, loving when he pushed back to meet my motions. "Let's go crash the other bachelor party?"

"The other...the movie watching?" His forehead wrinkled like he'd expected a different suggestion, but keeping him off balance was part of my grand plan.

"Yep. Ditch our crews, go find some PJs..."

"Pajamas are hardly what I'm thinking about right now." He gave a strained laugh.

"Tell me," I demanded. "Or better yet, show me."

His eyes sparked with wicked mischief that made him look younger. "There's limits to what we can get away with on the dance floor."

"Damn. Right. Screw movie night." I ground more deliberately against him. "Tell me you have a hotel room close."

"I shouldn't abandon my friends." He kept moving with me, eyes closed, hair brushing against the side of my face.

"I know. Me either. But I wanna. Let's be bad together."

"You're a terrible influence. I'm usually known as the solid friend. Everyone's favorite designated driver, middle-of-the-night rescuer, and crisis solver."

"Me too. Shocker, I know. But I'm the good friend."

"Rebound?" He rolled my name around like he was testing it, considering. "Yeah, I guess you would like to help your crew."

"I'm all in on being a helping hand. But right now, the only one I want to help is you. How about it, Lieutenant Butter?" My hands on his sides, I spun him so we were face-to-face again, so close our breath mingled. He smelled like clean sweat and an expensive, musky aftershave that was out of my price range. Out of my league, but damn, I *wanted*.

"I..." He inhaled sharply as I lined us up for more grinding, bodies pressed tightly together. "Damn."

Whatever he'd been about to say got lost in a mutual moan at how fucking amazingly we fit together.

"Or I could kiss you right here. You want that?"

Chapter Three

Monroe

Bossy guys, technically still young enough to be considered a twink, didn't usually do it for me. But something about the terribly nicknamed Rebound got my motor humming on every cylinder. I'd never been the bad friend before, the one ditching everyone to get laid in what would quite clearly be a one-and-done thing. But God, I was tempted.

So tempted.

"Maybe I should kiss you," I countered. I'd loved dancing with him, the way we melded styles until neither of us was leading, only two guys dancing, perfectly matched like our brains were plugged into the same outlet.

"You should." He maneuvered us to the far edge of the dance floor, a line of speakers against a wall near a hallway leading to the back of the bar. "Luckily for you, I'm a very flexible guy."

"I noticed." We were mere millimeters apart and so very clearly going to kiss, but I liked this drawing out, the anticipation continuing to gather as we bantered.

"What else did you notice?"

"Your smile. You've got a great one. And your ass." I threw that compliment in to avoid sounding too sentimental about his smile. And he clearly worked out. He knew he had a world-class ass. No sense in acting like I hadn't appreciated his hard work. "Smile. Ass. Eyes. All pretty amazing."

"Thank you." Leaning in farther, he ghosted his lips along my jaw. "Glad you like. Just FYI, I don't bottom, but you'll like my mouth even more than my ass. Guaranteed."

"Big talker." I let my lips hover next to his, hand coming up to rest near his chin. I was totally okay with no penetration. Like him, I rarely bottomed, and definitely not with a random bar hookup, so I respected whatever rules and likes he had for himself. If he wanted to show me what his mouth could do, I was more than game.

In the end, I wasn't sure which of us went for it first, going from all-but-kissing to actually kissing, warm lips against warm lips, every nerve ending I possessed singing the *Hallelujah* chorus as our mouths met for the first time in earnest. Rebound had full, soft lips that tasted like cola and mint, apparently my new favorite flavor combo on earth. I traced his lips with the tip of my tongue over and over until all I tasted was him, and I simply couldn't get enough.

His mouth parted with a gasp, welcoming my kiss like I was the last bottle of water at the finish line of a marathon. He chased me back to my mouth, a different layer to our dancing, taking turns, moving effortlessly together. We sagged against the wall, bodies no longer enough to keep us upright in the gale force winds of desire stirred up by this kiss to end all kisses.

Rebound didn't kiss like a one-night stand. I understood his stupid nickname now. Lord, rejected and dumped friends must have been lined up around the block back at his college, waiting for Rebound to cure their heartbreaks with kisses that felt like memories and promises.

He kissed like a third date desperate for a fourth, like U-Hauls and monogrammed towels might be in our future. I was years removed from my last ill-fated attempt at dating, another connection lost to long-distance and frequent deployments, but Rebound kissed like the boyfriend everyone wished they had: tender, kind, slow, sensual, giving. All that. He kissed like we'd have all damn month, not a few stolen minutes up against a sticky wall with a bass-thumping speaker next to us.

We ground together, bodies powered by the driving beat of the music. I'd never been harder, certainly never in public, and never this close to orgasm on the dance floor, but here we were, and still, I couldn't stop kissing this intoxicating man.

A clump of people stumbled too close to our little hideaway, and he pulled away with a groan.

"Hey, watch it," he said to the dancers before turning back to me. "Ready to get out of here?"

I nodded. I'd get Jorge half his damn registry as an apology for leaving early, but I needed more of those lips, preferably without an audience.

"Excellent." A slow smile spread across his face. Had I thought his smile was amazing before? I'd been so wrong. Turned out that was his B-Class smile, the one he gave friends, songs he liked, and strangers who made him laugh. The smile he turned on me now was nothing short of exquisite. That once-in-a-lifetime steak in Argentina or wine in Spain. An entire experience captured in a single moment.

Like his kiss, he was something else, and I was going to

treasure him like a meal that wouldn't come around again. I held out a hand, but before he could take it, one of his friends, who'd been near him earlier admiring the go-go dancers, came loping over.

"Rebound!"

"Kind of busy, Chaz."

"Yeah, well, X-ray turned his ankle." Chaz had blond hair that stuck up at a million angles and seemed way younger than Rebound, looking barely legal to drink. Or perhaps I needed to recalculate my estimate on Rebound's age. I dropped my hand as Chaz continued, "Gonna need your muscles to help get his drunk ass home."

"Seriously, dude?" Rebound didn't step away, but I swore I felt the rush of a breeze, him retreating. "Swear to God if this was anyone but X-ray..."

"Go. Help your friend." I was the one to break apart, away from the blissful heat of his strong body. He was a good guy and wanted to help his friend. He'd said as much, and I knew if the situation were reversed, I'd be cursing a blue streak but making my excuses nonetheless.

"Give me your number?" Rebound asked, pulling out his phone, which had a superhero case. Damn. Maybe the lighting in here really did suck. How old was this guy anyway? "Let me get my pal stashed safely in his bed, and then I can meet up with you."

"I'm not sure..." I hedged as I started patting my pockets for my own phone. I needed to check my number, but I also needed a few seconds to recover enough brain cells to ask his age before agreeing to a later hookup. My phone wasn't in my left pants pocket like usual. Or the right. "Crap. Where's my phone? Sorry, I don't have my new number memorized yet."

Which was the truth, but Rebound frowned like I was giving him the runaround.

"It's okay. Don't give me your digits if you're not down for it, but I really do have to go."

I nodded as he let Chaz drag him away back toward the front of the bar. Honestly, this might be for the best because even if he was twenty-five or whatever, he was still way too young for me, and more to the point, no way could a hookup match the intensity of that kiss. Chemistry that good didn't exist in the real world. I was saving us both an awkward moment at my hotel later.

"Monroe! We've been looking for you!" Jorge, his cousin, and a few others in our I Do Crew left the dance floor to head in my direction. "Somehow, I ended up with your phone, so we couldn't call you."

He held out the missing phone, which probably hadn't been three feet away from me in five years. It had to be fate. The hottest kiss of my life was destined to be nothing more than a memory.

Chapter Four

Monroe

I wasn't sure whether it said more about that kiss or my weekend, but by late Sunday afternoon, Jorge and Tyreece were mister and mister, I was back in Safe Harbor surrounded by boxes and to-do lists of repairs, and I had yet to get the memory of Rebound out of my head for more than a few moments. I could taste him. Smell him. Feel him. Every time I closed my eyes, I was right back on the dance floor, wrapped together with that gorgeous guy. Had I ever enjoyed dancing more? And each time I opened my eyes again, I was left wondering what kind of idiot doesn't have his own phone number memorized?

Me.

I was the idiot. My worries over the age difference and the actual hookup not living up to that kiss seemed silly in the lonely light of dawn. I could have had a few hot memories, at least. And now I was in for a long, dry summer because my stack of half-done lists kept mocking me. At this point, continuing my dry spell seemed a given. I might as well do Rob a solid and take on his kid for the summer. The sooner I got to the next phase of my life, the better.

I'd told Rob as much in a text, so I showed up at his home with a six-pack, a premade fruit platter, and a resigned attitude. Rob and his second wife, Jessica, lived on the newer side of Safe Harbor in a two-story nineties faux craftsman with a daylight basement and big backyard featuring a giant trampoline, play structure, two-level deck, and stone patio perfect for the entertaining they loved to do. With him serving as police chief and her as the head high-school guidance counselor, the two of them knew everyone and never seemed to lack company.

I'd been to dinner twice since my return to town, and both times had been loud affairs with other young families and assorted relatives. Rob had evolved into his parents, who'd always had room for one more at the dinner table and seemed happier with a house full of chaos. Hearing party noises from the backyard, I could have headed for the house's side gate, but I rang the bell out of courtesy, expecting one of the various guests would answer the door.

Heavy footsteps sounded along with kid laughter. I braced myself for needing to make small talk with some random dad-type. But then the door opened, revealing a smiling face. A *familiar* smiling face.

"Rebound?" My jaw flopped open, and I almost dropped the beer and fruit. Had I conjured him up from the sheer force of want? Was this a dream? A near-death experience? Like, any second now, I might lose consciousness sort of deal? My rapid pulse and pounding head sure seemed to think doom was near.

"Lieutenant Butter!" He smiled, not a bit alarmed. "You know my dad? Oh man, this is the best luck I've ever had. I've been thinking about you all weekend."

Best luck? More like the worst ever. Death was definitely imminent. Might as well have a stroke on the spot because otherwise, Rob was going to kill me himself.

"Your dad?" I croaked.

"Or Jessica? You a new teacher at the school?" Even Rebound's frown was hopeful. Dead. I was so very dead. And I couldn't even muster a headshake, let alone a reply, as he grabbed my arm. "Come here. You look like you're about to fall over."

He steered me into the living room, a cheerful space with lots of colorful throw pillows and pictures of the triplets. I'd barely registered the photos on my previous visits, but now I scanned the wall, looking for answers. Only a couple of pics with a scrawny teen with a bad buzz cut holding three babies. Not much resemblance to the buff, bearded guy standing in front of me.

"You okay? This is a good surprise. Well, at least for me." He gave a half-smile that faded into something more awkward when I failed to answer. "X-ray ended up having to go to urgent care. Hairline ankle fracture. But I spent all night in the ER with him, wishing I'd tried harder for your number."

"It's new." My voice came out numb, almost robotic. "I wasn't lying. I didn't have the number memorized."

"That's even better news. So you weren't looking to blow me off?"

I'd been looking to blow something all right, but definitely not my longtime friend's way-too-attractive, way-too-young *kid*. Assuming this was Knox, I was so, so screwed, and not at all the good kind. Twenty-three felt a hell of a lot younger than the twenty-five-ish I'd assumed. Of age or not, Rob would not forgive me if he found out.

In the light of day, Knox did look younger. Board shorts.

Sandals. Messy hair. Scruffy beard. No way would Rob accept any *"I swear he looked older"* BS, even if I doubted Knox got carded often. That was the sort of line creepers used. I was the one who was forty-freaking-one and should have known way better.

"We can't—"

"Monroe!" Rob came striding out from the back of the house where the big kitchen and family room were located. "I see you met Knox. Good. I was just telling him earlier that you said yes to the summer plan."

"You're Monroe?" Now it was Knox's turn to look stricken and confused. "I thought Monroe was some retired, older dude."

"Knox." Rob's tone was scolding, which somehow made everything worse. "Have some manners. Especially if you want a room for the summer."

Rob's dad voice had me waiting for the bolt of lightning to take me out.

Monroe, you idiot, I lectured myself. *Don't assume.* Ever. I was a fucking naval investigator. I was feared throughout NCIS for being relentless and finding even the tiniest connections between details. But not apparently when it came to my own life. I'd assumed Rebound—Knox —was older, and my loose hookup ethics hadn't bothered to press for an actual name, something I was kicking myself for, big time.

"Rob?" Jessica's voice sounded from the kitchen. "Did you move the pepper grinder?"

"Coming," he called back before he pointed at Knox. "Take Monroe out back to the party. Fruit can go on the food table, beer in the cooler. And try to make a better impression."

"Sure thing, Dad."

24

Dad. Death seriously couldn't come fast enough. Knox had an easy smile, but as soon as Rob disappeared to the kitchen, his expression transformed, face wrinkling with either pain or disgust, possibly both.

"I need one of those beers." He plucked the six-pack from my hand, pulling one loose as he led the way to the patio doors to the deck and backyard.

"You can't—"

"Twenty-three, remember?" He deposited four beers in the cooler and held out the last one for me after I set the fruit platter on the table with other side dishes. Below us, kids ran free while a few clumps of adults stood or sat talking.

"Don't remind me." I groaned. And damn it all to hell, why did he have to make flipping open the bottle cap sexy. He held out the bottle opener, and our hands brushed, every bit as electric as on the dance floor, and I wanted to groan for a whole different reason.

"Hey, I look older. You look younger. It all washes out. Cheers." He clinked bottles with me. "Let's start again. I'm sorry for the reaction. Dad made it sound like his friend with the hoarder house was old. Like Henri was. That kind of old."

"As opposed to my kind of old?" I shook my head, not sure I'd ever felt more ancient. "Henri was my great-aunt. You knew her?"

"Just the stories about what a character she was. I've never been inside the house, but I remember the metal reindeer she'd put on the front lawn every year until she got sick. I've always wanted to explore the place. I'm looking forward to that. Among other things." He gave me a pointed look I couldn't quite decipher. Or rather, maybe I didn't want to. If he was willing to pick up where we'd left off...

No. Better to assume he wasn't.

"No exploring. No way."

"What? You don't need summer help? Dad said it was a done deal that you had a place for me."

I bit back an exasperated noise. Because I so did have a place for him. Under me. Over me. Next to me. My body wasn't picky. But I couldn't. We couldn't.

"And *Dad* is exactly why this can't possibly work."

"Oh wait." He peered closer at me. "Are you not out? I just assumed..."

"I'm out. Your dad's known longer than the navy even."

"Yeah, he's cool." Knox had an offhand tone that reflected none of my panic and terror back when I'd told my friend group. Knox's casualness only underscored how much younger he was. Different world now and all that. Knox smiled easily. "I told him and Mom when I was in middle school. So, if we're both out, I'm not sure I see the problem here."

He sounded all reasonable, which only made me that much more frustrated.

"The problem?" I scoffed, voice too harsh, but the words kept tumbling out anyway. "There's too many to list, starting with I'm not afraid of much in this life, but I'd rather not trash one of my oldest friendships simply because I made a stupid mistake."

"Mistake. I see." Smile gone, Knox stepped back like I'd slugged him, wounded tone matching his pinched expression.

"Sorry, that came out abrupt." I paced away, shaking my arms, trying to keep my body language from mirroring my mood. Didn't need anyone glancing our way thinking we were arguing. Which we were. But we didn't need any questions, especially from Rob or Jessica.

"Or you were honest." Knox shrugged, but the tightness around his eyes and mouth said he was anything but carefree. "Don't worry, Lieutenant. I'm not looking to become another mistake on your flawless record. I'll figure something else out for the summer."

"Knox—"

"Damn. I thought I'd fall to my knees to hear you say my actual name. Apparently, that was a mistake too." He brushed past me on his way into the house, leaving me to lean against the deck railing. How in the hell was I supposed to make this right?

Chapter Five

Knox

I could feel Monroe's eyes on me. He didn't chase after me, but his intense, soulful gaze was a palpable thing as I went about helping Dad set up the grill and pushing the triplets and their friends on the swings. Damn it. When I'd opened the door to see Lieutenant Butter—Monroe—in the flesh, looking far more comfortable in a short-sleeve cotton shirt with buttons and pressed khaki shorts, elation had rushed through me. Like an *A* on a test that I'd expected to fail. Immediately, I'd had a plan. Live with the old dude Dad had lined up for me, seduce Lieutenant Butter all summer long...

And then, in even more of a shocker, my sexy-ass lieutenant, who could dance like he had a slinky for a spine, was also *Monroe*—a.k.a. the old dude. Apparently, my brain had forgotten that military dudes retired young. And hot. For all of five minutes, I'd had visions of the perfect summer fling. Fix Monroe's house. Get out of the basement. Spend all summer tangled up with the hottest guy I'd ever kissed. Seemed like the best plan ever.

Until he'd called me a mistake, voice all bitter, like the entire memory was tarnished now that he knew who I was. Sexiest night of my damn life, but just another *mistake* to him. One he didn't want to repeat. And yeah, I probably should have kept talking to him, tried to wrangle him into honoring the agreement for the summer, but there was only so much rejection a dude could take.

Kid duty and my usual role as chief gofer were easier, even if I did feel his eyes on me the whole damn time.

"Oh my gosh!" Jessica's mother, Edith, arrived, fashionably late as usual. Her Australian accent was way more pronounced than Jessica's, and she had a way of dominating a room, or in this case, a deck. I much preferred her quiet, American second husband with whom she traveled the country. They were nominally based out of Portland, but they seemed always on the go. Her husband trailed behind Edith as she admired Jessica's fruit-patterned sundress. "Jessica! You and the girls match!"

"I brought the matching dresses with me, Mum." Angie, Jessica's sister, stepped outside as the girls ran ahead of me to greet their grandmother. Indeed, the triplets wore identical dresses to the one Jessica sported, and they obediently twirled and preened.

"Let's get a family picture!" Edith suggested, never one to miss a photo opportunity, as proved by the crowded walls of photos of the triplets in every room of Dad and Jessica's house. Wedding shots. Maternity shots. Ultrasound pics. My mom's Seattle condo had been similar—pics of her and Candace and the pair of sisters they'd adopted from foster care. I assumed their new place in Chicago had even more of a shrine to their coupledom and Candace's pro basketball career. In both houses, I was on the periphery in a few shots —there at the weddings and birthdays, but not the focus.

Which was okay. I wasn't a center-of-attention type of guy, and I helped Jessica line up the triplets, getting fingers out of mouths and dresses straight.

"Rob?" Jessica called over to Dad. "Mum wants a picture of us and the girls."

"Sure thing, honey." Dad came loping over and dug his phone from his pocket. "Knox? Can you take one with my phone too?"

"No problem." I took pics with his phone, Jessica's fancy camera that seemed always at the ready, and then a few with Edith's of her and Jessica and the girls. The bright dresses would look cute on whatever scrap of wall Jessica found for these pics. I nabbed one with my phone at the end, the girls having run out of patience and acting all silly. I'd send it to a few friends to show how big the girls were getting.

"Knox?" Dad yelled from over by the grill as I pocketed my phone. "Can you bring up some towels? Some kids got into the garden sprinkler."

"I'll grab them." I turned to head back to the house, but Jessica touched my sleeve.

"Thanks. And remember, don't let that cat of yours out." She made a face that Angie, her sister, echoed.

"Are we even sure it's a house cat?" Angie had a laugh like an old parrot, and it was going to be a hell of a long summer with her in the house. She was training to be a doula, and I knew she'd help Jessica, but she sure could grate on my nerves. "Kitty looks like something we might throw on the barbie back home."

"He's probably a Maine Coon. They can get big." I hated how defensive I sounded. Who cared what they thought of my cat? I hurried downstairs to the laundry room to rescue an armful of towels from the dryer, only to turn and almost run into Monroe at the bottom of the stairs.

"Need help with the towels?" Mouth twisting, he held out his arms, eyes darting around as if he wasn't entirely sure what he was doing here. That made two of us.

"I've got it, but thanks." I didn't pass over the towels, instead staring him down, daring him to tell me why he was really downstairs.

"This your baby?" he asked, crossing over to my futon in the corner of the basement room. Beyond this unfinished space was a playroom for the girls and a small bathroom, but the laundry area itself was long and narrow with a cement floor, high-capacity washer and dryer, laundry sink, and exactly enough room for a futon for me and a couple of stackable plastic containers for my crap.

"My..." It took me a second to realize he meant Wallace, who was sprawled on the futon. I'd wedged his scratching post against the wall and his covered box in the corner. "Oh yeah, the cat. Meet Wallace." I shifted the towels so I could reach down and give him a scratch. He was gray and white striped with the classic shaggy Maine Coon fur and delicate lynx-like features. "When I found him after Christmas this past year, he was a lot smaller, more like four pounds. Now he's sixteen pounds, but he really is still a baby."

"So he might still grow more?" Unlike a lot of people, he didn't seem cowed by Wallace's size, giving him pets. When our hands brushed while giving Wallace attention, we pulled apart, but not before an electric shock zoomed up my arm. Damn, I wanted to be back on that dance floor so badly. But no, I was in this dingy basement admiring my cat and trying not to jump Monroe.

"Vet wasn't sure. He's probably close to a year now. I

31

saved enough to cover his vaccines and neutering, so he's all up-to-date." I scratched behind Wallace's big pointy ears. He rolled to show us his pale furry belly, and Monroe laughed.

"Someone wants a belly rub." He reached out to oblige the cat, and it took all my self-control not to make a crack about being willing to rub Monroe's belly too. His gaze shifted from the cat to my corner of the room. "This is a teeny space."

"It's fine." I readjusted the armload of towels. "I lived in dorms for three years and shared a tiny apartment for another two. I can sleep pretty much anywhere. At least if I stay here, I can help out."

"You seem good at that." His voice was solemn, not the jolly praise I was used to, but something more serious than the endless stream of compliments from outsiders who thought our blended family was adorable.

"I try." Somehow, I could be more serious with Monroe in return, letting a little struggle show in my tone. "The triplets came when I was in college, but that's partly why I needed a fifth year. I took a term off to stay here and help with the babies. Angie and Jessica's mom were around some too, but three babies were a ton of work."

"I bet." Our eyes met, conversation happening on a level so deep, I wasn't even sure what was being said, only that he understood far more than most. I took a step toward him, and he didn't back away. The air seemed to thicken, even Wallace sensing a seismic shift, fur crackling as he stretched and turned his back on us. Privacy. We had—

"Knox?" My name sounded from somewhere upstairs, and I groaned like I'd taken a punch. The moment lost, Monroe was already in motion, grabbing half the towels and heading for the stairs.

"We better get the towels out to the kids." He bustled ahead of me, and then I was swept up in a flurry of requests as the food came off the grill.

"Knox? Can you get me a platter?"

"Knox! Come push us!"

"Knox? The lightbulb in the guest bathroom just went out. Can you—"

"I'm on it." And I was, one task after another until I arrived back at the food table to several empty platters. Oh well, at least there was some of the fruit Monroe had brought. I was deciding what could go with the fruit when Monroe stepped in front of me, holding out one of the blue and white checked paper plates Jessica had set out.

"What's this?" The plate held a plain burger on a bun, but what I really meant was, *What the heck, Monroe?*

"You were running around so much that you didn't get to make yourself a plate when everyone else grabbed their burgers, so I snagged the last patty for you." Monroe shrugged, but there was tension around his eyes like he also couldn't figure out his sudden burst of helpfulness.

"You didn't have to do that. But thanks." I busied myself adding toppings to the burger and arranging fruit and some salad on the plate rather than allowing myself to continue the staring contest with Monroe.

Which turned out to be a good call because my dad came striding over, all smiles and a back slap for Monroe.

"Ah. Good to see you both getting along. Knox manage to not insult you again?"

"He's fine." Monroe's mouth curved, not quite a smile, but something almost fond nonetheless. "Not his fault I'm ancient."

"Knox, Monroe here can probably run a faster mile than either of us," Dad scolded me like I'd been heckling Monroe all night and not ogling all those lean muscles every chance I got.

"He does seem rather...fit." I looked directly at Monroe, not Dad, trying to beam Monroe memories of exactly how *fit* he'd been at the club.

"Military will do that for a guy." Dad was almost adorably clueless. "You should have seen him back in high school. Monroe was all elbows and knees, not an ounce of muscle. First guy from our school to ever get a Naval Academy scholarship. We were all convinced he wouldn't pass the fitness test, but a couple of years later, he turns up, looking all GI-Joe buff."

"We all grew up." Monroe shrugged, but hell if I didn't want to grab Dad's yearbooks, see Monroe's glow-up firsthand.

"And out." Dad patted his middle, which was getting a little thicker these days. "Swear I've gained sympathy pregnancy weight."

"That's what you said last time." I duffed his shoulder.

"Yeah, but weirdly, this time is more nerve-wracking. With the triplets, everything was so choreographed from IVF to the c-section at thirty-five weeks. This one was such a surprise."

I nodded along because biology was weird. I'd been a total accident back in high school for him and Mom, who both insisted they'd used birth control, then Dad and Jessica had struggled with infertility for years, only to have a post-forty shocker of a surprise bonus kid.

"Maybe you're still in shock?" Monroe suggested.

"I better get over it in a hurry." Dad chuckled, voice warm like it always was when he talked about Jessica or the kids. "Baby will be here around August."

August. The month circled on my planner, and the

month I was supposed to be counting down to like a second Christmas and birthday rolled into one. Grad school was waiting, and I had a billion open tabs on my browser for possible housing options and not one application submitted. And hell if I knew what was up with my reluctance.

"I'm glad we get one last summer with Knox close by." Like he could read my mind, Dad threw an arm around my shoulders. "You and Monroe figure out when you can move in?"

"I...uh..." Hell. I should have used some of that time running around doing favors to figure out a plausible excuse for Dad as to why the roommate thing was a no-go.

"Wednesday?" Monroe sounded way more confident than I did. "I need a day or two to clear one of the bedrooms for him and Wallace."

What the...? I had to clamp my jaw shut to avoid sputtering.

"Oh, you met the cat already." Dad made a dismissive gesture. "Should have known you'd fall for him."

Me. How about falling for me? But no, Dad was undoubtedly right, and Wallace was the reason for Monroe's abrupt change of heart. And I could get all up in my feelings over that, or I could seize the damn opportunity before he yanked it back.

"I can help with the bedroom clearing," I said quickly. "Tomorrow, I'm supposed to work a gutter install for Measure Twice, but I could come early on Tuesday and help get the room ready and Wallace-proof."

"That cat is a menace." Dad rolled his eyes before slapping Monroe on the shoulder again. "Better you than me, buddy. They're your problems now."

"I'll take good care of them both." Monroe sounded all responsible, which perversely made me that much more eager to tell him all the ways he could *take care* of me. And problem? Nope. I couldn't speak for Wallace, but I was determined to be the best damn roommate Monroe had ever had.

"Rob? Can you help with the ice cream?" Jessica came to the patio door.

"Oops. Gotta go." Dad gave her a dopey look before nodding at Monroe and me. "Glad everything's all settled."

I waited until he was back in the house before turning to Monroe. "*Is* it all settled?"

"Guess so. See you Tuesday. Not too early because that's one of the days I run in the morning, but it should work." Monroe sounded all businesslike, not at all the same guy who'd been no-way, no-how an hour ago.

"What made you change your mind?" It was a dicey question, but I had to know. *Please don't say pity.* People didn't understand how weird it was to be on the outside looking in with two families. However, the only thing worse than false praise or cluelessness was people who *did* understand.

"I felt sorry—"

"Don't." I held up my hands. I wasn't too proud to accept his offer of a place for the summer, but I didn't think I could bear another syllable of sympathy. "Please. I'm used to the weirdness that comes with a blended family."

"Me too. But that's not what I was going to say. I feel sorry for Wallace. Poor giant baby cat." He laughed, eyes going soft. He was lying. It wasn't about Wallace, but I let him continue. "Tiny laundry room. Hard-looking futon. I can't promise much better, but at least the cat won't get woken up by the dryer cycling on and off or someone needing a shirt."

"Yeah. Cat needs his rest." I kept my voice light, but I held Monroe's gaze firmly.

"He needs taking care of." To his credit, Monroe didn't glance away, instead matching my intensity with a message I wasn't sure I liked.

"Eh. He's pretty tough. Survived on the cold streets." I made a dismissive gesture before turning my tone more pointed. "So, I take it we're not telling anyone about Friday?"

"God, no." Monroe's voice dropped to a spooked whisper. Yup. I was still a mistake, just one he felt sorry for now. "Apologies. That came out—"

"Honest. I like that you're honest with me, even if I don't like being some shameful mistake—"

"I'm sorry I put it like that." Monroe huffed out a breath, expression pained, and for a split second, I thought he might touch me, but he balled his hand instead. "The club wasn't a mistake. And if there's any shame, it's that I probably should have asked more questions, but I was just having so much..."

"Fun?" I suggested when he trailed off. "And you don't want more fun?"

"We can't. You know that." His whole body slumped, military posture giving way to a defeat I absolutely hated for him.

"Do I?" I'd never wished harder to be older or from a different family. Something. Anything so Monroe would stop looking so kicked and see this as an opportunity instead of an obligation.

"You should. I would hate to come between you and your dad. You seem pretty close. I'm not going to be the thing that wrecks your relationship."

"Fair enough, but I know how to keep things on the down-low."

"Knox..." More of that pained voice, like my flirting might do him in. "I've done the down-low thing. I did my time under Don't-Ask-Don't-Tell. And it's not that I'm looking for serious, but I simply can't go there with you. I can't hurt you or Rob either one."

"Fine, I'll stop pushing." Much as I liked baiting him, I wasn't going to be a source of agony for the guy. "We can be just roommates if that's what you want."

"It is." Monroe firmed his jaw, eyes unnaturally still. He was a terrible liar.

"Well, cheers to a good summer, roomie." It would undoubtedly be a long one, and my lust might spontaneously combust at some point, but at least I was out of the basement.

Chapter Six

Monroe

"I hear you have a new roommate." Looking up from his laptop, Holden greeted me from his usual table at the coffee shop as I arrived for my post-workout coffee on Tuesday morning. At least this time, I'd made it through the front doors of Blessed Bean before being heckled.

"Good lord, the gossip mill in this town moves fast." I was low on groceries and craving cold brew, but maybe I should have skipped the coffee trip. Again.

"Have a seat." Our mutual friend, Sam, waved from behind the counter, signaling me to sit with Holden, which I did. Way back in high school, Sam had been the annoying eighth grader who kept showing up at the worst moments, but now he was a man with a mission and a coffee shop, irritating tween days long past. He'd also been the first to invite me to the regular trivia nights at the local sports bar he and Holden made a point of attending. I enjoyed the inclusion, although it did open me up for more teasing.

My hair was still damp from my post-run shower as I grabbed one of the colorful hand-painted wooden chairs across from Holden. I'd walked the short distance to Blessed Bean, which was in an older building on the edge of downtown Safe Harbor.

"Ha. Rob was in earlier, all happy you're freeing Knox from the laundry room." Holden laughed before taking a sip of his half-empty coffee. He was braver than me if he trusted Sam's drip coffee. Unlike the big national chains, Blessed Bean's quality could vary wildly from drink to drink. "And Rob also said to ask you to bring one of the cold cases you're working on to an episode of my podcast."

"You have a podcast now, Professor?" I was more than happy to grab any topic that wasn't gossip about my living arrangements. Holden was a professor of criminal justice at the nearby community college, a role he'd assumed after being injured in the line of duty as a police officer.

"Doesn't everyone?" Holden gave a smug smile. "*Mistakes Were Made* is actually rather popular beyond the usual criminal justice circles. We look at where various investigations went wrong. You have a case you'd like to bring on to dissect?"

"Hmm. Let me think." I wasn't afraid of public speaking, and an hour or two spent recording something with Holden was hardly a chore. Like in high school, I found him easy to be around. For all his extroverted, busy-body nature, he was also kind and nonjudgmental, and his sense of humor tended to make time pass quickly. "A couple of the cases I'm reviewing might fit. And I'm thinking of taking another look at the Stapleton case."

Holden sucked in a breath. "Yeah. That's a hornet's nest of a case, all right. Everyone around here just assumes the husband did it, but without a body for the wife, there's far more speculation than evidence. And, of course, rumors persist that the house is haunted."

"I know. I run by it every morning. It's sad, seeing it in such disrepair." The Stapleton house was down the street from Aunt Henri's place, another rambling turn-of-the-century home in far worse shape than Aunt Henri's, thanks to two decades of mystery surrounding what had happened to Mrs. Stapleton. She'd disappeared before her husband later succumbed to a massive heart attack, but some thought his death was also rather suspicious. And then there were those like me who missed their son, Worth, the most. Brilliant and friendly, he'd been a big part of my high-school years. "Do you ever hear from Worth?"

"Nah. He left for good." Eyes growing distant, Holden shook his head. Worth had been his friend too. "I heard he's an investment banker of some kind in California. Maybe you can look him up when you move?"

"Don't be so quick to ship Monroe out." Sam had an easy smile as he brought me my cold brew and a muffin, the same as the last few Tuesdays. "And yes, do that case for the podcast. It never sat right with me how fast everyone was to rush to judgment."

Sam might have been younger than us, but he knew exactly who Worth was. His puppy-dog crush on Worth had been so painfully obvious at the time, a stark contrast to Sam's current cautious and collected demeanor.

"People generally are." I picked at the muffin's wrapper. It wasn't only missing-person cases. People loved to judge. Not that I was going to act on the attraction with Knox, but it wasn't only Rob who would have an issue if we hooked up. Everyone in this whole town would have an opinion.

"I'll take a look at those case files and get back to you on a time for the podcast."

"Excellent." Holden toasted me with his cup.

"Oh, and congrats on the new helper for your house." Sam wiped down the table next to ours.

I groaned. "Not you too."

"Hey, Knox is a good one. Beyond looking like some superhero who moonlights as a pro-surfer, he's smart and a hard worker."

"Is *looks like a pro-surfer* Sam-speak for Knox is easy on the eyes?" Holden teased. At odds with his besotted younger self, Sam seemed contentedly single and devoted to his charity for at-risk teens who ran the coffee house. If he dated, I hadn't heard about it.

And he might be closer in age to Knox, but the thought of Sam crushing on him had me making an indignant noise. "He's a kid."

"Chill. He's twenty-three. More than legal. And looking isn't a crime." Holden rolled his eyes like I was the unreasonable one, and even Sam laughed.

"Kind of hard not to look, but he could be sixty-eight, and I still wouldn't want to face Rob's wrath." Sam headed back to the counter. "Want me to ring you up?"

"Sure. I better head out anyway. I have to let Knox in." I glanced down at my phone. Crap. I was cutting it kind of close. Only a few months off-duty, I was already falling away from the early-to-everything habit. And showing up with my half-full to-go cup felt a little rude. "Maybe I should grab Knox a coffee too. What does he drink?"

"Depends on his mood, but iced chai is pretty reliable." Sam rang up the order and took my card. His memory for various details about his customers and the young workers from his teen charity was impressive. "I'll grab Knox's drink for you."

"Thanks." As soon as he prepared the drink, I headed back to my house, a brisk walk in the cool early-summer morning. June in Oregon was nothing short of spectacular, something I'd forgotten during my years away, the riot of colorful flowers and green gardens in front of the other, better-kept historic homes near downtown.

I reached Aunt Henri's place to discover Knox already on the wide wrap-around porch.

"Hey. I was just looking for the bell." He stepped out from behind a large overgrown planter, which served as a good reminder to add a landscaper to my to-do lists. Next to Knox was a neat stack of bags and a box.

"I'm not sure there is one." I'd only ever noticed the old-fashioned heavy door knocker on the front door.

"No camera? How do you check for deliveries?"

"Surprisingly, we ancient folks survived long before smart houses and wired everything." Chuckling, I held out his drink. "Brought you a chai."

"Thank you." Accepting the cup, he took a sip. His lips did things with the straw that made me regret the impulse to get him a drink. I had to look away before he caught me staring. My gaze landed on a bag with a big clear dome containing a very unhappy cat.

"Is that a cat backpack? Poor Wallace." I opened the door to let us in before setting my drink on a low ledge to help with Knox's bags.

"Yeah, I know." Knox carefully carried the cat in like he was an alien explorer in a spacesuit. "He barely fits in it anymore."

"You need to get him a leash."

"Oh!" Knox made a delighted noise, and his excitement

43

was possibly even more distracting than his lips on the straw. "That's a great idea. Then I could take him on walks."

He knelt to soothe the cat, who let out a plaintive whine as Knox tapped against the dome. I understood Wallace's pain. Hard plastic was no substitute for Knox's touch, not that I'd admit that aloud.

"How about we get him in your new room, and then he can be safe in there while I show you around?" Grabbing the box that held a jug of litter and a covered litter box, I led Knox down the long front hall. After turning into the kitchen, we passed through the breakfast nook, the sun porch, and then into a small room that might have been a canning kitchen once upon a time. At some point decades ago, the space had been fashioned into a sort of guest suite with wood paneling, shag carpet, and a narrow cabinet with a dorm-sized fridge of dubious origins and a sink. "Darn it. I aired it out all day yesterday, but it still smells stale."

"Old pot and cigarettes." Knox made a face as he switched the bag with the cat to his other hand. "And why do I get the feeling this is where they stashed the house-keeper back in the day? Or some much-hated mother-in-law?"

"Possibly," I admitted. The room actually looked worse in the sunshine. The carpet was several shades of brown, none of them natural, and the grayish tinge to the paneling was more obvious in the light. At least there was a decent-enough bed. Though even that looked shabbier today. Maybe I could get Knox a mattress topper as an apology. Or would that be too much?

Gah. Only I could obsess over whether bedding was too close to a romantic gesture.

"And let me guess? It's farthest from your room?" Knox gave me a pointed stare.

My face heated far more than I liked. That was indeed exactly why I'd picked this one for Knox. "A coincidence."

"I bet." He carefully set Wallace's bag on the bed and unzipped it so Wallace could sprawl on the faded quilt.

Reaching down, I gave the cat a scratch. "Tell you what, if you see one of the other rooms you like more, you can switch. I suppose I could take this one even. Right now, I'm back in the guest room I used in high school. I haven't tackled Aunt Henri's room and attached bath yet."

"Oh, that's right. Forgot you lived here." Knox rubbed Wallace's furry belly, putting his hand way too close to mine.

"Year and a half." Tone identical to the one Knox used the other day when talking about the perils of a blended family, I made a dismissive gesture. "Aunt Henri was my mom's aunt. Mom died when I was young, then Dad remarried. He got deployed to Guam, and I wanted to finish high school in the states. I stayed with Aunt Henri while he and my stepmom were stationed overseas."

"Wow. That must have been hard on you." Knox's expression held far too much sympathy for my liking. "I bet it was a hard choice."

"Yeah." Not everyone understood that. Part of me had wanted to go with Dad and Carolyn, but I'd felt stifled by their rules and tired of feeling on the outside of their tight partnership. Aunt Henri had been an unknown factor. At sixteen, I hadn't wanted to admit being afraid to anyone, but I'd been plenty nervous on the plane to Oregon.

"Did she already have the rep of being a recluse? The way Dad and his friends always talk, I bet staying here got you teased."

"Some," I admitted.

"When I visited, it was always a toss-up which house was spookier, this one or the old Stapleton place." Knox crossed the room to open an old dresser, which sent up a cloud of dust. "This house is just old, though, while that one's cursed. Buyers keep falling through or something."

"Yeah, I jog past it often, and it's sad. Used to be a pretty cheerful place. Holden wants me to come on his podcast, talk about the Stapleton case."

"Because you knew their kid along with Dad and Holden?" Moving on from the dresser, Knox quickly set up the litter box for Wallace.

"Yeah, Worth was a big part of our friend group, but also, I'm a criminal investigator. I was with NCIS in the navy. I'm looking at some cold cases for your dad while I'm here working on the house. Keeps me busy until I can land with the San Francisco PD or possibly the FBI field office. I've had offers from both." I wasn't bragging as much as reminding us, me especially, that I wasn't sticking around.

"So, the plan is to flip this place and then return to city living? Not a fan of small towns?"

"Nope. I've got my eye on some sweet condos near the Castro in San Francisco. Between all my dad's moves growing up and my own various duty stations and deployments, I've seen enough small towns."

"Darn. I was gonna offer to spring for Pie in the Sky pizza tonight as a thank-you for letting me stay. But maybe you're more of an anonymous chain sort of guy." Knox's eyes sparkled, but there was a message there about how readily I'd been down for a no-name hookup.

"I remember that place." I didn't rise to the bait. And the smart thing would probably be not sharing food with Knox, but pizza sounded better than trying to squeeze in a grocery run. "I could go for splitting an order with you. I always liked their house specialty pizza with all the meats and red peppers and olives."

"That's my go-to." He beamed like I'd answered correctly to some quiz. "There's lots of cool stuff here if you know where to look."

"Says the guy headed East to the Ivy Leagues." I'd paid enough attention to Rob's bragging to know that much, at least.

"Don't remind me." Knox headed to the door to the room. "Let's see more of the house."

"What? You don't want to go to graduate school?" I asked as he shut Wallace in the room.

"Yes. No. I don't know. It's fine." He threw up his hands. "Anyway, moving on, tell me about your vision for this place?"

He stopped in the center of the kitchen, surveying the large space, which sported evidence of various remodels over the last hundred years or so. It opened onto a sunny nook with faded yellow wallpaper and had a door to the dining room, which had dark wood wainscotting and an ancient chandelier in dire need of dusting.

"Vision? Uh...flip it for the best return?" I pursed my mouth, trying not to sound like a complete heel for not wanting to keep this place. Regardless of my desire to get out of town, it was way too much house for a single guy used to small officer's quarters. "I figure I'll hire out what help I need in addition to you. Paint will go a long way. Get all the wallpaper stripped, then white walls throughout. No more carpet. Refinish the hardwoods. Just get it sellable and clutter-free."

"White? Like an empty box? You're no fun." Knox shook his head like he was genuinely sorry I lacked more imagination. "That might work for the condos you want in the Bay, but people come to Safe Harbor partly for the historic homes. You have to show people the Victorian charm in-house. Encourage them to look past the age and quirks and embrace the details. Come on, just for fun, what are your favorite features?"

"Hmm." I took a moment to consider the question, thinking less like my forty-one-year-old self and more like the sixteen-year-old exploring the place for the first time. What did I notice? What seemed cool when I took away the pressure hanging over me to sell? "The clawfoot tubs in two of the bathrooms. The line of built-ins in the upstairs hallway. And the dumbwaiter." I pointed to the far corner of the kitchen.

"There's a dumbwaiter? For real?" Knox gasped like a kid finding one last present on Christmas.

Damn it, why did he have to be so expressive? And why did I have to keep noticing? It was one thing when my attraction had mainly been physical, but all the ways I kept finding him appealing were distinctly unsettling. Made my back tight, knowing I'd have to spend the entire summer resisting.

"It goes all the way to the third floor." Opening the old metal door, I demonstrated the raising and lowering features.

"Show me," he demanded, already heading for the back stairs, another feature I liked. It always felt like using a secret passageway, the squeaky boards of the dark wooden staircase adding to that sense. Knox barely paused at the second floor to arrive at the third, a main airy space with several built-in cupboards and closets under the eaves and a small bathroom tucked into the furthest corner.

"Whoa. You gotta let me and Wallace stay up here."

Knox looked around like he'd landed in a fairytale. I tried to see the place through his eyes. Old woven hammock swing chair hanging from the ceiling, crowded built-in bookshelves, and metal storage containers full of ancient paints and brushes. There was a white daybed against the far wall with a rag rug in front of it.

"I'm pretty sure this was Aunt Henri's distant cousin's art studio. Aunt Henri rarely came up here because in the winter, it gets too cold, and in the summer, it gets too hot. Like sweltering," I warned.

"This is me not caring. Look, there's a fan." He pointed to an oscillating one under the drawing table.

"Why do you like this room so much?" To me, it was an attic, but the way Knox's face lit up had me wishing I could see the magic. Or perhaps be the one to put that look there —a dangerous line of thinking.

"There's a story here. A reason for the dumbwaiter. Probably some art waiting to be uncovered and other treasures." Knox's voice was all breathless. "It's got the best energy in the house."

"It's yours." I couldn't give him much, but I could give him this, and at least it smelled far better than the other guest suite, musty but not unbearable.

"Give me until pizza time, and I'll have it livable for Wallace. You'll see." He grinned at me, gaze flitting around like he was already full of plans and schemes. Damn, he was adorable. And infectious.

"Okay, tell me how I can help. What do you want moved first?"

"I get to be the boss?" Knox made a show of exaggerated skepticism, eyes wide, mouth soft, hands open, and hell if I didn't want to kiss him silly.

"I'm just coming off twenty-odd years of taking orders.

And giving them. Pays to be flexible." I realized a moment too late that it sounded dirty, and Knox laughed knowingly.

"Uh-huh. I do appreciate a *flexible* man."

"Knox." I groaned.

"Sorry. No flirting. Got it. Work only. Hi-ho, hi-ho." He whistled softly. The attic temperature wasn't all that was rising. It was going to be a long, hot summer, one I might not survive.

Chapter Seven

Knox

"Oooh, it's so tight." I grunted as my back muscles protested my awkward position.

"Knox." Monroe's tone was even more pained than mine.

"What?" I faked innocence. "This container is really wedged in here." I finally pulled the last bin of art supplies free from its hiding spot under the eaves. "It's not flirting if it's literal."

"We can literally put that whole box right into the trash." He held out a trash bag. We already had a big stack of bags near the stairs, along with a smaller tower of boxes for donation.

"No way! The paint is dried up, sure, but there's usable brushes and some things like pastels that don't go bad." I quickly picked through the bin, removing a few good finds from the unsalvageable bits.

"Remember, anything worth saving, you can have."

He'd made the same offer when we started our work several hours earlier.

"Thanks. We've found so much more than I can use by myself, so I'll give some to Sam for teen activities with his program." I added some colored pencils, pastels, and empty sketchbooks to a box I had going for Sam and the shelter.

"Good idea." Monroe's voice was just this side of too sharp.

"You don't like Sam?" I wasn't aware it was possible to dislike Samuel, who was kind to absolutely everyone and had a smile that was impossible not to return.

"He's great." Monroe made a choking sound that didn't sound entirely involuntary. "Sorry. Dust."

"Here, let me sweep up the dust." Done with the bin, I grabbed the broom and swept the now-empty corner, working my way backward to the center of the large space. My internal soundtrack clicked on, and I ended up doing a second pass on most of the room as a pulsing pop tune played in my brain.

"Knox." Voice strained again, Monroe looked up from the shelves he'd been dusting.

"What now?" I hadn't done a single flirty thing in at least ten minutes.

"Do you have to dance with the broom?" A dusky flush rose on his defined cheekbones.

"I was dancing?" I chuckled, but I wasn't entirely surprised. "Oops. Hazard of having a wicked bass line in my head."

"Sure seemed that way from how you were shaking... never mind." He resumed dusting with quick, aggressive movements before taking a couple of hilariously deep breaths. "You like art, huh?"

"I always have." I'd let him have the change in subject

because he'd hit upon one of my great passions. "Despite the sibling influx in the last five years, I was pretty much an only kid my whole childhood. Lots of time on my own, and art supplies were far cheaper than electronics for keeping me occupied. Art. Legos. Building things. I liked things that kept my hands busy." I paused to laugh at how Monroe's gaze dropped to my hands on the broom. "Sorry. Not trying for innuendo there. It's true though. I get all fidgety, and making things calms me down."

"Ah. I usually run. Or pound out some reps in the weight room. If it's late at night, I'll read something super dry to quiet my brain."

"Well, next time you're antsy, try coloring something." Putting a teeny bit of flirt on the word *antsy,* I grinned at him. "Or painting. You'll see if you help with the painting. Something magical about transforming a room."

"You're something else." He shook his head, but his fond tone felt more like a hug than a rebuke.

"Does that mean you'll let me use more than plain apartment-white paint?" Might as well use the brief moment of affection to press my case.

"Have at it. Whatever you think will sell."

"Awesome." I flicked the broom back and forth like I was painting the bare hardwood floor. "So, I'm thinking camo trim..."

"Camo?"

"What? That's not your favorite color, Lieutenant?" I knew perfectly well he wasn't the type to go around off-duty in head-to-toe camo and GO NAVY T-shirts, but if I'd asked him point blank for favorite colors, he would have protested. A little subterfuge was way more satisfying.

"Blue. Which I know is so boring and predictable." A smile teased the corners of his mouth.

"Yup. But I can tell from how your eyes got all dreamy that there's a story there. Tell." I leaned forward on the broom, chimney-sweep style.

"Well, my folks usually lived in typical military housing. But when we were stationed in Pensacola the year I started kindergarten, we had a landlord who let Mom paint —my bio mom, who died when I was young, not the stepmom who came later. Mom did my room light blue with baseball accents. The color was close to her eyes, so whenever I see sky blue, it makes me happy." He smiled softly, then straightened as if irked at himself for being emotional. "Sorry. That's cheesy."

"It is not." I crossed the room to lightly tap the back of his head. "It's sweet. And I'm sure you get tired of hearing it, but I'm sorry you lost your mom as a kid. I love Jessica a lot, but she's not my mom, and I get that difference, you know?"

"Yeah. Dad and Carolyn retired to Arizona together. They're a tight team with Carolyn's kids from her first marriage, and I'm glad they're so happy and going on three decades together, but...yeah. Not the same thing." He exhaled hard as I dropped my hand from his head to his shoulder and rubbed the tense muscle. "Thanks."

"And you had your Aunt Henri. I'm sure she missed your mom too."

"She did. And her distant cousin, the one who was an artist and reportedly spent all her time up in this studio. Never quite understood her link to the family tree, but she too passed too soon. Fuck cancer."

"Word." Stepping away from him and the dangerous temptation to offer more than a sympathetic touch, I pulled three canvases from behind the shelf Monroe had been cleaning. They'd been stored with the art facing the wall, and when I flipped them over, I couldn't help my gasp. "And, heck yes, she was an artist."

"Oh my." Monroe's eyes went wider than a paint can as I revealed the artwork. Each was a male nude done in vivid colors, lush textures, and an unabashedly erotic gaze. "Maybe there's a reason Aunt Henri didn't display more of her cousin's art."

"I love it. We gotta find more. I've got a professor at the university who knows people with galleries. But in the meantime, I'm hanging this one up." I carried my favorite of the three large canvases to the wall above the daybed, which conveniently already had a nail centered on the wall.

"What?" Monroe trailed after me, wringing his hands as if he'd never seen a sweaty naked man before. "Why would you hang it there?"

"Because I love it. And it deserves some wall time." I gestured widely with my hand. "Not like I'm planning on bringing visitors up here—"

"Thank you," he said a little too quickly, and I had to chuckle.

"Monroe. Give me some credit. Not like I'm gonna hookup right under your nose, okay?" I didn't let him protest what he'd meant. We both knew the truth. "Anyway, the paintings are great. I'll take them down if you have a showing for the house, but right now, I'm gonna admire that ass."

Monroe mumbled something under his breath that sounded suspiciously jealous, like his earlier tone about donating supplies to Sam.

"Would you prefer I ogle yours?" I waggled my eyebrows at him.

"No."

"Liar." I danced away to hang the remaining two paintings while Monroe finished wiping down the empty shelves and desk.

As I stepped back to admire the paintings, Monroe groaned and stretched his arms, nearly brushing the low ceiling. "Man, this is work. I'm used to exercising, but I'm still getting quite the workout."

"Yup. Don't get me wrong. I love my gym time, especially in the winter. But there's no substitute for the way construction uses all your muscles." I joined him in a big stretch, not missing how his eyes followed my every move. "That's what I love about working with Frank and Leon at Measure Twice, honestly. Dad doesn't get why I love remodeling so much, but I love coming back home exhausted. Put me on a roof for eight hours or doing three coats of paint in a grand living room, and I'm a happy sweaty mess."

"The navy could use a few more hard workers like you."

"Nah. Trust me. I'm way too much of a free spirit for Uncle Sam, Lieutenant Butter." I danced with the broom again, deliberate this time.

"I can see that too." Monroe's intense look had me seconds from pushing him onto the daybed and showing him exactly how *free* I could be. But I could also be good, so I forced myself to stick to bland topics. "Look at all the bags of trash. See? Unlike at the gym, we've got immediate proof of all our work. I love that about remodeling. Something tangible to admire at the end of the day. Makes the work that much more satisfying."

"It does look way different now." Monroe glanced around the space, which seemed far larger with all the trash and clutter removed. Brighter, too, thanks to the discovery of a teeny balcony and several windows hiding behind decades-old coverings. The paintings further brightened and gave personality to the space, and I couldn't wait to bring Wallace up and spread my belongings around.

"Yup. And we're gonna do this to the whole place." I swept my arms wide, energized from the day's work. "You'll see. You won't recognize this house by the time I'm done."

"Good." He grinned at me, a genuine wide one with enough appreciation to add to my ego. "And I have a budget. While we eat pizza, I'll show you my lists, and you can add your ideas, and we can talk about what to outsource and what to DIY."

"You're gonna listen to my opinions?" Much as I liked being appreciated, I remained shocked that Mr. Officer Dude intended to take advice from me instead of charging ahead like most bossy types. He'd taken direction from me all afternoon, though, and it had been incredibly validating.

"Why not?" He shrugged. "You're the construction expert, not me."

"I am." I preened. What else might Monroe let me take charge of? My body hummed with delicious energy.

"And the one with vision. I could never have imagined this space so transformed." Chuckling, he shook his head. "I still think you're going to be too hot up here, but I see now why you like it."

"I'll just wear fewer clothes."

"Knox." The way he groaned made me want to strip right there.

"I kid. I kid." Dancing away from him, I moved a little too quickly and tripped over the box of art supplies for Sam. "Whoops."

"Careful." Monroe righted me before I could hit the floor, bringing our faces much, much too close to each other. And he kept his grip on my upper arm even after I had my footing again. Time slowed, the light in the room shifting,

57

the air thickening, the beat of my heart getting louder and louder. Or maybe that was his. I inhaled, eyes locked on his full lips. Waiting. And waiting. This had to be his call. His head dipped, and my pulse sped up, and...

"We can't." Releasing my arm, he moved away quickly, shrinking back against the bookshelves.

"I know." I let the full force of my regret lace my words, but I didn't chase after him. "I better go check on Wallace again, bring him up here to see his new home."

Monroe made a sound that was part cough and part gasp.

"You okay?"

"Yeah." Straightening, he regained his ever-present composure. "You just...switched directions so easily there."

"Were you wanting me to go for the hard sell, Lieutenant? That's not my style. You know perfectly well I'll go there with you in a heartbeat, but I'm not gonna beg, and I'm not gonna coerce. You want me, you know where to find me."

Chapter Eight

Monroe

My body was woefully ill-prepared for the energy Knox brought to our first morning as roommates.

"Today, we're taking on the primary bedroom." He wandered into the kitchen, looking remarkably breezy for the early hour in shorts, a T-shirt with a picture of a snoring cartoon cat, and bare feet.

"We're doing what?" Even in the service, I hadn't been the best in the morning, and I tried to shake the cobwebs from my brain. "Sorry. My head's still foggy. The coffee should be ready in a second. I need to do groceries, but I think there might be cereal."

"No problem." Knox opened the fridge to peer at its limited contents. "Here. You have two eggs with a decent date. I'll make us something."

Moving around like he'd lived here forever instead of less than twenty-four hours, he grabbed a skillet, cutting board, knife, and spatula.

"Thanks." It was weird how, after years of being the one

in charge, the highest-ranking person in the room, it was remarkably easy to let Knox take charge. Yesterday had worked out well, following Knox's lead on cleaning up the third floor and going along with his favorite pizza order. "So, what was that about today's plan?"

"Master bedroom is an outdated term of dubious origins," he explained as he chopped the lone potato and onion from the fridge. "But that suite is what needs our attention. Because right now, you're staying in a room that seriously has baseball posters so old the stars can now collect social security."

"Hey, now." I made an indignant noise. "And you looked in my room?"

"Wallace followed me down the stairs from the third floor, so I went around shutting doors on the second." Knox gestured with the spatula as he dumped the potato and onion into the heated skillet. "Your door was wide open. I didn't go in. I just closed the door for you so Wallace wouldn't get any ideas."

"Ah. Thank you."

"No problem." Knox stirred the skillet with a casual offhandedness that was rather sexy. After years of chow halls and officer clubs, a guy who could cook was a novelty. "Anyway, you, my friend, are sleeping in a twin bed."

"It's temporary." I couldn't deny that my old room was small. It was an interesting shape with dormer windows and a built-in desk, but the narrow bed was a definite detractor.

"Staying in the primary suite would also be temporary, but at least you'd be comfortable in a realtor-ready space. Better for the psyche than being among your high-school stuff. Trust me, I know."

"This is true." I nodded as I poured us each a cup of coffee. "Probably better for my back too. If we can do something about the explosion of pink currently in there, I suppose I could switch."

The main bedroom was also marginally farther from the stairs to the third floor, but I didn't need to point that out. Not like I'd lain awake last night calculating the exact number of steps to where Knox lay in the daybed.

"Excellent." Knox grinned like I was giving him permission for an amusement park ride, not agreeing to a ton of work. "I told Frank and Leon I'd work here today because I'm helping Measure Twice on a garage remodel Thursday and Friday. Drywall. Can't wait to get muddy. But today, let's strip."

"Excuse me?"

"Wallpaper." He rolled his eyes at me as he deftly cracked the eggs into the skillet. "From what I could see from the hallway, that wallpaper must go. We'll clear the room, investigate what furniture can stay, and prep for painting this weekend."

"Sounds like a plan." As soon as I said it, I couldn't help but laugh loudly enough that Knox turned his attention away from his skillet. "Sorry. It's just that you make this seem so much more manageable than it was even two days ago."

"One room at a time, Monroe. Just take it one room at a time."

"I'm trying. I'm used to big projects with finite deadlines and concrete steps. This has felt like an ever-growing hydra."

"I can provide the steps. We'll slay the hydra." Knox's cocky confidence was utterly infectious. "You provide the muscle."

"I think you're doing fine for muscle," I said before I could think better of sharing the compliment aloud.

"Why, thank you." Spatula in hand, he flexed his biceps. "But four hands are always preferable to two. Or one for that matter." He waggled his right fingers, making his meaning that much more obvious.

"Damn it. I walked into that one." My groan was softened by the arrival of a steaming plate of potatoes and eggs. "Thank you."

"Hope you're hungry." He winked at me, and I *so* was hungry. Famished. Starved. But not only for food. I dug in, and so did he. In short order, we were done with breakfast and heading upstairs, and Knox was back to bouncing with excitement.

"Come on. Let's go see what we're working with." Loaded with empty boxes and trash bags, Knox strode toward the main suite, throwing the heavy wood door open. "I only peeked in."

"Pink. We're working with pink. Aunt Henri really, really liked this peachy-pink shade." The peach wallpaper, peachy-pink satin bed cover, gauzy window coverings, and shelves of knickknacks seemed even more garish in the morning light with Knox beside me. "And empty perfume bottles."

"Those are collectibles." Knox gave an airy wave of his hand. "The donation place will know if they're worth anything. Same with the creepy dolls."

He pointed at one of the shelves in the corner of the room, lined with Victorian-style dolls with vacant expressions and fancy dresses.

"They are creepy, aren't they?" Like most things in the house, the faint layer of dust added to the haunted-house vibe, like we were one spooky encounter away from a bad teen flick.

"Yup. The triplets have some cute dolls, but those are just spooky. People will collect anything, I guess." His pragmatic tone made him sound older than twenty-three. His maturity was one of his most attractive—and tempting—traits. "I've done enough renovations to know everyone collects something."

"Not me."

"Ha." He made quick work of stripping the bedding from the queen-size bed. "Even you, Lieutenant. Come on. Tell."

"I've had too many moves for much collecting." Frowning, I tried to think as fancifully as Knox naturally seemed to. "I don't date enough to collect broken hearts. Had some baseball cards as a kid but never stuck with it. Takeout menus don't count. And fortunes don't either."

"Fortunes?" He finished bagging up the bedding and gave me a pleading look.

And damn it, his puppy-dog eyes worked. I fished my wallet from my back pocket and showed my small stack of white papers, which testified to my Kung Pao chicken addiction. "I like Chinese takeout. And it's silly, but I keep my favorite fortunes."

"I love it." Knox smiled like my little quirk was brilliant, and hell if I didn't love his praise. "I collect playlists, but that's digital. And art supplies, obviously. Too many old Lego sets I can't let go of. And it's a good thing I don't have a house this big, or I'd collect pets. But my weirdest collection is flat pennies."

"Wait. Like the smashed ones from tourist traps?" Still holding my wallet, I flipped open the coin pocket and revealed a couple of flattened coins. "These are from a couple of family trips. Good luck charms, I guess."

"Yup. Mine too." Knox's grin transformed into something warmer, more like a shared secret. "We might even have some of the same ones. That's cool."

"It is." Having something in common, even a minor thing like collectible pennies, made the gulf between us seem far narrower than at Rob's barbeque when I'd felt nine hundred to Knox's fresh-faced twenty-three.

"Okay, that's the last of the linens." He moved over to the small bookshelf next to the bed. "Oh, nice. Aunt Henri was a reader."

"Yeah, mysteries and British cozies. She used to read on the nights she didn't watch TV crime dramas." I cleared all the creepy dolls in one swoop into a box.

"These aren't cozies." Shaking his head impishly, Knox held up a stack of what could only be termed bodice rippers —long-haired heroes holding half-dressed heroines in close cinches. "I love your aunt more and more. She was one cool old lady."

I gulped. "I'm almost scared of what else we might find."

"Maybe you should turn around while I do the night-stand." Voice merry, he motioned for me to spin.

"What do you think you'll find?" I couldn't help my alarmed tone.

"Turn. You can't unsee some things." He could be plenty commanding when he wanted, so I obeyed, facing the far window until he exhaled hard. "Okay. We're safe. No ancient personal items, promise. More books though. Three with barbarians in the title. And two sapphic anthologies."

"Sapphic?" I blinked rapidly, trying to line up my memories of Aunt Henri with all the new revelations. It was rapidly becoming apparent that I hadn't known her well at all, and that was a damn shame. And my own fault, all the years I'd spent away and in sporadic contact. But she'd been so much more than her sharp voice, steel-gray short hair, and smart sweater sets. And more than her eccentricities too. My chest panged for all I hadn't seen when she'd been alive.

"Oh, and there's a pic," Knox added.

Pulse strangely erratic, I crossed to peer down at a much younger Aunt Henri with her arm around a shorter, plumper woman with paint smears on her face and arms holding a dripping brush, affectionate look on both their faces.

"Yeah, that's Aunt Henri. And that must be her cousin. They don't look much alike, do they?" Aunt Henri looked a lot like me—pencil-straight hair, long lean limbs, high cheekbones, narrow nose, and defined lips. The cousin had wild, frizzy hair, elfin features, a squat build, and freckled skin.

Knox's eyes narrowed. "You certain they were blood-related?"

"Distantly, I think? I never entirely understood their roommate arrangement. Henri and my grandmother grew up here, then Henri took care of their elderly parents when my grandmother moved away. Henri never married. The cousin turned up at some point, took over the attic, I guess."

"Uh-huh." Knox adopted an arch tone like I was the naive one.

"What? Are you suspecting there's a mystery there?"

"You kiss any of your cousins?" He revealed a strip of photo booth pictures, one featuring them kissing in a distinctly non-familial way.

"Wow." My voice came out all weak.

"You're the investigator, not me, but I think her life is

65

fascinating." Knox moved to box up the empty perfume bottles.

"She never said anything to me." I replayed my memories, looking back with adult eyes and decades of investigative experience. She'd favored mystery dramas with female sleuths, never wore skirts, was happier with cats than humans, and had misty eyes when discussing "Dear Florence," the long-lost cousin. Should I have suspected? "Hmmm. One time, on the phone, she was teasing me about girls chasing navy officers, and I told her there wasn't a missus in my future. I'd come out to a number of people at that point but not her. And she laughed, said that was fine, and there was no mister for her either. And that was that. But you think she meant...?"

"Maybe." Knox looked at the picture again before gently laying it in the box he'd labeled KEEP. "It's neat that she was cool about you regardless. It's hard to predict with older people."

"Oh, she could certainly be cool in her own way. And she likely knew something before the conversation, honestly. I kept quiet in high school but not silent."

"Like my mom and how she was always bi." Knox added one of the barbarian books to the keep box with a cheeky grin.

"Petra? Yeah, I suppose I wasn't shocked when I heard she married Candace. Probably her agreeing to go to homecoming with Rob was the bigger shocker." I wasn't sure I should admit that to Knox, but he laughed.

"Ha. She's said as much over the years. I took a guy to my first dance. Funny how much has changed in only a couple of years."

"More than a couple." The earlier bonding over the

pennies seemed further away than a matter of minutes. A sour taste coated the back of my throat.

"Quit trying to paint yourself as ready for assisted living." Knox rolled his eyes. "We both know my folks had me super young. They were only kids themselves. My friend X-ray dated a thirty-eight-year-old last year. Another friend has a forty-two-year-old guy. Forty is the new gay twenty."

"Hardly."

"Says the guy who had his tongue—"

I cut him off with a long groan. "Don't remind me."

"Fine. Fine. Let's gather the wallpaper-stripping supplies, and I'll get my portable speaker from upstairs. We can listen to music while we strip." He had another enticing smile for me.

While talking was dangerous because I was coming to appreciate Knox as someone I truly enjoyed being around, music proved even more deadly over the next hour or two. Knox twerked around the room to a wicked club mix, scoring both wallpaper and my self-restraint.

"Knox." I made a pained noise as he did things with his glutes that were probably illegal in six states. "You're dancing again."

"So I am. It's a good song." Shrugging, he kept right on dancing, this time closer to me. I could smell him, warm and sexy, putting me right there back in the club, wanting him more than air. He beckoned me forward. "Come on. Dance with me."

Chapter Nine

Knox

"Come on." Winking at Monroe, I kept my voice light, but I wouldn't ask again. I'd promised not to go for the hard sell, and as much as I wanted to dance with him in the summer sunshine in this big empty bedroom, I wasn't going to beg.

I fully expected him to turn me down flat and was bracing myself for the inevitable brush-off when he stepped forward. Maybe the song was more magical than I'd thought.

"Maybe a dance break won't hurt," he said so softly I strained to hear him. "Just one dance."

"Aye, aye, Lieutenant." I chuckled because I was down with whatever he needed to convince himself. For all our differences, we shared surprisingly similar musical tastes and had easily agreed on a playlist. Monroe moved like he and the music were in spiritual communion, as though he truly enjoyed dancing for the sake of dancing. Of course, he'd needed a little coaxing to let go, but once he started moving, he quickly found a rhythm, body undulating like he'd physically melded with the tune.

No awkward swaying or shuffling from him. His sultry movements kept a healthy distance between us, but there was a clear invitation there, a seductive give and take as we moved closer. Slowly, we morphed from dancing near and around each other to dancing together, bodies brushing, hands tangling, the scent of his shampoo overpowering the dust we'd stirred up while clearing the room. He filled my every sense—clean scent, warm skin, the rasp of his khaki shorts against mine, the soft cotton of his gray T-shirt, his strong grip when his hands finally found my hips.

"Damn. The way you move." He made a noise like he wasn't sure whether to be pleased or annoyed at how well we fit together.

"You're not so bad yourself, old man." Tone teasing, I met his gaze, letting him know I saw him as anything but old right then.

"Old, huh?" He pulled me snugger against him, and I adjusted to the closer grind with a happy sound. He made me feel closer to flying than dancing, high on him and the song. I'd always loved dancing, but he took it to the next level. Forget one song, I wanted to keep dancing until the stars came out, wanted all future work breaks to involve moving with this man exactly like this.

Accordingly, when the first song shifted to the next, I held him tighter, distracting him with more deliberate bumps of my hips until we were both hard and panting from the exquisite friction. We rocked together in time to the music, which moved through us, carrying us higher until he pressed me against the nearest wall, tripping over the scattered supplies on the floor. But I couldn't care less about our remodeling work. All I wanted was to get closer. And closer. And closer still.

"Oh my god, this is madness." His breath came in little huffs against my neck before he licked me there. He used his tongue to trace the cord that ran past my Adam's apple, stopping to tease the line where my scruff started.

"Yup." I tilted my head to give him better access. "Let's go crazy together."

"You make me forget every damn thing." He groaned but kept grinding against me, hard cock pushing insistently at mine through our shorts.

"Good." I gasped as he kissed right below my ear. "Nothing else matters. Only this. Right here. Right now."

"Yes." Monroe shuddered against me. "This. Just this. Need it."

"Me too." I stroked his strong back, mashing our torsos together, close enough to put delicious pressure on my nipple ring. "Need you. Been a long damn time."

"You? *Rebound*?" He scoffed and lightly bit my earlobe, the sting gentling his words.

"What? I can't have dry spells too? Maybe I'm getting pickier in my old age. Wiser too."

"Mm-hmm." He did magical things with his tongue along the shell of my ear, sending sparks darting down my neck.

"Maybe we both need this." I palmed his ass, making us both moan.

"Yes. God. Yes." Eyes fluttering shut, he inhaled. And as he exhaled, he sagged against me, finally fully giving in. The tension left his back and ass as his mouth went slack. His grip on me loosened, more trusting. Not like I was going anywhere, not with his mouth headed right for mine.

And apparently, every damn kiss with this man was

destined to be pizza-oven hot. No little warm-up or teasing brushes of his lips. *Need.* Pure, combustible lust and need sparking, making us kiss like ravenous beasts. Like we'd never had it and never would again, so we needed to gorge on each other.

I feasted on his mouth, loving the effortlessness of kissing him. Like with dancing, we fit together, taking turns leading and following until the kiss had a life of its own, dragging us both along for the ride. Monroe sucked on my tongue like he was starving for my cock, but hell if I could stop kissing him long enough for anything else. This endless kissing was both too much and not enough and everything in between.

We were on a collision course with a climax, and every time he thrust against me, my cock pulsed so hard it hurt.

"Need." I wedged a hand between us, desperate to touch him.

"Yeah. That." We shoved our shorts down, but before I could jack him, he pushed me back against the wall, thrusting hard against my belly. Our cocks rubbed together, warm skin meeting for the first time, making us gasp and moan.

"Fuck." I met him thrust for thrust, grinding myself against him in time with the music. We had our own pulsing beat, one I'd be hearing in my memories forever. He swallowed my every moan, kissing me with an intensity that seared those same memories into my brain. *Bruise me. Mark me.* I wanted it all, every needy suck and bite, every greedy thrust. I loved how fucking ravenous he was for it, and it only served to make me that much hungrier.

"So close." Monroe grimaced, face contorting with the effort of holding his orgasm back.

"Do it. Now," I ordered, yanking him even more forcefully against me. Holding back was the last thing I wanted. Rather, I needed every damn thing he had to give me. His cock painted a damp stripe on my stomach, and still, I wanted more. "Come on."

"Kiss me." Monroe's voice was ragged, and I was powerless to do anything other than comply, devouring his mouth with a ferocity that surprised even me. I sucked on his tongue and rubbed his ass. My abs tightened, hamstrings straining, every muscle waiting. And then he broke, thrusting fast and hard against me, dragging me along for the ride. "Oh fuck. There. Right there."

"Me too. Me too." And what a ride it was, like catching air off the biggest ramp at the skate park, that feeling of badass triumph and near-flight and reckless energy all rolled together, and I never wanted to come down.

However, Monroe was already stepping back, mouth twisting. "Fuck. Fuck. We—"

Still feeling tingles in my hands and feet, I groaned. "Can't you have thirty seconds of afterglow before the we-shouldn't-have-done-that speech?"

"I was going to say we're a total mess. But yes, that too. Hell, Knox. We can't let that happen again."

"Why not?" Having had the barest of tastes, I wanted the whole damn buffet, every hour I could wring from this most confounding man. "Despite what you keep insisting, we're both consenting adults, rooming together for the summer, and who the fuck cares what we get up to here? Neither of us is looking for forever. Why not have some summer fun?"

"*Because.*" Stripping off his T-shirt, Monroe mopped at his come-spattered stomach. And damn, he had one fine chest. Fit. Lightly hairy. Perfection. And I'd happily tell him if he'd stop listing all the reasons we weren't already onto a second helping of orgasms. "Your dad. My friends. It's complicated."

"You've never done anything on the down-low before?" I gave him a pointed look because he'd previously mentioned Don't Ask, Don't Tell, and for a guy who didn't do relationships, he had to have had his share of secret hookups.

"You know I have. And I hated it. Hated hiding. I'm not..." He paced away, then spun on his heel to stare at me, eyes heated but mouth tense. "*Hell.* You look all fucked out, and all I can think is how I want you again."

"So?" I smiled but kept my tone bored. I was tired of all his reasons. Anything as good as what we'd done needed dozens of repeats, not excuses. "Have me."

"It's not that easy." He made a noise that echoed my own. Damn it. Even our frustration was in sync. "I...need to clean up. And think. Mainly that."

"Okay." I shrugged. I'd said I wouldn't beg, and I was going to stick to that. Either he'd come around, or he'd keep throwing up barriers. Regardless, he had to make his own choices. I'd deal no matter what, but I sure hoped he'd get out of his own way while we still had time to make it the best damn summer of both our lives.

"I...um. I'll figure out some late lunch for us. Might have to run to the store." Still clutching his shirt, Monroe backed toward the open door. "I'm sorry."

Funny. The excuses didn't faze me, but the apology *hurt*, landing square on some tender spot in my chest. I didn't want him to be sorry. I wanted him warm and willing and desperate for more. Nothing had ever felt as good as dancing and making out with Monroe had, and it was the

73

kind of wonderful I refused to apologize for. I'd kissed and danced plenty, but the kind of connection I'd found in his arms was rare indeed. Sorry felt like the worst kind of brush-off, and as he retreated down the long upstairs hall toward his room, I both wanted him to stay gone a good long while and to come racing back. Fuck. I truly was a mess.

Chapter Ten

Knox

"You need to eat." Monroe strode into the primary bedroom, where I'd stripped off the last of the wallpaper and was working on wall prep and priming. The walls were in poor condition after years of wallpaper, so the primer was necessary. And, as usual, I'd gotten into a groove working. I supposed it was past dinner time, but I was still surprised by Monroe holding a plate of steaming food.

"What's this?" I gestured at the plate, but I meant him. He'd been scarce all afternoon since our little dance-party orgasm fest. And now he was back, neatly pressed short-sleeve shirt, jeans in far better shape than any I owned, and loafers rather than sneakers. I had no idea how to interpret the food gesture, and confusion made my voice sharp. "You made me dinner?"

"Well, to be fair, the pork chops came in a package of two. It's rather basic. Pan-seared chops. Rice. Broccoli." Monroe looked downright sheepish as he passed over the plate. His gaze kept flitting about like I might seriously reject his offering. I wasn't sure when someone had last cooked specifically for me, and while I was sure the bribe was intended as a peace offering, I wasn't going to toss it at the wall. "I'm a pretty novice cook, to be honest. Far better sous chef than chef, but you've been up here for hours. You need to eat."

"I like cooking. Mom and Candace were gone enough that I got decent at it, then when the triplets came, I did a fair bit of cooking for Dad and Jessica. I can't do much fancy, but I know a bunch of stir fry variations and pasta dishes."

"I got pasta at the store too. And some of the beer you liked the other night. You're welcome to any of the food I brought in."

"You got groceries?" I had been so deep in the zone, stripping wallpaper, that I hadn't registered him leaving. And dinner plus beer? Monroe had to be feeling crazy guilty over what had happened earlier.

"The presence of fresh vegetables on the plate didn't give me away?" He laughed a little too loud. "Yeah, I did a quick run to the store. Earlier."

"Earlier." I drew the word out, layered it with all my vivid memories of our wall-thumping encounter. I glanced over at the speaker. I'd moved from dance music to dreamy alternative tracks, channeling my overly emotional state of mind.

"Look, I know things are awkward..."

"They don't have to be." After giving him a pointed stare, I took a bite of food to show I appreciated his gesture and distract myself from reaching for him.

"Can we at least try being roommates? Friends?" Monroe's smile looked far closer to a grimace. I made a scoffing noise because we both knew that friendship was the barest tip of what we both wanted.

"You really don't want a second helping of that titanic orgasm?" I asked as I scooped up some rice. It was either eat or try to kiss some sense into Monroe.

"I want to be friends more." He was lying through his perfectly white teeth, and I'd had enough of his martyr routine.

"Grab a roller." I pointed at the pan of primer I'd left on the floor, paint rollers on a plastic drop cloth nearby.

"What?" His eyes went wide and startled like I was asking him for a dirty favor. Not that I wasn't sorely tempted, but I'd said all along I wouldn't go for the hard sell, and I meant it.

"If we're friends, I'm going to put you to work while I eat." I settled my ass on the ladder in the corner.

"Okay." Monroe headed to the primer, and damn if his ease with taking orders wasn't one of the sexiest things about him. I loved that, for all he appeared to be a stereotypical military alpha male, he seemed to have zero interest in posturing or being bossy only to prove a point. "I'm ashamed to admit I haven't painted before."

"Long, firm, even strokes, Monroe. Long, firm, even strokes." I winked at him.

He groaned and laughed at the same time. "I guess I walked right into that."

"You did." I grinned at him. "You should take your shirt off."

"Knox."

I held up my hand, the picture of innocence. "Because it's a nice shirt, and you don't want to ruin it. Paint tip number two: drips happen."

"Oh. Yeah. Be right back." Adorably, Monroe skedaddled from the room as if showing me his bare chest was somehow more scandalous than grinding together earlier. Or like I couldn't be trusted to not jump him if I spied nipples and chest fuzz. He returned a minute or so later in an older shirt advertising a charity 10k run in DC.

I had to chuckle at the mirrored ball and eighties font on the front of the shirt. "You did a disco-themed 10k run?"

"It was for a good cause." Monroe's tone was between embarrassed and defensive as he started rolling primer onto the bare part of the wall. "And I like music."

The memory of how well we danced together hung heavy between us, a potent crackly energy I could have exploited. But I was good and didn't even flirt. "Me too. I pretty much always have an internal soundtrack going."

"I've noticed. It's cute." That crackly energy turned warm and welcoming. For all Monroe kept insisting we were roommates and friends, he sure looked at me with the same fondness lacing his words. "For me, it's less an internal soundtrack and more that certain moments trigger musical memories. And vice versa."

"Oh, that too. Any time I hear this one hip-hop NBA jam, I remember the first time I met Candace, my mom's wife. And there's this sappy country love song from Dad and Jessica's wedding. Other times, I smell coffee, and this jingle comes into my head."

Monroe hummed the iconic morning wakeup-ad tune, but given all the various brands of coffee, it was rather remarkable he hit the right one on the first try.

"That's the one. How did you know?"

"That ad campaign has been around since *my* childhood, and my mom used to hum all the time. Commercials. TV theme songs. Cheesy kid songs. Certain tunes will always take me right back to her in the kitchen, humming while washing dishes or making brownies. She made great brownies." His tone turned distant, and my heart twisted. Damn it. I was good with Monroe turning me on. And okay, in theory, with us being friends, but I didn't want to care. But every time we hung out in the same space, every story he shared, and every sentimental look that crossed his face all increased the risk he posed to my feels.

"She sounds pretty wonderful."

"She was." Monroe quirked his mouth, and damn it, here came more of those feels. "I wish..."

"Go on." Apparently, I was actively courting the same emotional attachment I should be running from. Monroe wanted to be friends, and even that might be a stretch, an offer born of awkward post-orgasm guilt.

"It's silly, but I wish I could go back and ask her what she knew about Aunt Henri and hear her stories about Aunt Henri and the so-called cousin. I know Mom was Aunt Henri's favorite niece, but I was too young to ask many questions. Sometimes I wonder about all the stories I missed out on."

Well, that did it. Unwanted feelings cascaded over me, sure as a can of paint and equally hard to clean up. There was only one thing to do. Leaving my empty plate on the ladder, I crossed the room to hug a very startled Monroe from behind. I ended up with a smear of primer on my arm, but hell if I cared.

"Don't look shocked." My voice came out too gruff. "We're friends. Friends hug."

"Thank you." To my utter amazement, he leaned into the hug. "I've talked about Mom more today than in years."

"Tell me more." I released him rather than push my luck. "It's not the stories you never got to hear. It's the ones you get to keep and share."

Monroe's face scrunched up with concentration. "She gave me my first flattened penny. Cross-country drive from one base in California to another duty station in Florida. Dad had to report earlier, so it was just the two of us in our old station wagon. Cliché oldies on the whole trip. When I hear certain songs play, I swear I can smell truck exhaust, and my skin gets sticky like summer in Texas with poor air conditioning."

"I like her already." I gave him an encouraging smile. I wanted every damn story he was willing to share. "So, she liked blue, the oldies, and was brave enough to drive alone with her kid to a new state. What else?"

"She didn't like chicken. Never met a berry she didn't love. And we probably tried most of the ice cream places along our trek that summer. She loved strawberry ice cream, but she'd let me get whatever wacky flavor I wanted."

"Dessert." After slapping my thigh, I started cleaning up the wallpaper and painting mess.

"Pardon?" Monroe was so darn cute when he was confused. And I loved that he didn't cover his confusion with bravado like so many men would.

"I'm taking you for dessert." I squeezed his shoulder as I passed him. "Finish that section, then we're going to Dairy Mart on the other side of town. It's June. One of the specials is strawberry shortcake-flavored ice cream."

"Aunt Henri loved that one too." Monroe's tongue darted out as if he could taste a decades-old flavor. And damn, I wanted to kiss him again. Instead, I busied myself with getting rollers ready to clean as he continued, "Guess she and Mom had that in common. Wonder if they still have that fluffernutter flavor—the banana-peanut butter-marsh-mallow one."

"Only one way to find out." I grinned at him. "First scoop is on me."

"I should change shirts." Nose wrinkling, he looked down at his T-shirt. "Funny. I'd forgotten, but Mom was always casual: T-shirts and shorts and sundresses. But after she died, my dad made a point that I looked neat and clean, especially if I was leaving the house. Couldn't risk people gossiping that we weren't coping."

"You lost your mom. You could have worn the same shirt for a month, and people would have forgiven you."

"Possibly." He shrugged. "But my dad was a huge believer in appearances and routine. Showers. Laundry day. Fresh clothes. Anything to keep grief at bay."

"Well, I think your shirt is perfect as is." I kept my tone light, but inside, my internal soundtrack had shifted to a ballad about hopeless crushes. The shirt wasn't the only thing perfect. Monroe, with his ease of following directions, tender heart, and wounded soul, was catnip for my inner caretaker. I did favors for everyone, took care of all those I held close, but the one thing I truly wanted for myself was Monroe. I might be younger, but I wanted to wrap him up, keep him safe. Damn it. Being friends was going to do me in.

Chapter Eleven

Monroe

I could pound out miles in a grueling run. I could prime acres of bedroom walls. But try as I might, I couldn't outrun the memory of Knox and me dancing, grinding, *coming,* the hottest climax of my life. We'd been clothed, and the entire encounter had lasted only a couple of songs, but it had seared my soul.

Thus distracted, I arrived at the weekly trivia night at Harbor's Edge, the sports bar-style tavern downtown across from a bank and on the same street with some other small eateries.

"So...how's the roomie?" Holden greeted me with a grin, rolling to the side to let me in so I could claim a chair at our usual round table. Funny how I hadn't been back that long, yet I already had a regular spot at the table. Holden and Sam had recruited me during my first visit to Blessed Bean because they'd recently lost a few trivia team members.

"Fine." I signaled a passing waitress for the microbrew lager I favored.

"No wild parties yet?" Holden was having way too much fun with the teasing, waggling his eyebrows before sipping his pale ale.

"Nope."

"What's with the shifty eyes?" Holden tilted his head as he passed me the basket of fried pickles from the center of the table. We'd split a few different appetizers over the course of the evening, settling up at the end. "Did you catch him with weed or something and don't want to tell Rob?"

"Nah. It's not that. He's a good...person." Damn it. I hadn't meant to pause there, mentally reframing Knox from *kid* to *man* and dialing it back to *person*. But that brief hesitation gave Holden more than ample opportunity for more ribbing.

"Oh my god, you like him."

"Holden." Sam hurried in, still in a Blessed Bean T-shirt, nabbing the seat next to me right as the waitress returned with my beer and an iced tea for Holden. "Perhaps he meant Knox is a good person, full stop. Not everything has a want-to-get-in-his-pants subtext."

"Thank you, Sam. A vote for sanity." I saluted him with my drink. Sam regarded me with quietly speculative eyes like he saw far more than he was letting on.

But he'd succeeded in tamping Holden down, and for that, I was grateful. We put an order in for cheese sticks, Buffalo-style cauliflower, and honey hot wings before the emcee started the quiz game. It didn't take long for us to fall behind in the standings, thanks to a spate of questions all relating to various professional basketball stats.

"Darn it." Holden groaned as the electronic leaderboard updated to show us in last place after the emcee announced a ten-minute break before the next round. "We really need a sports trivia person."

"Knox likes basketball," I shared absently before I could think better of it.

"Does he now?" Holden sounded more than ready to resume his earlier teasing.

"You should bring him around." Sam made the offhand suggestion with an easy tone as he nabbed another cheese stick.

"I don't think so." My voice came out too sharp.

"What?" Holden scoffed. "He can drink. And we need more warm bodies."

"You can socialize with Knox," Sam said to me, far gentler than Holden. "It's okay."

"Maybe." After taking a bracing sip of beer, I deliberately tried for a change of topics, turning toward Holden. "So, when do you want to record the podcast? I've been thinking about the Stapleton case more. It's a good one to explore, and not only because of the Worth connection. So many early missteps in how it was handled."

"Yep. A good example for the need to approach every investigation seriously." Holden stretched his heavily muscled arms over his head. "The initial theory was she'd taken off after a domestic argument with the assumption that she'd be back soon. But the lack of a money trail has always made me doubt that explanation."

"A lot of the first interviews were also sorely lacking." I shook my head. "I'm supposed to go to a wedding in California later this month. I might try to look up Worth, get his perspective."

"That's a good idea. Doubt he'll talk, but might as well try."

"I know I was younger that summer, but they went to our church." Sam's cheeks were surprisingly pink, and his words came more quickly than usual as if speaking fast would stop us from remembering how he'd followed Worth around.

"And you had a monster teenage crush." Holden laughed, but his voice was kinder than when teasing me.

"Maybe." Sam's full lips thinned to a narrow line. "But the family always seemed happy. Which is no guarantee, but I've never bought the theory the husband killed her and hid the body."

"Statistically—" Holden started, but now it was Sam's turn to groan.

"Yes, Professor. We know. But I prefer to give people the benefit of the doubt. Some marriages are actually happy."

"Not many." I tried for a pragmatic tone, but all the divorces, remarriages, and divorces again I'd seen over twenty years in the navy gave my voice a bitter edge. "God, I'm not sure why anyone tries a long-term relationship. Even the happy ones always have cracks."

"Cynical much?" Holden rolled his eyes, but Sam took on a more thoughtful expression.

"Maybe some couples truly are in love. Touch. Support. Connection. Those are legitimate human needs."

"Maybe." Unbidden, an image of Knox beckoning me to dance popped into my head. I'd never thought of myself as touch-starved or the sort of person who needed that intense spark of connection, but then there he was, and there we were, and all I could feel was *need* on some fundamentally primal level.

Our trivia team lost again in the second round, and as we headed out into the cool summer evening, I kept coming back to that need. Want was easy and simple. I'd wanted Knox from the first moment I'd seen him standing in the club, but need was messy and complicated, something I'd always tried to avoid. Need was the precursor to hurt every time.

But as I climbed the porch steps at Aunt Henri's house, my pulse quickened. Knox's little compact was in the driveway. The scent of something Italian—saucy and cheesy—greeted me, but the kitchen was empty, dishes neatly stacked in the drainer, counters wiped, the remnants of a pasta dish in the fridge, and a very irritated cat perched on the breakfast nook table.

Meow. Meow. Rawr. Wallace did an excellent impression of a pissed-off bobcat, with vocal complaints and restless pacing.

"What's the matter, kitty? Hungry?" I checked the cabinets, which held more people food than the day before, but no cat chow or cans. Knox must have taken the cat-feeding supplies up to the third floor.

"Knox?" I called out, but there was no reply.

Meow. Meow. The cat was increasingly desperate, marching to the back stairs, looking back over his broad feline shoulders to ensure I was following.

Hmm. Was something wrong? I took the steps faster, calling out again, only to be met with more silence. No Knox anywhere on the second floor, including the main bedroom suite, but the priming I'd spent all afternoon on was finished, brushes washed and supplies in organized piles.

Fine. I supposed I had no choice but to investigate the third floor.

"Knox?" I yelled at the base of the stairs. No answer. Wallace zoomed ahead, making more angry meows. But his feline pleas didn't reveal Knox. The daybed was carefully made with a colorful comforter I hadn't seen before. A biography of Frida Kahlo lay near the pillow and a stack of sketchbooks sat on the drawing table, one of which was open to a photo-realistic drawing of Wallace lounging on the daybed while another showcased an impressive free-hand floor plan of this house. Despite Wallace's continued complaints, two bowls full of water and cat chow were placed on a woven mat in the corner.

Huh. Feeling slightly ridiculous, I peeked into the bath-room and opened the little closets tucked under the eaves. No Knox. Maybe he'd gone out, a thought that unsettled me. He'd said he wouldn't hook up *here*. But what about elsewhere? Bah. He was a grown adult, something I kept wanting to ignore, and if he wanted to go out by foot or in someone else's car, that was his business. I hated the way my abs clenched like I had any claim to Knox and his time.

I was about to head back downstairs when I saw a shadow outside the largest of the attic windows, the one with a narrow mock balcony.

"Knox?" I raised the cracked window.

"Lieutenant Butter." He lay on his back, looking up at the glittering night sky. "How'd you find me?"

"Your cat misses you," I said, like that justified barging into his room.

"I'm sure he does." Wiggling slightly, Knox adjusted his position, but he kept his gaze on the sky, not me. "He wanted to come out here, but it's not safe for him."

"I'm not sure it's safe for you either."

"I'm fine. This section of the roof is plenty sturdy. I won't lean against the railing, but the view is worth the minor risk." His voice had an off quality about it, too mechanical, too flat, too dismissive, too *something*.

"What's wrong?"

"You mean other than the hot guy I made out with yesterday doing his level best to avoid me?"

Oops. Apparently, my efforts to be distant hadn't gone unnoticed. "Sorry. I...I'm not trying to be rude."

"Oh?"

"Guess I failed there. I'm sorry. You deserve—"

"I am so over hearing about what I deserve. I deserve someone my own age. I deserve time to have fun and explore. Getting warmer?"

He was dead-on, and he likely knew it. "Sorry."

"It's not only you. Everyone has opinions. I deserve one of the best architecture schools in the country. I deserve a well-paying career, a life in some big city, a suit-and-tie job in a high-rise, paid-off student loans, a nice car. I'm too smart, too talented, too...everything for anything less."

I was going to regret this later, of that I was certain, but nevertheless, I climbed through the window, praying the roof ledge could hold us both. I couldn't ignore the pain in his voice, the tension in his body, the way his fists were balled and his heels dug into the roof. He needed a friend, the one thing I absolutely couldn't be for him, and still, I clambered onto the balcony.

"Wanna talk about it?"

Chapter Twelve

Knox

"Not sure there's much to talk about." I wasn't about to send Monroe back inside, but I also wasn't sure I wanted to unload the messy toolbox that was my brain right then, a random collection of screws and bolts and competing wants and wishes.

"Stars sure are pretty." Monroe stretched his arms overhead as he settled next to me on the narrow balcony. "The sky always seems so much more vibrant in Safe Harbor than elsewhere."

"If you think this is good, I need to take you camping." I didn't have to work to make my voice warm. Monroe earned major points by not forcing me to talk about what was actually bothering me. "Middle of nowhere, like out in central Oregon. The stars make this glittery canopy. It's pretty awesome. I could look at the sky for hours, soaking in the quiet and stillness."

"Yeah." He shifted his legs, voice sounding vaguely aroused like he was picturing us on said camping trip. "The navy sent me to some pretty remote locations. The night sky was one of the few bonuses."

"What's your north star?" I rolled slightly toward him so we were face-to-face. "The thing that never fails to make you feel at home?"

"Not sure I've ever had that." The wistfulness in Monroe's tone made my chest tighten. Not sure what it was, but Monroe plus emotion, like when he talked about his mom, was going to be my utter downfall.

"That's a shame. Mine is this town. I pass the *Welcome to Safe Harbor* sign, and I know I'm home." I had to stop and swallow hard, emotions rising. A muscle worked in my jaw, the same as whenever I tried to put into words what Safe Harbor meant to me. "And when I'm away, the sky always seems to point me back here."

"Is that what you're worried about?" Monroe asked gently. "Being too far away on the East Coast?"

"That's part of it, yeah." Because he hadn't pushed, instead easing into the topic, I rewarded him with a piece of my truth. "With Dad and Jessica's new baby coming, the kid might be walking or at least crawling before I make it back to visit. The town itself changes more slowly, but things are still different every time I go away and come back."

"Why not go to an architecture program closer?" His tone was the type of reasonable that had me groaning.

"It's not that easy. Ever since high school, I've heard how talented I am, how I deserve a shot at the best programs, almost all of which are out east. Want to work for one of the best firms? Design the biggest, best buildings? Better go to one of the best schools."

"You *are* super talented. I've only seen a couple of your sketches and listened to you talk art, and I can already tell that much. But I also know a little something about expectations." Monroe's mouth twisted, light from my room behind us giving him an otherworldly glow.

"Oh?"

"I come from a military family. My dad, my uncles, my grandfather, a couple of great-uncles too. A long history of naval service. And because I got good grades, the whole family started talking about if I could get into the academy, go in as an officer rather than enlisted."

"No one asked your opinion." I didn't bother making it a question because I knew the answer all too well.

"Nah. It was simply assumed. Rebelling would have been going to West Point instead of Annapolis. And at the time, way back in the dark ages, I wasn't out to my dad, and I was reluctant to use my sexuality as a reason not to go."

"Makes sense. Sometimes it's just easier to go along with others' plans." I sighed heavily, both out of personal experience and empathy for Monroe's younger self, trapped by so many competing forces. "But what would you have done after high school if you could have done anything?"

"Not sure. English seemed intriguing, the idea of reading literature all day. I always liked to write, but everyone said there was no security in being an author. Well, everyone other than Aunt Henri. She'd tell me I'd be a great thriller writer because I always solved the TV murders faster than her. But everyone else was down on the idea. Even so, I had a couple of brochures from these liberal arts colleges..." Monroe's voice drifted off, a fondness there that made me wish I had a time machine to pack him off to some ivy-covered campus. "Anyway, that life wasn't for me."

"Twenty years is a hell of a long time to do something you hate." And with those words, my own dilemma gained clarity. Did I really want to be miserable? Decades and decades of a barely-tolerable life?

"Oh, I didn't hate NCIS." Monroe's dismissive tone pushed back on my conclusion. Maybe I'd been hasty there. And heck, now I was right back to my endless internal debate. "I love investigating, finding facts, carefully piecing together events, and coming up with conclusions. But I'm not sure I would have ended up there without the familial push."

"Yeah. I get that." I rolled my shoulders against the hard roof, accidentally moving closer to Monroe. "My dad is always going on about how the community college was his only choice because of me, how they had to scrimp and save, and how lucky I am to have options."

"Options are only good if you want them," Monroe said with a sageness I felt all the way to my soul. In fact, I didn't need Monroe's wisdom. I was drowning in options, and my yearning for simpler choices had plagued me over the months since the acceptance email landed in my inbox.

"Amen."

"What do you want, Knox?" Monroe touched my upper arm, fingers brushing the bare skin at the edge of my T-shirt, contact making my skin spark like the stars above us. "Not what everyone keeps saying you deserve, but what do *you* want?"

"Frank and Leon of Measure Twice want to retire soon." I sidestepped the question to get to the heart of my dilemma. "They've offered me the chance to take over the business. It's the sort of opportunity that doesn't come along very often. An established small business, loyal clientele, operating in the black."

"Wow. But Ivy League graduate school is also a rare shot. The sort that might not come again."

"I know." I drew the *know* out into a long groan, heavily emphasizing the *ow*.

"Close your eyes," Monroe ordered, and for a second, I could totally picture him as the commanding lieutenant. "Picture ten years from now. Where are you?"

Here. Right here. With him on this roof. But, of course, I couldn't say that even if I could see it so clearly. A shiver raced up my back. Something had changed the night Monroe told me more about his mother and let me buy him silly ice cream flavors. I'd gone from wanting him in my bed to wanting him in my whole life. Apart from my never-ending lust for this man, I wanted to stay here, talking and sharing secrets. There was nothing I didn't want to know about Monroe, and if hanging out with him delayed my inevitable decision, so much the better.

But Monroe was waiting on an answer, so I took another deep breath, this one full of his ocean-scented cologne. He'd looked nice for his quiz-night outing, light-colored polo and khaki pants, but his patience was possibly his sexiest quality, the way he didn't press.

"I could be in a fancy condo, I guess. Chicago. Boston. Nice car. Maybe a hot boyfriend in advertising and a host of architecture awards on my loft's walls. Or..." Eyes still shut, I relaxed my facial muscles, letting go of all the *shoulds* and *coulds* that had defined my last few years. "Or I could be here in Safe Harbor. The triplets would be almost in high school, and the surprise baby would be the perfect age for some of the summer rec league camps. Maybe I'd volunteer to help. And Frank and Leon would be retired and holding court at the senior center. I'd drop off their groceries and tell them about the jobs we had on tap for the week. There would be some college kids on summer payroll, maybe a big job at the nice homes over on the bluffs. Plenty of gossip to share. It would be a good life."

"It would be," Monroe said so softly the words felt like a caress, a brush against my cheek. No, wait. Those were his very real fingertips ghosting down my cheek. "You paint a damn pretty picture."

"I do, don't I?" I couldn't keep the sadness out of my tone as I leaned into his touch.

And then Monroe, he of the honey-sweet voice and tender fingers, said the most seductive words I'd ever heard. "I trust you to figure it out."

"You do?" Pushing onto an elbow, we were now nose-to-nose, faces mere millimeters apart. "You're not going to tell me what to do?"

"As you seem to love telling me, you're a grown adult." His tone was as fond as the caress had been. "You don't need permission or direction. I figure you've had enough of that."

"I probably already know the answer," I admitted.

"I know." His eyes, always so expressive, were deep enough for a man to drown in. And then he kissed me, pulling me even further under his spell.

Chapter Thirteen

Monroe

I had no idea why I was kissing Knox, only that I was. Kissing him felt less voluntary and more like an order from the commanding officer in the sky, and I was a hapless recruit powerless to do anything other than comply. And it wasn't pity, nor was it only desire. It was the night, the spell he wove over me, how he'd trusted me with his dilemma. All of it combined to a level of intoxication where all I could do was kiss him.

The stars glittered above us, the moon a pale sliver in the dark night sky, the dim light from the house the only reminder we weren't in some remote wilderness. He tasted sweet and a little spicy. The same addictive flavor as that first kiss a week ago on the dance floor. Had it seriously been only a week?

Felt like a lifetime. A lifetime of kisses and touches, but also like the barest of seconds, everything still brand new and as sparkly as the sky above us. Our hands tangled, holding fast against the rough wood of the narrow balcony.

And that point of contact was almost more intimate than the meeting of our mouths. His grip tightened on mine, and I moaned as much from that delicious pressure as from what he was doing with his talented tongue.

"Want you," he growled against my lips, and I moaned low, hips shamelessly seeking his cock, desperate for pressure. He pushed down on my hands, levering himself up and over me, a blessedly welcome weight. Not exactly holding me down. I could have rolled him off with little effort, but my abs trembled, a seldom-indulged desire surging to the front of my brain.

"Want you too." I hooked a leg around his hips, holding him fast to me. Knox shifted, settling between my legs, forcing them wider—

"*Whoa.*" He clutched me hard as my foot connected with the creaky railing, making the whole balcony wobble and moan louder than we had. "Let's not die tonight."

"Let's not." I gave a shaky laugh.

"Yeah, plummeting three stories would be less than fun." Knox regarded me through wary eyes. "Is this where you tell me that kiss was yet another mistake, and we both crawl off to our respective beds?"

"No. Nothing that good can be a mistake." He'd trusted me with so much of his own truth that I felt compelled to be honest on a deeper level. "And I know I didn't handle the other time well."

"You think? This thing doesn't have to be complicated, Monroe." Scrubbing at his hair to readjust his topknot thing, he sat up, moving back from the edge of the balcony.

"I like when you say my name. And you're right." I nodded sharply as I too scrambled away from the railing and toward the open window.

96

"I am?" Knox paused halfway through the window, expression going from quizzical to cocky. "Wait. I am."

"Don't sound so smug. But yeah, I'm done fighting this pull between us. I've never felt chemistry quite like this."

"That makes two of us. So now what?"

"Now we get off the damn roof because dying while coming is less than sexy." I followed him back into his attic room. "But coming is definitely still on the agenda."

"And where do you want to come, Monroe?" He turned toward me, expression so seductive I would have followed him right off a damn cliff edge, let alone that balcony.

"That's quite the question." Unbidden, an image flashed in my brain of myself flat on my back, come painting my stomach, Knox inside me, thrusting deep and hard. But I rarely bottomed, and there were so many other intriguing possibilities. Mouths and hands and acres of skin to contemplate.

"There's a definite shortage of usable double beds in this house." Laughing, Knox peered over at the daybed, which was only a twin like the bed in my room.

"That there is." I was desperate enough to be willing to squeeze our two very adult-sized bodies on the nearest horizontal surface. Bed. Couch. The drawing desk. I glanced around the room as Knox chuckled again.

"Luckily, I have a healthy imagination." He steered me to the hammock chair in the corner, pushing lightly on my shoulders until I sat, careful to not tip myself onto the hardwood floor.

"And what precisely are you imagining?" I looked up at the bolt affixed to the ceiling. The ropes were sturdy enough, as was the rainbow-striped canvas fabric, but I was still a little shaky after the near-fall on the balcony. "No way is this holding both of us."

"Nope. But you're going to sit right here and let me blow your mind."

"In the swing?" I frowned. "Not sure this is any less likely to do me in than the rickety balcony."

"Well, I haven't killed anyone yet with my mouth. Happy to try though." And with that, Knox sank to his knees in front of the hammock chair with a wicked grin and an eager mouth. Hell if I could do anything other than sit back and let his deft fingers undo my fly.

"Feels like I'm getting the better end of this idea." Even as I said the words, I shifted in the chair, leaning back to make his work easier.

"Oh, trust me, you're not." His expression went from mischievous to feral as he withdrew my cock, both of us moaning softly. "I've been fantasizing about this exact scenario for two days now. And there's nothing I love more than oral. I've waited a solid week now to get your cock in my mouth."

"Well, don't let me stop you." I tried to sound ambivalent, but my harsh breathing gave me away. His firm grip felt so damn good. "This weekend, we're remedying the bed situation."

"Are we now, Lieutenant?" He stroked my cock with a lazy touch. He peered down at it with a hooded gaze, the sort of anticipation in his eyes usually reserved for six-layer chocolate cake. "You planning repeats already?"

"You keep looking at my dick like that, and I'll keep you around indefinitely." I hissed in a breath as his grip tightened. "But I meant what I said. I'm done fighting this. A down-low summer fling, whatever we call it that gets me more of..." I had to trail off as he delicately licked at my cockhead. "That. This. Everything. Oh god, more of that."

I stopped making sense as his featherlight tongue traced

every ridge and vein. My dick had never felt bigger, harder, or sexier, the way he treated me like such a delicacy.

"Damn, I love reducing you to babble, Lieutenant."

"Monroe. Say my name again. Please." I shuddered, ass clenching, the subtle motion of the swing intensifying each soft lick and touch.

"Mmm. *Monroe,* you taste so damn good." And then he moaned my name around my cock, and I nearly lost my damn mind. He took me deep, millimeter by sexy millimeter.

"Jesus. You're a miracle." I arched my spine, trying to get more delicious contact.

He laughed as he slowly slid back up the length of my shaft. "Nah, I'm just Knox."

"More, Knox. Please." I wasn't above begging when he teased me with only his breath across my cockhead.

"You like it deep? Fast? Slow? Show me." He moved one of my hands to his head, and my fingers instinctually tangled in his hair. Sometime I wanted to pull his ponytail bun thing loose, luxuriate in all those satiny curls framing his scruffy jaw, but right then, I was more obsessed with guiding him into my favorite rhythm, slow but deep.

He caught on quickly. A gradual, tortuous downstroke, faster on the upstroke with more suction and pressure. I wasn't porn-star huge, but I was probably north of average, and Knox still deep-throated me with impressive ease. He did this little huffy exhale against the fabric of my pants every time he bottomed out, and it was sexy as fuck. I could see yet again why they called him Rebound, why his friend group relied on him to get back on the dating horse.

Unlike those Rebound groupies, I didn't have a broken heart, but Knox's mouth felt like the softest blanket ever, swaddling all the sore and tender spots I hadn't even been aware of having. But I did. I ached for this man. For his mouth, for this connection. For how damn good he made me feel.

He established a consistent yet devastating rhythm, tongue, lips, and roving hand all working in concert. The sway of the swing was one more layer of sensation, the rocking motion taking the pleasure and spreading it down my hamstrings and up my abs. The weightless sensation was new for me, nothing to tense against like with a mattress or floor, nothing to do but lie back and let Knox have his way with me with his mouth. I loved it.

Absolutely loved it.

Earlier on the roof, I'd had the sort of vague restlessness that had led to ill-advised experiments in bottoming before. An unspecified want I could never quite place or perhaps an itch that never seemed to get scratched, but with Knox, sex was already so different.

Knox made it effortless to hand over the reins to him with the house projects and with sex. An epic orgasm was all but guaranteed, and I trusted him to get me there.

Make that get both of us there. When I returned my gaze to him, he had his own cock out and was idly stroking it with his free hand.

"If you wait, I'll help you with that." I was torn between leaning back and closing my eyes or keeping my gaze locked on him until the very last second. He was so hot, the entire picture: wild hair, full lips stretched around my cock, big hand holding my thigh steady while the other played with the tastiest cock I'd seen in a very long time.

"No way. Coming with a cock filling my mouth is one of my favorite things. Not gonna miss my shot." As if to prove his point, his grip on his dick tightened, stroking becoming more purposeful.

"Oh, someone's shooting, all right." I groaned as he resumed sucking.

"You better." He grinned up at me before taking my cock even deeper. The hand on his dick sped up in tandem with his mouth, erotic vision mingling with the hot pleasure zooming all over my body. Everything enhanced the rising sensations—the swing, the sight of Knox on his knees, cock out, for me, the sounds he made as he sucked and slurped and moaned around my cock, the soft lighting, and even the unabashedly erotic paintings on the wall. Instead of lewd as they'd originally seemed, now the paintings added a decadent air like this was our own private orgy.

In fact, everything was in such perfect concert that I almost missed the warning tingles and rising tension in my muscles. My breathing hitched, tightness extending to my lungs, oxygen in shorter and shorter supply until I was panting with each shallow exhale.

"Close. Going to..." I tried to warn, but my barely-distinct words were mainly moans.

"Gimme," he demanded roughly, sucking harder and faster, hand on his dick blurring, and then I was coming, no holding back, no resisting, letting go on a level I never had before. But I'd craved this. The freefall, the quiet support of Knox's left hand on my thigh, tethering me even as I relinquished all pretense of control to tumble into the hardest, longest orgasm of my life.

"That's it." Knox sucked more frantically, low moans escaping his lips with a few drops of my come as he shot all over his fist and shorts. The vision of him climaxing, eyes shut tightly, hand moving fast, built biceps flexing, jets of come erupting from his cock while he continued to suck like I was the best thing he'd ever tasted pulled a few final rough spurts from my cock.

And my soul. Lord, my abs burned. Thighs too, like the climax had taken all I had to give: come, sweat, brain cells, all of that.

"Wow." Pulling back, he grinned at me, licking stray drops of come from his full lips. "You're incredible."

"Come here." I yanked him up to my level for an awkward, off-balance kiss. "Pretty sure I should be the one doling out praise."

My voice came out croaky. Had I shouted when I came? Most likely, although the cat was over on the daybed entirely unperturbed by our exploits.

"Oh, by all means, praise me." Knox grinned before giving me a longer kiss. The faint taste of come had my body humming and my sex-addled brain already thinking about round two.

"If you want praise, that was the best I've ever had."

"Yeah, the swing was a rather inspired idea." He shrugged, but his rapidly darkening cheeks said he liked the compliment a lot.

"Not the swing. *You.*"

"Nah. I'm not that good. Just enthusiastic." He pursed his lips, glancing thoughtfully at my still-out half-hard cock like he was also considering going again.

"Hardly. I mean, enthusiasm always helps, but there's something about you…" I let myself trail off because I was perilously close to an emotional declaration I had no business making.

"Something good?" Knox suggested, eyebrows waggling as if this were all a big joke. "Something amazing?"

"Yeah, let's go with that. Amazing." *Special.* I wanted to say special, but I couldn't. This was too new, too temporary, too forbidden for all the feelings surging through me like potent aftershocks. Far beyond any physical reminders of how damn much I liked Knox.

"Fabulous. Maybe my superpower is making you come." Grinning widely, he whipped off his T-shirt to wipe off his hand. "The shower situation is also rather dire. Nothing big enough for two unless you want a bath in one of the claw-foot tubs."

"Not tonight." I managed to fake a casual, slightly tired tone. The sudden craving for a shared bath was almost too potent. I shouldn't start wanting more than Knox could give.

"Fair enough. So this weekend. Primary suite. We'll paint. Hit the discount place outside of town for a big bed. Fluffy linens and see what we can do to bring the attached bath into this century."

"That sounds like a lot." I accepted his hand to help me out of the hammock chair.

"Nah. You finally giving in to Operation Secret Summer fling? That's a lot." He shook his head, pleasure sparkling in his eyes like I'd truly done something note-worthy instead of finally letting my cock—and the rest of me —have what I'd wanted from the first glance. I might have to live without my brain for a few months, but it would be worth the loss of my logic and reasoning to have a little more Knox in my life.

Chapter Fourteen

Knox

"You're a magician." Monroe stood in the doorway to the primary suite, and the marvel in his tone was something I never tired of. I loved how he turned ordinary DIY projects into wonderous transformations. The dude had been part of an elite naval division, leading critical investigations, yet he always acted like I was the impressive one.

"Nah." I paused in adjusting the bed's position to shake my head at him. "I'm just a guy handy with a drill and a paintbrush."

"If this were one of those complete a remodel in a weekend shows, you'd win every time." He continued to glance around, taking in the now sky-blue walls, gleaming white trim, new ceiling fan that replaced the decades-old dusty fixture, and refreshed furnishings. He'd made the barest of protests over my color choices, but the small smile he got every time he stepped through the door was worth the fight.

"Ha. I could have my own show. *Knox Knocks it Down.* I could be a star."

"You could." Walking into the room, he carried the lamp I'd sent him to fetch from downstairs. By cobbling together unused items from various rooms in the house, I'd created a whole new look with very little cash outlay.

"Your belief in me is admirable. And sexy." Being able to openly flirt with Monroe while we worked was a new pleasure, and his blushes were almost as good as his compliments.

"I'd call you a praise whore, but most of it is well-earned."

"Most of?" I adjusted the lamp from where he'd set it, centering it on a small end table I'd repurposed as a nightstand. A quick ten-minute touch-up with turquoise spray paint had given it a more modern look, and the art deco lamp completed the mix of old and new that gave the whole space a fresh vibe.

"Okay, okay. All of you is worthy of praise." He gave me a heated look that made my bare toes curl against the fluffy rug I'd found lurking in the spare bathroom's closet. "And don't make me think about sex right now."

"There's a bad time to think about sex?" I located the bags of bedding waiting to make up the bed. We'd cut more costs by adding a premium mattress topper to the existing older bed in the room and swapped out the eighteen hundreds-looking brass headboard for a more modern blue fabric padded number I'd spotted in the clearance aisle of the discount place.

"We're almost done, right, boss? Then we can break and have all the sexy thoughts you want." Without being asked, Monroe joined me in opening the sheets, mattress pad, and pillows packages.

"I do love being the boss." My smug tone had him laughing with me.

"You're good at that too." Monroe's expression went from heated to more thoughtful. "You'd make a good boss of a small business."

"I would." I liked how he'd stated it as a fact, not a question about my intentions regarding my dilemma over my future. So far, Monroe was the only person I'd truly opened up to about my decision, and he reinforced my trust by the way he seemed to have complete faith in me to work things out. "I'm leaning in that direction for sure."

"Follow your heart with open eyes. Listen to your intuition, then back it up with clear facts and supporting reasons."

"Good advice." I fluffed a pillow that had been vacuum-packed. Dreams were kind of like that. Stuffed tightly down, covered in layers of plastic, but when they escaped, they tended to expand and expand, changing from abstract potential to a seductive landing spot. But like with pillows, some dreams were firm and supportive while others were cheap, easily squashed cotton.

"I do have well-earned wisdom." Monroe groaned like he was eighty, and I rolled my eyes at him.

"Don't act all old, Mr. Threepeat yesterday." Saturday, we'd spent most of the day painting. There had also been some well-timed orgasm breaks in there, more fun with hands and mouths, and Monroe had been more than eager for each round.

"That's because I know how to pace myself," he said archly.

"And pace yourself, you did." I gave him an appreciative glance. He liked to heap praise on my mouth, but I was quickly becoming addicted to his large hand and how perfectly it fit my dick. And speaking of pacing, the man was an absolute edging master, capable of bringing me close over and over before finally letting me come.

"I needed to prepare for the shopping marathon with you. Remind me again why I need piles of bedding?" Monroe shook out the hotel-quality puffy white comforter we'd chosen at the discount place.

"Staging." I adopted a superior tone, but actually, a number of the purchases had been for Monroe's comfort. Like, sure, we could have each settled for scratchy twin blankets all summer and made do with an ancient mattress, but I couldn't deny my urge to pamper Monroe, treat him to colors and textures he'd otherwise deny himself.

"I'm not sure buyers will notice the thread count of the sheet set."

"No, but they'll notice the overall ambiance of a seductive retreat and look beyond the older bathroom fixtures." I gestured toward the attached bath. We'd scrubbed the cream tile until it gleamed, painted a darker aqua on the walls to complement the bedroom color scheme, swapped out ancient fixtures for new stainless ones, and replaced the plastic shower curtain with a glass door. But the overall layout had remained unchanged, the sort of big refresh rather than full-on remodel I loved doing for those on a budget and time crunch. "Now help me make this bed."

Monroe dutifully helped me put on the sheets and comforter, but as we finished, he gave me a look that was two parts heat and one part frustration. "Why do I get the impression we're just going to unmake the bed later?"

"We?" I faked surprise, even though things had been trending in that direction all weekend. "I get to sleep here tonight?"

"I think you know you do." He came around the bed to

hug me from behind, the sweetest gesture. Ever since Thursday night's balcony talk, he'd been far more handsy in the privacy of the house.

"Do I?" I leaned into his hug, tipping my head back against his. "Maybe you should try asking."

"Ah. Yeah. That would probably be more polite." Chuckling, he lightly nipped my ear. "Knox, would you please sleep here with me tonight so we can finally try this thing we've got going in an actual bed."

"I'd love to. And just for asking so pretty, you can have anything you want in said bed."

"Anything?" He kissed his way down my neck, from the edge of my scruffy jaw to the top of my T-shirt collar.

"Within reason. Like I said that first night, I don't bottom." I kept my voice light but firm.

"Me either, or at least not often, but I want that with you," he said into my hair.

"Yeah?" I turned in his embrace so I could look him in the eyes. My dick was suddenly very interested in the proceedings, but my brain exercised far more caution, even as I teased, "You want me to rail you through your new bed?"

"Apparently," he mumbled, cheeks adorably pink.

"Why, Monroe, are you blushing?"

"I don't usually ask for this." And that admission was why I wasn't already pushing him down on the freshly made bed.

"You don't have to go there with me. No requirements if that's a no-fly zone for you."

"I know. But something about you makes me want to try bottoming again. When we were on the roof, and you were on top..." He gave a happy sigh that went right to my still-intrigued cock.

"Pinning you down." My hands tingled with the memory. The way he'd let me hold his hands back had been intoxicating, the way he'd yielded to me, strength meeting strength. "You liked that?"

"And how. You make it safe to just completely let go, like floating in a warm pool."

"I want to do that for you, make you float away so you forget everything other than how it feels." Now it was my turn to wrap him in a hug. I had limited experience topping because I was all in on hands and mouths after the two times I'd bottomed myself had hurt and been pretty damn awkward. I'd never want to make a sex partner uncomfortable, so I'd set out to make myself amazing at oral and hands and frot. I absolutely loved focusing on the other person, losing myself in their pleasure rather than my own. However, if Monroe wanted me to fuck him, I would certainly do my best. "I love making people feel good. I wanna make you feel good, Monroe."

"I know. And you're damn good at that already. I trust you."

"Say that again." I kissed the back of his neck.

"I trust you." And with that simple sentence, Monroe lassoed my heart, ensuring I would do everything in my power to be the person—the man—he needed, to give him whatever he needed, to fully earn that trust because I knew damn well what a gift it was.

Chapter Fifteen

Monroe

"Forget magician. You're a damn wizard." I strode out of the bathroom into the bedroom to find Knox shirtless and lounging in close-fitting black boxers in the center of the new bed. The covers were turned down like a posh hotel, the low lamps provided a cozy glow, and Knox himself was as inviting as a cool pool on a hot summer day. "How is this the same room?"

I couldn't get over how different the bedroom and attached bath seemed now. Thanks to low-odor, fast-drying paint and Knox's impeccable clean-up habits, there wasn't even much evidence of our efforts over the past few days. He'd talked me out of my original goal of a serviceable, neutral space and created what he kept calling a seductive retreat. And he'd succeeded because not only was this the sort of room to escape to after a long day, but even without a Knox in the bed, the room was alluring, inviting naked lounging and pillow talks and all sorts of other things I'd never had time for.

"Here you are marveling at my decorating skills, and I'm just over here trying not to swallow my tongue at you in a towel." Waving a hand, he motioned me closer.

"Flattery will get you everywhere tonight." Never one to be particularly modest, I let the towel drop. Knox had seen the goods a couple of times now, but neither of us had made it to the completely undressed stage yet. Having the time, freedom, and space to get naked and explore was a novelty. My pre-Knox hookups had tended to be quick and furtive, so the blatant appreciation in Knox's eyes was welcome on multiple levels. His expression was hungry as he shimmied out of his boxers, promising a long, long night. I shook my head at his adorable eagerness. "You certainly seem to have made yourself at home here."

"Complaints?" He leered at me, rolling to his stomach, showing off that perfect ass of his: twin muffins I couldn't resist dropping a playful bite on.

"None at all." I'd retrieved supplies from one of my unpacked bags in my old bedroom, and I tossed the condoms and lube next to Knox. Rather than join him, I took a moment to step back and appreciate how damn sexy he was, tanned skin against the white bedding, blue accents in the room making him look like the star of a dirty surfing calendar.

"Then why aren't you in this bed yet?"

"Maybe I like looking at you." I kept my voice light, but inside, I was well-aware this was the moment that might not come again. The whole weekend had been pretty damn perfect, yet we were only just now making it to an actual bed, the fruits of our hard work framing a memory I was going to keep close.

"Take a picture?" He gestured at my phone next to his on the newly-painted bedside table.

"I've been part of too many investigations to risk sexy phone pics."

"Then take one for me?" He tossed me his phone instead. "I want to see what you see."

"Well, I could stand here all night cataloging your muscles." I didn't open his phone. Still wasn't risking a pic, no matter how much I wanted one. "But that's not what I want a picture of. I see your swagger. It's in your smart mouth and cocky grin and the way you carry yourself, even in bed."

"I'm not over the novelty of me in a bed either." He grinned up at me, but there was a sentimentality in his eyes that hadn't been there before.

"Hush. I see your hands which, in addition to working like crazy here at the house this weekend, managed errands for your dad and Jessica and even some hours for Measure Twice. You're always doing something for someone, Knox."

"That's how I like it."

"But what do you want for yourself?" I held his gaze.

"If you're asking me to be selfish, you might want to come here and get your cock within sucking range."

"I'm serious. I see your strength and selflessness and kindness and smart-assed self, Knox. That's what I want a picture of."

"Oh wow." Inhaling sharply, he rolled back over, expression soft and open. "You might have missed your calling as a poet. The navy wasted your talents."

"Oh, my reports were poetry, all right." I laughed as I gave in to the urge to stretch out next to him after placing his phone back on the nightstand.

"Finally." Knox wrapped himself around me, a most welcome barnacle. "You want me to want something for me? I choose you." Reaching down, he groped my ass.

"And this. You did say that was your request tonight, right?"

"It is. But I don't want to be another favor or errand for you." I turned to peer into Knox's eyes, trying to tell him something I didn't quite understand myself. "I want to treat you, not require you."

"Aw, Monroe, that's the sweetest thing anyone's ever said to me. Yes, please, treat me to your ass." He tickled my sides lightly, and laughter barked out of me, rusty but true. I couldn't remember the last time I'd been tickled, but I liked it.

"It's a rare enough gift."

"I know." Sobering, he stroked my jaw. "And that's why I *do* want this. It turns me on that you chose me for this, that you're trusting me with your body."

And everything else. But, of course, I couldn't admit that, not even close. "You're easy to trust."

"Thank you." Knox gave me the softest of kisses, a sweetness I neither deserved nor could keep, but I was going to soak up anyway, add to my memory banks. "I'm gonna make this so good for you."

Knox easily flipped our positions, as nimble as any special forces warrior, and immediately started kissing a determined trail south.

"Better not." I shoved at his shoulder. "I'm already hard enough. I don't wanna come yet, and you're too damn talented."

"Did I say I was heading for your cock?" Expression impish, he shoved my legs farther apart and ducked under my thighs, a move worthy of a college wrestling crown. His hot breath gusted across my rim, and I shivered. "If you haven't figured it out yet, I love pretty much everything I can do with my mouth."

I made a noise that was part protest, part need. This wasn't something I'd had the sort of time and space to indulge in, and the unfamiliarity made my abs quiver. I wasn't sure I'd ever been this open—or wanted to be—but then Knox dropped a gentle kiss on the inside of my thigh.

"Let go, Monroe. That's what you said you wanted, right? Let go, and let me make you fly. Please?"

"Yes." The please was what did it, the way he seemed to need this every bit as much as I did. He seemed to crave my pleasure as much as his own, and I couldn't gift Knox much, but I could gift him my surrender.

And what a surrender it was. I forced myself to relax, to banish the restless tension from my muscles, and as soon as Knox teased a circle around my rim, my entire body went pliant, putty for him to do with as he wished.

"Oh, Monroe." His fond tone was going to be my utter undoing. "You're sweet as hell."

"No—yes. Yes. That." Whatever protest I'd been about to make was cut off as he attacked my hole in earnest, licking and sucking, the same devious tongue my cock adored doing devilish things to my ass until I was rocking up to meet his mouth. "Please."

"More? I can do that." The happy noises Knox kept making went straight to my pulsing cock, and the more enthusiastic he became, the better his attentions felt until my belly was streaked with precome. I didn't dare reach for my cock because I was that damn close.

"Please. Fingers. Now." I fumbled for the bottle of lube, nearly lobbing it at Knox's head. "Don't wanna come from your mouth."

"Is that even possible?" Knox's eyes gleamed like I'd just confessed to a secret horde of diamonds. God, he was such a fucking delight.

"With your talents? Yeah, probably."

"Damn. I love that." He went right back to rimming me, totally ignoring the lube and my pleas.

"Quit trying to test that theory." I pushed at his shoulder again, getting more purchase this time, and he made an adorable frustrated puppy noise before sitting back on his heels and slicking his fingers.

"You'll tell me if I go too fast?" Knox asked as he eased the tip of one index finger in.

"Continental drift is faster than you." I arched, trying to take his finger deeper. I'd never wanted it this bad before, never been this mindless, this consumed by need, this aware of every nerve ending.

"Complaints, complaints." Sighing like I was a demanding princess, he did a nifty little maneuver with his finger before sliding a second in beside the first. I saw stars as he used both to press directly on my prostate. No searching, no more questioning, only the exact pressure and depth I'd craved. Perfection.

"Oh fuck. Jesus. More like that."

"There you go, forgetting my name again." Knox made a clucking noise as he eased back enough to take care of the condom, slicking himself with an alarming amount of extra lube. But his attention to every detail, his care and concern, was a huge part of the appeal of doing this with him. With Knox, I didn't have to worry, and that was its own pleasure and release. And with him, I could laugh, even as my body strained toward his.

"*Knox.* If you don't fuck me in the next five seconds..."

"You'll what?" He matched my laughter as he pushed my legs up and back, as confident as ever, so damn appealing the way he had no problem taking over or manhandling me to both of our satisfaction.

"Cocky..." I gave up on words temporarily as he pushed forward. More of that glacial slowness and care, but man, his steadiness was so welcome. *Trust.* I'd said that earlier, and it was so true here. I trusted Knox to go at the right speed for both of us, to take me to the edge of too much without ever tipping into discomfort. The initial stretch and subtle burn faded into deep pleasure as he connected with my prostate, perfect angle and pressure yet again. "Fuck. That's good."

"Yeah?" Knox sounded slightly unsure, which, if anything, made him that much sexier.

"More." I pulled my legs up farther, quads burning like I was running a steeplechase. I met him thrust for thrust, power for power until my head and then my hands fell back, every rational thought and voluntary movement ceasing. I sagged against the mattress, taking it, taking him, taking every last thing Knox had to give me.

"God. Monroe." Knox stared down at me with undisguised wonder. "You're so fucking hot like this."

"I was gonna say the same thing about you." I managed half a laugh before I moaned again. Knox truly was spectacular, rippling muscles, sweaty chest, hair falling out of its ponytail, cock in tune with my every breath. He was strong, so strong, and I really did feel like I was flying, just as he'd promised.

"Going to come for me?" His voice was huskier now.

"Nah." I pretended to think it over. "Want it to last forever."

"Come on, Monroe." He wrapped a slick hand around my dick, firm strokes that would make a liar out of me in a hurry. "Please."

"You want that?" My eyes fluttered shut, all my concentration on not coming right that very second. I was drunk on the power I held over him, on how much he needed me. Knox was such a giver. He gave and gave to everyone, but here, in this place, I could give to him. I could reduce him to growls and snarls and low moans as he fucked me harder and harder.

"You know I do. Not gonna go till you do."

"That's..." I started a tease, then had to abandon it in favor of moaning. He hammered me hard enough the new headboard shook. Hell, my teeth might have rattled, and still, I wanted more. I was going to drown in how damn good every thrust was. "Not fair. Fuck."

"That's it." Knox's sound of pure triumph was what did it. Not his slippery fist. Not his unerring thrusts. That noise in the back of his throat, the gleam in his eyes, the quirk of his lips, the lift in his shoulders. He was so fucking proud of himself, and so was I. Something gave way inside my chest. Not orgasm. Bigger. Scarier. More all-encompassing. It truly did pull me under, but I basked in the sheer overwhelming sensations.

"Coming. God." Like Knox needed my warning. I shot so hard I hit my chin, painting my stomach and chest with ropes of come. He fucked me right through the orgasm, speeding up as his climax claimed him.

"Me too." And wow. I was so damn glad I had my eyes open as he came, joy transforming his features, all that earlier wonder and triumph giving way to pure joy. It was beautiful, no other word for it other than, perhaps, humbling. And tender, the way he ran a hand down my chest, chuckling at our mess before taking care of the condom.

"Okay, I hereby declare this room officially christened." Still laughing, Knox retrieved my towel from the floor, swiping halfheartedly at the mess before giving up and letting me take over.

"Is that what we were doing?" I couldn't help laughing too. And perhaps he was right. Because I'd fucked before. Had sex before. And this wasn't that. It wasn't even in the same ballpark. *Christening.* Something sacred. Yeah, that sounded more like it.

"Yep."

"Are we going to have to do this in every room?" I faked alarm to watch him chortle harder.

"Have to? No. Get to? Hell yeah." He tickled my still-sticky side, teasing loose yet another belly laugh.

"God bless Aunt Henri and this giant house." For the first time, I saw the house's appeal. Knox's obvious pleasure at transforming this suite had revealed possibilities for the rest of the house. Maybe I'd been burdened before by a lack of imagination. I still wasn't entirely sure why Aunt Henri had picked me, but with Knox looking at me with those twinkling dark eyes, I sure was grateful.

"Lots of rooms." He beamed at me. "Lots of summer."

Not enough. Not enough. I nodded, but it wasn't ever going to be enough time, enough weeks, enough *Knox* to suit me.

Chapter Sixteen

Monroe

"Okay, this one is my favorite." I took another bite of ice cream, mentally adding two miles to my morning run. But the treat was more than worth any worries over the caloric splurge.

"You say that about all the flavors." Knox laughed and swung his feet back and forth. He was perched on the edge of a large wooden picnic table while I sat on the bench. He, too, was worth the splurge. I was rapidly reaching a point where I couldn't deny him anything. When he'd proposed pizza and ice cream after a long day stripping wallpaper downstairs at the house, I'd readily agreed.

"They're all good." I forced a laugh. When he'd suggested dining in rather than takeout so we could escape the musty heat of the house and paint fumes, I'd agreed to that as well, even if my gaze did keep darting around to see who might be watching this gorgeous young man and me. Could strangers guess we were more than friends? The intensity of my feelings made me lose the ability to judge.

Trying to make myself relax, I licked the back of my spoon. "But this time, I mean it. Bigfoot caramel crunch is addictive."

"You should taste mine." Knox scooped a generous amount from the untouched side of his dish. "The coconut fudge ripple tastes like melted candy bars. So good."

He held out the bite, and I might have taken it had we been anywhere other than downtown Safe Harbor. I spotted Sam's parents on the other side of the parking lot, along with others from the church. Couldn't risk starting gossip.

"Not now." I waved the spoon away, hating how his face fell.

"What?" He frowned, then followed my gaze. Beyond the church group of retirees, several young families were sprawled on the grass, kids running around them. At least some of those folks had to know Rob and Jessica too. "Oh. Public. I forgot. I'll save you a bite for in the car."

"Thanks," I said tightly. In a different world, or at least a different spot in this world, I would be proud to touch Knox, share his food, bump shoulders sitting side-by-side, walk back to the house together holding hands. The need to touch him was palpable, and knowing I couldn't was almost a physical pain.

"It's okay." Knox sighed, then smiled at a group of young girls practicing a cheer. The line for ice cream snaked around the small building, and clumps of people waiting greeted new arrivals to the line with smiles and waves. "The people-watching is almost worth being unable to touch you."

"People-watching?" I didn't agree. The only thing better than touching Knox was touching Knox naked. "You mean the tourists?"

"Better watch it, or you'll sound like a longtime resident." Shaking his head, Knox gave an easy laugh. "And it's easy to see why tourists on their way to the coast love it here. Eighties nostalgia over that one movie filmed here, historic homes, and best ice cream on the planet."

"You're cute happy." I wasn't sure I agreed with Knox that this was the best small town ever, but I sure did love the sound of his laugh, the dimples almost obscured by his jaw scruff, the bounce of his messy ponytail, the curls escaping around his temples. God. There wasn't anything I didn't like about him.

"Hey, what's not to be happy about?" Knox beamed. The sun was starting to set, pinks and oranges streaking the blue sky, but the sun inside Knox never dimmed. It wasn't that he never had bad days or got moody, but even at his most melancholy, he still glowed with an indescribable inner energy. "I love summer nights in Safe Harbor. Pizza. Ice Cream. Sounds of kids playing. Hard to beat that."

"You're an easy date," I said without thinking. This wasn't a date, couldn't be a date, yet damn, how I wanted it to be one.

"Ha. Lucky for you, I'm also an easy roommate." The truly lucky thing was Knox not picking up on how badly I wanted to date him for real. Roommates. We were roommates. Friends sharing an after-dinner treat, nothing more. "And I can't say as I've ever done that."

"Gone out on a date?" I shot him a critical look.

"Not really. I never did any activities in college that had formal dances or dinners, and sure, I went to prom with a dude, but it was more as just friends because he'd recently broken up with someone."

"Rebound." I rolled my eyes at him. Someone needed to take him on a real date. Dinner, a nice shirt, strolling hand-in-hand, snuggling at a show—I had to work hard to not sigh longingly.

"Yep. I'm predictable."

"What if someone asked you out? What would be your ideal?" Clearly, I was a glutton for punishment, going down this line of thinking, but I wanted to know more than I wanted to finish my double scoop.

"Hmm. Like you said, I'm easy. And you've probably been on way more dates. You tell me. What's good?"

"You'd be surprised. Not many here either." I pursed my mouth, thinking. Various wedding dates. A charitable function or two. A couple of sporting events. Lord, Knox and I were quite the pair.

"A second date." Knox gave a sharp nod.

"I'm trying to follow you, but I'm confused."

"My ideal date would be one where I know there's a second date coming. Like no first-date jitters, no one-night-stand vibes, just...comfortable. I guess that what we do isn't as important to me as how I feel." He bit his lower lip, staring off into the dusk. I could give him that, a date that didn't feel like a first date, one that guaranteed other dates. We were already that comfortable. But not in Safe Harbor. No way could I date him here.

"You want to feel special," I said softly because as comfortable as we were around each other, I wanted to make him feel special. Treasured. Not taken for granted. And not merely desired for sex or escape either, but valued for himself, for being Knox.

"Yeah."

"You deserve that." Now it was my turn to look away. There had to be a way. Weekend in Seattle? Portland might be too close, but maybe Seattle. I mentally reviewed what I knew about our schedules. Too bad I had an upcoming trip for a friend's wedding.

Wait. Maybe...I opened my mouth to share my brainstorm with Knox, but he was already chortling.

"And I deserve the leftover pizza when we get back."

"You're a bottomless pit." I chuckled fondly. My big idea could wait.

"You're the one who keeps giving me reasons to work up an appetite." He waggled his eyebrows at me.

"Not gonna complain there."

"Yep. Gotta squeeze in all the sexy times while we can."

We did. Much as I didn't want to think about summer ending, we were already in the middle of the season, with hot weather, ripe fruit, and a ticking clock. We did need to squeeze in every moment we could, and I was for damn sure going to make one of those moments an actual date.

Chapter Seventeen

Knox

"Have you seen Wallace?" I asked Monroe. I'd been reluctant to bother him. When I'd come in through the back earlier, I'd spied him in the living room, two laptops open, piles of paper everywhere, deep in concentration. So, I'd headed upstairs to greet Wallace instead, but the cat was nowhere to be found.

"He's kind of hard to miss." Monroe looked up from his computer, his seldom-seen reading glasses perched on his nose, giving him a professorial air. And ordinarily, I'd be down with playing hot professor and naughty TA, but right then, I was more concerned with finding my cat. Playtime could wait. Monroe frowned, head tilting. "Actually, no, I haven't. Shooed him out of our bedroom earlier this morning, so I could shut the door, but I haven't seen him since then."

Our. I was thrilled at that casual use of the word. I couldn't help but smile, though I was still concerned about the cat. The weeks were flying by, and I'd take *our* as long as I could. However, my smile faded as I calculated the hours between morning and five o'whatever now.

"Heck. I put out food before I went to work, and it's still uneaten, which is not like Wallace, and I can't find him anywhere."

"Here. I'll help." Leaving his glasses on a stack of papers, Monroe stood. "Where have you checked?"

"You don't have to get up. You look deep in work." I gave a halfhearted protest because I really was grateful for the help. "I haven't done a deep search yet. I can do that now on my own."

"Nah. I'm happy to take a break. I was reviewing my notes for Holden's podcast. Trying to look over everything with fresh eyes, see if I'm missing something in plain sight."

"Thanks." I led the way from the living room to the smaller front sitting room where Wallace sometimes liked to lay in the sunny front window seat, but the room sat empty, frozen in time with its older furnishings, vintage books, and rose wallpaper. "When do you record?"

"Tomorrow. We had to push the time once already because Holden got called to consult on an urgent case."

"He's in demand." I laughed on my way to the dining room. No Wallace flaunting the no-cats-on-table rule. "Guess that's what happens when you write the literal textbook."

I had some friends who had taken classes from Holden, and apparently, he was an amazing professor. Bigger schools kept trying to poach him, but he stayed on in Safe Harbor.

"Yep." Monroe stepped into the kitchen, glancing around. "Wallace? Here, kitty-kitty."

His use of kitty-kitty had me grinning despite my

Annabeth Albert

worries. And for a brief moment, I entertained a fantasy where Monroe might go the professor route. Stay here, find a place at the college like Holden. "You ever think about going into teaching like Holden?"

"Nah. I'm too restless for much time behind a lectern. I like getting up to my armpits in facts and evidence on a case. That's why I keep going over the details surrounding Worth's mother's disappearance. There has to be something I'm missing."

"Want to talk it through with me later?" I kept my offer light, covering any disappointment with an easy smile. "I'm a good sounding board."

"You really are." The fondness in his gaze went a long way toward making me feel better. After peeking behind the curtains, he bent to look under the breakfast nook table. "Yeah, after we find the cat, we can search out some food, and I'll run through the sticking points with you."

"Awesome." The kitchen and breakfast nook yielded no cat, so I headed for the back stairs. "I saw my dad at Blessed Bean. He mentioned you're doing an amazing job with the cold cases. Said you've been a huge help, especially with him busy more."

"Well, I'm trying. How is Jessica this week?"

"She's okay. Tired. Like with the triplets, the doctors are worried about preterm labor, so Dad is trying to do stuff around the house to allow her more rest."

"That's good. And he's a good guy." Monroe stopped at the second-floor landing. Frowning, he let out a frustrated sigh, as if my dad being a decent person was a problem. And maybe it was. I got where Monroe was coming from— sneaking around was no fun for either of us.

"He is. And he said you've been wrapping a record number of things." I deliberately backed away from reminders about what we were doing with this secret fling of ours.

"Well, a lot of that is advancement in forensics." Shrugging, Monroe methodically opened the row of built-in cupboards in the second-floor hall. "But yes, it's always fun to close things."

"You could do that full-time. Be a detective." If not a professor with Holden, maybe there was a chance Monroe could...

"Yep, that's the plan in San Francisco." Boom. There went any spark of hope. "Speaking of—"

"Wallace?" I called out, interrupting whatever poetry Monroe was about to spew about his future single life in the Bay. I opened the nearest door, a guest room we still hadn't touched. I peered around the cluttered space. "Sorry. You were saying?"

"Oh, nothing, just that I have to go to San Francisco soon. Summer of navy friend weddings, apparently."

"Ah. I see. Yeah, all my crew keeps getting hitched too." I tried to sound indifferent, maybe even bored by plans that only underscored how finite our time together was. "Wallace?" I opened the next door, Monroe's old room. My chest pinched as it always did at signs of his younger, far more vulnerable self. The sports posters. A few random school awards on the walls. Tickets from a concert. Photos he wasn't in, and lord, could I identify with that mood. I forced myself to look away. "You don't think Wallace could have escaped outside, do you?"

"No. I've been working here all day, and I was careful with the door when I opened it to get the mail, promise. It was warm today, but all the windows have screens other than the balcony in your room."

"Balcony." I rushed up to the third floor, Monroe close

behind me. My heart pounded, but the balcony window was firmly shut, and no sign of Wallace on the daybed I hadn't used in a week or more. Monroe checked under the desk and the low cabinets while I opened the bathroom door.

"Surprised we didn't pass him on the stairs. I always seem to find him lounging there, taking up an entire step with his massive self."

"Yeah, he's big," I agreed absently. Stairs. Stairs. Where else? "Wait. What if he didn't take the stairs? Dumbwaiter."

I rushed across the third floor to open the dumbwaiter. *Meow.* A distant cat noise sounded, and I pounded down the three flights of stairs and wrenched open the door to reveal Wallace sitting in the middle of the dumbwaiter cabinet in the kitchen.

"Oh my god, *Wallace.*" Much to his feline indignation, I scooped him up and cuddled him close. "How in the hell did you get in there?"

"Oh no." Monroe made a distraught noise, making me turn to where he was holding on to the dumbwaiter door.

"Wallace is okay." I shifted the cat so I could pat his arm.

"No, not the cat. Look." He pointed at where the dumbwaiter door had pulled loose from its frame. And it wasn't a matter of old wood or loose screws. Nope, this was unmistakable damage.

"Oh crap. That's—"

"Don't say it." Monroe groaned like I'd punched him in the belly, complete with bending forward.

"Termites. That's a problem you can't ignore." I shook my head because I'd seen this enough in other old houses to know how serious the damage was, even when one couldn't see the bugs. "You'll have to get the whole place extermi-nated and then deal with repairing the damage."

"Hell." Straightening, Monroe petted Wallace in my arms as if Wallace might have a better prognosis for him than I did.

"You'll probably need a hotel while they fumigate." I was nothing if not pragmatic about house disasters. "I can go crash at Dad's."

"San Francisco."

"What?" I studied Monroe more closely, unsure if he was in shock.

"That's what I kept trying to say earlier. Come with me to San Francisco."

"Because you feel guilty leaving me?" I needed some-thing to do. Right that damn minute. I set Wallace down and quickly washed my hands at the kitchen sink. Jerking open the fridge, I scanned for something to chop. Or pound. "Yeah, your trip would make sense for the fumigation if you can get someone with an opening then, but you don't need to drag me along out of guilt. The laundry room at Dad's isn't that bad."

"I'm not dragging you anywhere." Monroe made a frus-trated noise as he accepted the package of chicken I handed him. We always cooked so effortlessly together, Monroe grabbing a skillet without being asked and me dicing the ever-loving hell out of an onion. "I want to bring you with me because I can't date you here."

"You want to date me?" I stopped mid-chop before I accidentally lopped off a finger. That fickle hope I'd had earlier, the glowing ember of something real and lasting we'd had for weeks, sparked again. *Dating* had to be a step up from secret fling, right? But I couldn't seem too eager. "I mean, you're already getting—"

"And it's spectacular." He gave me a lopsided grin, the slightly shy smile he used whenever he hinted that he might be open to fucking that night. Even with my confusion and churning emotions, heat still licked at the base of my spine. God, I wanted this man with everything I had. I smiled back as he continued, "But sometimes a guy likes to go out to dinner with the person he's doing that with. Walk together. Leave the house. Call me old-fashioned, but all this sneaking around is depressing. I'd like to hold hands, maybe dance somewhere other than in the rooms we're painting. We could do that if you come with me to the Bay. I've been trying to ask you all week."

"Oh." My mouth fell open, but I quickly buttoned it again. I added my pile of pulverized onion to the preheated skillet he'd already added olive oil to. "So you're not just asking because of termites?"

"No, but I'm not going to lie. It's a convenient excuse for why you're also leaving town that weekend." He used the same pragmatic tone I'd used earlier. Fair enough. The sneaking around was a regrettable but inevitable part of our reality.

"The lying sucks."

"It does." He slid the chicken in among the browning onions. "I mean, you suck better..."

"I do." I preened at the praise, then sobered. "And I'm in. I'll tell anyone who asks that I'm going to California that weekend to see friends. Not that far from the truth. I'll sneak in a coffee with a friend interning at city hall in down-town San Francisco, add some credibility."

"Thank you." Monroe pulled me close enough to kiss my forehead. We were very nearly the same height, but his subtle stretch was endearing as hell. "Thank you for giving me this."

"No problem." Oh man, if he only knew I'd give him my best drawing, my luckiest penny, my favorite shirt. Whatever it took to keep him. If I thought it would work, I'd give him my whole damn heart.

Chapter Eighteen

Monroe

I was doomed. I was going to be done in by a rare sighting of Knox's dimples and his always-present boundless enthusiasm. We'd had a late arrival in San Francisco thanks to a flight delay and had barely had enough energy to tumble into the hotel bed the night before, but given a couple of hours of sleep and wake-up blowjobs, Knox was chipper as ever. And as we entered a downtown coffee shop near the financial district, Knox bounced on his feet like we were at an amusement park, not on a hastily arranged coffee date with a profoundly reluctant Worth Stapleton. Sharing none of Knox's enthusiasm, Worth had been entirely monosyllabic in his text responses.

"So, am I the good cop or the bad cop?" Knox asked as I scanned the Saturday morning coffee shop crowd.

"Pardon?" I was distracted because I didn't see anyone who looked like the Worth I'd known. He'd been skinny like the rest of us as teens but a true golden boy with blond hair, dark soulful eyes, and peach skin. It was no wonder he'd made a young Sam swoon.

"Well, we're here to gather information from Worth, right?" Knox was also glancing around the coffee shop. The place was full of well-dressed patrons, yoga clothes and Saturday morning designer sweats mingling with suits and ties of those unlucky enough to have to work weekends. "This isn't strictly a friendly catch-up."

"Yeah, I've got some questions." I'd gone over the case individually with Knox, Holden, Rob, with anyone who would listen.

"And I've got ideas." Knox had been by far the best audience for my hypothesizing, going so far as to sketch me both a timeline and a rough layout of the Stapleton home. Knox's energy was already my favorite part of this trip. Dealing with the exterminators for the house had been a pain. The flight delays had been a drag, but Knox was a stubborn ray of sunshine that refused to be diminished. "I could play it as the bumbling but adorable boyfriend who keeps stumbling onto topics he shouldn't. Or I could be a gossipy brat who asks too many annoying questions. Or maybe I could pretend to be a reporter..."

"Maybe I want you to be Knox." I pulled him in close to my side. Less than twelve hours in this city, and I was already drunk on the freedom of touching Knox in public, sniffing his hair, grabbing his hand, or simply staring with wonder that this marvelous creature chose mine as the bed to share. I hadn't ever craved such things before, but with Knox, everything was different, and I hadn't known how badly I needed to publicly claim him until I couldn't.

"That works." He returned my look with one of his own, so much adoration in his gaze my breath caught. But then his eyes darkened. "Heck. Just realized. I can't be Rob's kid if I'm here with you. I know you can't risk gossip getting back to the town busybodies."

"Yeah." Deflated, I dropped my hand from his side. The easiest solution would be to send Knox back to our hotel, but that option had a razor edge of guilt. This was supposed to be *our* weekend, damn it. And I didn't want to risk hurting him, even if he had a darn good point. *Think, think, think.* Knox turned slightly as if already bracing for me to ask him to leave. But in his profile lurked that sexy guy I'd first seen at the club. *Bingo.* "You can be Rebound. My too-young, too-good-for-me guy who lets me ask the hard questions."

"Not too young. Definitely not too good." Snuggling back into my side, he grinned at me. Our eyes were level, and even that small detail pleased me. He was tall and strong, and I'd give anything to freeze time right here, never risk cutting him down or dimming the spark in his eyes. "And letting you talk is easy. I'll try to let you lead. For once." He gave me the naughtiest of smirks. "And I'll try to stop thinking about the size of that hotel bed."

"Oh, I have plans for that bed. Don't you worry." I returned the leer as I led the way to the lone free table in the back of the coffee shop. Right as we sat, I spotted a medium-height man in an expensive suit with a rumpled shirt, an askew tie, and a two-day beard. "I think that's him. Man, he doesn't look the best."

"Maybe that's what a career in finance does." Knox narrowed his eyes as he studied the man more closely. "Or perhaps he's dealing with the reminder of the past?"

"Hell. I don't want to make things worse for him."

"You won't." Knox gave my hand a quick squeeze as Worth headed in our direction.

"Monroe. Long time, no see." Worth had broader shoulders, darker blond hair, a thicker build, and a deeper voice. But his eyes had remained the same, fathomless and haunted. My gut clenched. I might not have seen my old friend in years, but I truly didn't want to be the source of more pain for him.

"It's so good to see you. Sit." I motioned at the empty chair. The *good* part was a stretch. Worth looked like shit, clearly didn't want to be here, and I'd give anything for the meeting to be under different circumstances. Taking a breath, I turned toward Knox. "This is..."

I hesitated, more because I'd never used the word *boyfriend* about anyone before. Luckily, Knox was as social as ever, giving Worth a wide, easy smile.

"Everyone calls me Rebound. Silly name, long story." He waved a hand. "And you look like a guy who needs the biggest cold brew this place offers and one of those cinnamon rolls in the display case."

"Uh..." A muscle worked in Worth's jaw. I sympathized with his overwhelm. Knox truly could be a force of nature. In this case, though, his take-charge energy was a welcome thing, and he collected our drink orders before striding off.

"That's your guy?" Watching Knox join the long line at the front counter, Worth shifted in his chair, looking less like he was sitting on a porcupine. Like Rob, he'd known I was gay long before my family and the rest of the world. At the time, Worth confessed he was unsure about his own orientation. I hoped he'd gained some clarity about his identity over the intervening years, but those same years created a distance where I couldn't pry.

"Yeah. I'm not sure I deserve him, but yes." I'd longed to claim Knox, but the words still felt odd on my tongue, and I had a pang of anxiety as to what Worth might do with this confession. "We're a new thing though. Haven't mentioned him to Holden—"

"Wait till the wedding to tell Safe Harbor's gossip king." Shaking his head, Worth smiled for the first time.

I, however, gulped. Hard. "Doubt we're headed..." I glanced over at Knox in line. My heart twisted with things I had no business wanting. "Probably not in the cards."

"Too bad." Worth shrugged out of his suit jacket, let it fall back on his chair. "No one's ever looked at me like he was staring at you."

I stifled a groan. Things were so much easier when I assumed I was the only one fighting a daily tidal wave of emotions. Knox returning my growing feelings was another complication neither of us needed. But I couldn't dwell on that then. I needed to keep the focus on Worth.

"No one? You've never had...a person?"

"I'm crappy at relationships." He shrugged, a distant look in his eyes.

"Hard same," I said, even as I couldn't take my eyes off Knox.

"Maybe at least one of us has changing luck." He offered me half a smile before his face sagged again, a heaviness in his eyes I recognized from battle-hardened military personnel. Worth had seen some shit. "God, tell me something good, Monroe."

I had to think because everything good in my life over the last month began and ended with Knox. But most of those were acutely private moments, sharp and new. I didn't want to prick Worth with romantic musings, so I went for humor instead. "I exorcised all the peachy-pink from Aunt Henri's house."

"That's something." He didn't even crack a smile. "Big

houses. So much work. I remember. No idea why my folks loved that crappy old Victorian."

"Are you okay?" Something in Worth's tone had me leaning forward. I'd known enough navy friends with PTSD to recognize all the signs of someone struggling. "Do you need anything?"

"No." Gaze distant, he shook his head. "Just ask the questions you came for."

"What?" My concern for him had trumped my original purpose, but Worth pursed his mouth and set his shoulders.

"Don't play dumb. Heard you did a podcast with Holden. You're both on the trail of answers that don't exist. But go ahead, like you always used to say, shoot your shot." His voice was as wooden as his expression.

"What do you mean don't exist?" The investigator in me warred with the part of me who'd always been Worth's friend. I had a thousand questions, all tempered by concern for Worth's mental state.

"He did it. Everyone knows he did it. Open and shut case. Tie a fucking bow on it." Each of his words had a brittle edge, like Worth himself was on the verge of crumbling.

"And here's your coffee." Knox arrived back at the table, toting drinks and food, breezy tone like he hadn't heard Worth, but a wariness in his eyes indicated he'd heard enough. "And a cinnamon roll."

"Thanks." Worth accepted his drink and food from Knox without a smile.

"Not everyone thinks your dad was guilty." Leaning forward, I tried again for a congenial demeanor. "Sam—you remember Samuel Bookman, the kid who always tried to tag along with us—he's always said he never believed that assumption. Holden thinks there's room for other theories too."

"It's not a theory," Worth said flatly. "He did it."

"What do you know?" The investigator in me took over, tone hardening, the friend part of my brain taking a back seat.

"They fought that summer. One of the times, he said... some shit. Anyway, at the time, I told the cops things were fine because I didn't want to believe..." Mouth twisting, he trailed off. "Fairytales, man. They rope us all in."

"But you changed your mind?" Much as I hated it, I had to press.

"When I came back from college to help with the search and he wanted me to return to school, we argued. I accused him of knowing more than he was saying. Then I asked him point blank if he did it. And he just walked out of the room."

"That doesn't mean he did it," Knox was quick to point out.

"Fairytales." Worth scoffed like Knox was hopelessly naïve.

"What were they fighting about?" I asked before the two of them could get the conversation too far off track.

"Stupid shit, but the arguing was more than they ever had before. My mom was deep into this pyramid scheme thing, and Dad hated it."

"A business?" I mentally reviewed my notes, all of which had pointed to Worth's mother being a homemaker with no outside income.

"Not exactly. She never made any real money at it. That's also why I never mentioned it. No need to tarnish her rep." Worth's mouth twisted like he knew that was a lost cause. "Wasn't relevant that she was into that multi-level mass marketing shit. Selling kitchen supplies and gourmet food through parties."

"Investigators looked at the bank statements," I pressed. And I had, too, looking for even the smallest hint of a money trail. "No big red-flag transactions."

"She used mattress money for her start-up."

"Mattress money?" Knox asked before I could.

"Dad's folks lost a lot in a down market back in the day, so he always kept a certain amount of cash on hand. Called it mattress money. She used that for her buy-in for the kitchen crap. Didn't tell him. Hence the yelling."

"What was the name of the pyramid scheme? Do you remember?" Eagerness rolled off Knox as he pulled out his phone. He'd be a terrible poker player, but I'd had that exact question.

"Fuck if I know." Mouth pursing, Worth looked about five seconds away from telling me where to shove it. "There was a picture of a big chef hat with a crown and a white dude with a beard stamped on every item."

"Is this it?" Knox held up his phone. "Kitchen Kingdom?"

"Yeah." Worth exhaled hard. "Haven't seen that logo in a minute."

"That's because they went under." Knox was about to wiggle right out of his chair as he spoke quickly. "My mom is obsessed with true-crime shows. There was this whole exposé movie that came out a couple of years ago because this kooky dude in Florida connected with the company and offed like three women in different Florida towns who'd worked for the scheme."

"Fuck." I whistled low as I grabbed for my own phone to take notes.

"I'm done here." Worth pushed away from the table and

stood with jerky movements, hands visibly shaking. "No more rabbit holes. Florida's a hell of a long commute, even for a serial killer. Some tangential relationship to a stupid money-grubbing scheme isn't going to change what I know in my heart to be true."

I held up a hand to stop him, standing as well. "Worth—"

"I just can't. I can't. I'm sorry." Voice breaking, he stepped away from the table. "Chase whatever leads you and Holden want, but I'm done."

And with that, he was gone, striding off, past the crowd at the register, not stopping until he was outside the double glass doors. I collapsed back into my seat, not sure what the heck had just happened.

"Oh my god, Monroe." Knox held up his phone. His eyes were big, like Wallace's when he spied a treat. "The mass-level marketing murderer—that's what they call him— did a year of college in Vancouver, Washington. That's not that far from Safe Harbor. And he got kicked out for harassing and stalking a fellow student."

"Show me." I grabbed his phone, taking notes on my own as fast as I could type. "Hell. I need to call Holden. But we've also got to get changed for the wedding and reception."

"I'm on it. I'll handle finding us a ride and all the other details. You focus on the case." Knox gave an emphatic nod as he patted my hand. "Leave it to me."

Leave it to me. There wasn't a glimmer of sexy intent in his words, but something stirred in my chest. *Trust.* That's what we had, and it was seductive as hell, to the point I wasn't sure how I'd lived without it.

Chapter Nineteen

Knox

I absolutely loved being Monroe's Mr. Fix It. Ride back to the hotel? On it. Emergency iron of his dress shirt? Got it. Forgot a card for the wedding? Already handled it. Need directions from the church back to the hotel? All over that. And need to duck the reception to take Holden's return call? No problem.

"Your wine." I handed Monroe a glass as he sank back down next to me. The dinner and toasts were over, and the tables were starting to clear. After Monroe sipped his wine, I reached over to straighten his collar. "And your tie is crooked."

"Thanks." He glanced around the silver-and-purple decorated room. The wedding party held court near the front as the DJ encouraged guests onto the dance floor. "Think anyone noticed I was gone?"

"Nah. It's a small party, but I told the grooms you had a call, and they understood. And I kept up on all the gossip for you. Kenny and his wife are expecting twins. The

Darrens are adopting. The one groom's brother is hot for the other groom's sister, but that's destined for heartbreak."

"How do you figure?"

"She keeps checking her phone." I nodded toward the front table, where a bored younger woman in a purple sheath dress was looking down at a shiny pink phone. "She's searching for a better option, and he's looking for forever. Poor dude, but guess he needs to shoot his shot."

"Don't we all." Monroe's voice was distant and resigned. "And how is it we both love that expression?"

"Because we share a brain." I laughed, but he didn't. "You okay?" I put an arm around him, grateful for a setting where I could touch him as much as I wanted. Returning to Safe Harbor after the luxury of all this PDA would be difficult. "How did the call go?"

"Holden agrees the multi-level mass marketing murderer is a promising lead. We're meeting with your dad Monday. If he agrees, I'm going to seek an interview with this suspect at the Florida prison where he's housed."

"Awesome." I made my tone as bright as possible. This was a huge break for the case and a potential big win for Monroe's efforts. My losing out on a few days with Monroe was a small price. "I'll hold down the fort on the house projects for you."

"You're the best." Monroe gave me a look so sentimental it bordered on dopey.

"What?"

"Nothing," he said the word gently, like a kiss. "Just thinking how much I'll miss you."

Same. I inhaled, savoring his spicy aftershave scent. "It'll likely only be a couple of days. We'll be fine."

Even as I said it, the ticking clock in my brain increased its volume. Sure, this trip would be quick, but there would come a time when missing would be all we had. Stomach souring, I slid Monroe the piece of cake I'd nabbed for him while he'd taken Holden's call.

"You even saved me a piece of cake?" His smile softened further, which perversely only made my stomach that much sloshier. To distract us both, I stole a bite of the icing, eating it super slowly off my index finger while holding his gaze. Monroe let out a long groan. "Don't look at me like that. I've skipped enough of this reception. We probably need to linger a bit longer before I drag you to our room."

"Who says you're doing the dragging?" I gave him a hard, hot stare.

"Good point." His cheeks colored nicely. "I do love it when you take charge. Like how you handled all the details today."

"I like that you let me." I meant it too. I loved that this big, capable navy lieutenant trusted me enough to let me take charge of certain things and was willing to accept my help to make things easier for both of us. "We make a good team."

"We do." His voice turned wistful as if he was also thinking of that not-so-distant future when we wouldn't be a team. "Dance with me?"

"Anytime." I was more than happy to grant him the change in subjects, and I was never going to turn down a chance to dance with Monroe. The easy way we moved together had only improved over our weeks together, dance break after dance break, to the point where we quickly found our way to a slow, sultry waltz.

"Hey, what do you know?" I smiled at him as we made our way around the edge of the dance floor. "Apparently, we don't need a club jam to get our groove on."

"We do fit together perfectly." Monroe beamed back

before tilting his head. "Man, this song takes me back. This was Worth's favorite in high school."

"I hope he gets help." I matched Monroe's thoughtful tone. "He needs someone to talk to."

"That used to be me." Monroe sounded pained before turning more pragmatic. "My own fault, I guess. Fleeing for the navy, not keeping in touch the best."

"Don't beat yourself up. Doesn't sound like Worth has exactly been eager to hear from Safe Harbor friends."

"Nope. But you're right. He needs something." The lines around Monroe's eyes deepened. "I'm worried. I texted earlier, but no reply. Predictable, but I hate knowing he's in a bad place."

"We'll check on him again tomorrow before our flight."

"We?" Monroe pursed his lips like he wasn't sure whether I meant the promise.

"We," I said firmly. "You don't need to deal with this on your own."

"I..." Shaking his head, Monroe leaned in for a fast kiss on my cheek. "I'm not sure I've ever had a...friend quite like you."

"Ditto. But I mean it. You don't have to go it alone." I held him tighter as the song shifted to a more romantic one about fields, firsts, and forever. Monroe wasn't my first or my forever, but he sure would be seared upon my memories, coloring everything that came after. If we were a song, it was a wistful lament, but as we swayed, I couldn't help but wish we could instead be a sappy ballad without a hint of sorrow.

We nestled together, dancing slower, but eventually, the song came to a close, and in a playlist fail, a stupid group dance number followed. We drifted to the edge of the dance floor, where the happy grooms found us.

"Monroe! There you are." The taller groom, a skinny bald man named Kale, slapped Monroe on the back. Kale had been someone important in NCIS, and I hadn't sorted out whether Kale was a navy nickname or his given name. "We were wondering where you snuck off to."

"I had—"

"A business call. Knox told us." The smaller groom, Eric, an accountant with a jolly laugh, smiled at me before turning to Monroe. "You've sure got a keeper here."

"I can't wait to make that pasta dish you told us about." Kale nudged my arm.

"And I'm going to hold you to that pickup game," Eric added.

"Anytime." I grinned at them. While they were closer to Monroe's age than mine, I liked them and their easy good humor a lot. We made some more small talk before the grooms decided to dance, leaving Monroe and me to head back to our table for our water glasses.

"Well. You certainly made quite the impression." Monroe's tone held a fair bit of surprise before he took a swallow of water.

"Sorry. Was I not supposed to circulate while you were gone?"

"I love that you didn't need me to socialize." Monroe pulled me snugly against his side before kissing my temple. "Your independence is one of the sexiest things about you."

"Yeah? What else?"

"You're tall, jacked, and have great hair?" He let out the closest thing to a giggle I'd heard from him, and I couldn't help laughing myself.

"Flattery will get you everywhere."

"Including back to our room?" He waggled his eyebrows at me, and I didn't need to be asked twice before I grabbed his hand. We made a fast exit and raced to the bank of elevators outside the hotel ballroom. A group of bridesmaids from a different function joined us in the elevator, so I settled for merely holding Monroe's hand tightly.

Once in our hotel room with its big, fluffy king bed, I was momentarily distracted by the bay of glass windows giving an unparalleled view of downtown San Francisco. The city hung glittery beneath our nineteenth-floor room, captivating and magical, and as much I wanted to push Monroe down on the bed, I had to take a minute to appreciate the perfect summer night and the once-in-a-lifetime view.

"Wow. Just look how gorgeous the city is," I marveled as I stepped onto the narrow balcony, which housed side-by-side lounge chairs.

"I'm looking." Monroe did an exaggerated leer, checking out my ass as he followed me.

"I'm serious."

"So am I." He pulled me against him, nuzzling my neck. "Well, at least this is sturdier than the last time we were on a balcony together."

"Yeah, wouldn't want to plummet to our doom when I kiss you." Turning in his embrace, I gave him the soft, romantic kiss the night seemed to cry out for. Tender and slow, our lips fit like we'd had decades together, while my heart still sped up like it was the first time all over again.

We kissed and kissed, city noise a faint roar beneath us, a cool breeze washing over us even as my skin heated more and more from each lingering caress. As with dancing, it ceased to matter who was leading. Monroe had started it, I'd continued it, and now the kiss ebbed and flowed like the traffic below, neither of us controlling as we let the kiss take on a life of its own.

Monroe dipped his head, kissing my jaw, which I'd shaved smooth for the occasion, and my neck. He loosened my tie before unbuttoning my collar.

"What are you up to?" I stretched my neck, nothing if not helpful as he continued down my torso until my shirt hung open.

"It's not obvious?" Eyes sparkling, he released me long enough to grab a pillow and throw from a chaise just inside the door, tossing both onto the nearest lounge chair.

"Here?"

"You sound so scandalized, Rebound." He laughed warmly, wrapping me in a tight hug before starting on my dress pants. "Aren't you the one who very nearly made me come in public within a half-hour of meeting?"

"Did I?" I tried to sound shocked.

"You know you did. And there's something about being up this high, late at night, an anonymous city below us..."

"Okay, I can see the appeal." Chuckling, I got in on the action, undoing his tie and shirt and unbuckling his pants, but I stopped short of pushing them down. "Are we seriously going to do it out here?"

"Yes." Lightly nipping my ear, he sent my pants to the balcony floor to join our shirts. "You'll have to be very, very quiet for me."

"I'm not the screamer," I reminded him, but he grinned, looking far younger out here under the moon, naked and naughty with me. And once we were both naked, he led me to the lounger, urging me to stretch out, him spooning me from behind. His hard cock pressed into my back, and his breath was warm on my ear. My stomach quivered, not with fear precisely, but not exactly eager want either.

"Monroe—"

"Shh. I know." He skimmed a hand down my side. "You don't bottom."

"You have me thinking more about it," I had to admit. Every time I fucked him in our bed back at the house, I became that much more curious about what he was feeling. "The way you love getting fucked is a hell of a turn-on. But my first times..." I had to stop and bite my lower lip hard.

"It's okay." He dropped a soft kiss in the middle of my neck. "You don't have to tell me."

"I want to. I'm known for being accommodating, right? So the first time someone at college asked, I said sure, I could bottom. But it sucked. I tried it twice. I wanted to like it. But it hurt, and both encounters were totally awkward on top of that."

"Oh, Knox." Monroe shuddered, hand tightening against my abs. "I'm sorry it happened like that for you. Honestly, my own first times weren't that much better. But I'm glad I tried again with you."

"Me too." Tipping my head back, I met him for a lingering kiss.

"And I'm not going to be that dude who tells you it would be different with me. Because I don't know that. Not everyone is wired to enjoy getting fucked. But I will say that if you ever did want to try, I'd do everything in my power to make it good for you like you always do for me, and I'd stop the second you asked."

"I know you would. You're...safe." Safe was as close as I could come to encompassing how deeply I trusted Monroe, how close I felt to him, especially right then.

"Safe is good." He kissed me, long and deep, with a new level of solemness to his touch and lips. "So, you trust me?"

"Always." I snuggled more securely against him, deliberately pushing against his erection rather than shying away.

"I want to go like this, between your thighs." He reached over to our pile of clothes, retrieving something from his pants. I had to laugh as he slicked up his cock.

"You were seriously packing lube?"

"I seriously want you." He chuckled with me before adjusting our positions so he was spooned behind me, cock nestled between my legs, riding right below the crease of my ass and nudging against my balls. "Not fucking, I promise. But I like being close to you like this."

"I like it too." I relaxed into the embrace, enjoying how tightly he held me, lower arm snaking around my chest, hand right over my heart. His other arm draped over my hip, his hand stroking my cock from intrigued to raring to go. Turning my head, I sought his mouth until we were kissing, at first languid, a gradual build of desire, then demanding as pure need took over.

"God, the way you kiss me." He kept his lips right next to mine. "You reel me in."

"You saying I caught you?"

"Yep. Didn't even know I was falling..." He sounded all dreamy, and knowing I did that to him made my dick that much harder. And made it that much easier to be honest.

"I'm falling too." I matched his dreamlike tone, but I was deadly serious. I was falling hard for this man. The landing would suck, but until then, I wanted to stretch out, enjoy each second of freefall. Reading the signals in his breath and grip, I pushed back against him, tensing my ass and thigh muscles.

"Yeah, do that again." He groaned, and I did too as his strokes sped up on my cock, the exact tempo and pressure I craved. "Shush. Can't be too loud."

"Says the moaner."

"I am not." His indignant tone made me laugh.

"Nah, you're more of a screamer."

"Am not." He released my dick long enough to tickle my side until I wiggled and chuckled.

"Hey, that's my signature move." I did a terrible job of faking upset, making us laugh harder.

"I stole it."

What he was really stealing was my heart, with each kiss and touch and silly word. I stopped wriggling and pulled him as close as two people could be. Forget fucking. This right here was making love. Each slide of Monroe's cock between my legs, each tender kiss, each meaningful caress.

"Fuck. Knox. So good." Monroe sounded both pained and awed, exactly how I felt too. He stroked my cock faster, adding the thumb action that always brought me closer to climax.

"Love your hand." My breath came in harsh pants. "More. Faster."

But instead of pushing me over the edge, he backed off, slower thrusts and lighter strokes. "We'll get there. Not ready for it to be over."

"Me either." I meant so much more than the inevitable end of the fuck, and judging by the way he kissed me, he did too. So I let him set the pace for once, gave up any pretense of being in charge, and floated, luxuriating in that freefall. Fuck the landing. The fall was too damn good. I let it go on and on. Or rather, we went on and on, no let about it. This thing between us that was bigger than either of us.

Climax snuck up on me, a scary rush of sensation that had me clutching at his wrist. "Monroe."

"I've got you." He added to the promise with soft kisses and firm touches.

"Fuck me." I had to say it, test out how it felt, let the quiver in my abs become the warmth of want.

"Yeah. Feel me?" Monroe adjusted his angle so his cock dragged hard against the underside of my balls, and I groaned, no longer in control of my volume. "Shush. Quiet."

"Kiss me." I was all need and breath and reckless want, and as soon as his lips met mine, I was pulsing in his hand, body shuddering.

"That's it, Knox. Let go." Monroe grunted, also not nearly quiet enough, as he came in a warm rush between my thighs. And as it turned out, the landing wasn't deadly at all, instead soft as a cloud. My internal rhythm shifted, the song that always played in my head becoming a sweet lullaby to drift along to in a post-orgasmic haze.

"God. You're beautiful." Monroe kissed me with so much tenderness that he had to be hearing the melody too. "Love your face when you come."

Love me. Love me. Love all of me, my heart chanted, the refrain of a song so sweet it hurt.

Chapter Twenty

Monroe

In all my years with the navy, I'd never had a real homecoming. Sure, my dad and his wife had attended my graduation from the academy, but it wasn't the same as a special someone waiting at the docks or hangar for a return stateside. And when Knox beamed at me, glowing with pure pleasure, I finally understood what I'd been missing.

"You're back." Looking freshly showered with damp hair, Knox was almost to the bottom of the back stairs as I entered the kitchen.

"I am." I had to brace because he launched himself into my arms for the tightest hug ever. Like I'd been gone three weeks, not three days. Warmth spread from my chest, down my arms and fingers, every spot that touched Knox melting like ice in July.

After giving me a sound kiss, Knox scooped up the cat lurking near the stairs. "Wallace missed you. See?"

"Just Wallace?" I was tired and in dire need of a shower, a beer, and a bed. And Knox in said bed. But then Knox made the cat wave at me, and I couldn't help grinning, my tiredness replaced by a near-giddiness at being back in the presence of the guy I...

And there I had to stop. There were words I couldn't let myself think, let alone feel.

"You know I missed you too." Setting the cat down, Knox gave me a longer, deeper kiss that made me forget all about being hungry and thirsty. "Hotel room phone fun notwithstanding, it was too damn lonely in the big bed here. I had to go sleep on the third floor last night."

"Aw. Poor baby." I chuckled, mainly at Knox's blush at the mention of the phone sex we'd had two nights ago. "I had to turn a pillow sideways on the left side of the hotel bed."

"We're a pair." He shook his head at me, expression fond but exasperated, exactly the one all the happy long-time couples I knew used. And I'd never wanted that either. No homecoming. No attachments. No wedding bells. But then I'd danced with Knox at Kale and Eric's wedding and watched Knox climax on the hotel balcony, and I could have sworn I heard distant chimes. The entire weekend in San Francisco had made me long for everything I'd never wanted before. I held his gaze, trying to soak up another few seconds of undiluted happiness until he rolled his eyes and kicked at the tile. "So...when are you going to tell me what you found out? I'm dying here."

Knox was now as invested in this case as Holden and I, demanding updates, offering suggestions, and celebrating the breaks along with us. While in Florida, I'd reviewed a bunch of case records not available online, interviewed a few people connected with the case, and been granted a short, frustrating visit with the chief suspect.

"The threads are tenuous, but they're there, and they

keep adding up." I leaned against the counter as Knox moved to the fridge. He passed me a sparkling water before studying the contents of the vegetable drawer. I took a sip of water before continuing. "The main thing is the tangential connection to this region, roughly around the same time frame. I've got some interviews set up with a few of the original witnesses here, like her friends, to see if anyone recognizes this suspect."

"Sam's mom. If she wasn't on the original list of interviews, she should have been." Knox nodded sharply as he stacked an onion, zucchini, and two peppers on the counter. "She knows everyone and everything going on in this town, and she's both sharp and honest. My grandpa was on the original case, of course, but my grandma is another one who knows everyone coming and going."

"Good ideas." I still had a hard time thinking of Rob's parents as a grandma and grandpa, but it was true that they might have some valuable insights. "I can't wait to share with Holden. Need to tell him about the suspect interview too. Tried calling him on my drive from the airport, but I think he was teaching his summer class."

"And now he's probably getting ready for trivia night."

"Trivia night." I echoed Knox, adding a long groan. "Hell. I need to beg out of that—"

"No, you don't. You should go." He waved at the door I'd only just entered.

"But you were about to cook."

"It can be for me." He shrugged, but the way he'd been pulling out ingredients said he'd been planning on feeding us both. "And I'll save some for your lunch tomorrow." He waved again. "Go on. If you hurry, you'll get there before the first round. I know you want to tell your friends about the trip."

"But I want to tell you more." I sounded like a whiny ten-year-old, but Knox's small pleased smile at my lament gave me an idea. He was so used to being not included and an afterthought, which had never sat right with me. After the past few weeks, I wanted him to come first, not be left out entirely. "You should come too."

"To trivia night?" He pursed his mouth like I'd handed him a lemon, not an invitation.

"We need a sports expert. We keep missing basketball questions and stuff like that. And Sam said it wouldn't be weird to bring you. We can socialize with each other. No harm in that." It wouldn't be as fun as San Francisco, where I could touch and love on Knox as much as I wanted, but it would be better than nothing.

"Well, we are roommates." His face remained as unreadable as his tone.

"Exactly." I put an encouraging hand on his arm. "We're friends."

"Buddies might be pushing it." He chortled like there was a joke I wasn't understanding.

"Come on. I don't want you here alone. I've missed you. At least this way, I can see you while we count down to being alone later."

"I like the sound of later." He returned the vegetables to the fridge and the cutting board to its rack. "Okay. I'll come. But mainly because I want to hear about your interview. The greasy fried pickles are a nice bonus."

After promising Knox all the fried pickles he could want, I locked up the house before we decided to walk the short distance to the sports bar. We didn't need to run, but it took a fast trot to get there before the first round started.

"You brought a sports guy!" Sam was first to greet Knox while Holden scooted over to make room for an extra chair.

"Hey, Knox. Sit here." Holden gestured at the empty chair, leaving me to find my own. "Remind me if you eat meat. We usually get a couple of kinds of wings."

"And fried pickles," Sam added. "I remember how you love those."

"Sounds great." Knox smiled widely, but I had a tough time following suit. It did not sound great. It sounded like my friends were poaching my territory. If my friends got any more enthusiastic about Knox's appearance, I was going to sharpen my teeth on the salt shaker. But it was my own damn fault, both for inviting him and being unable to claim him with a well-placed hand or sharp look for Holden's barely-disguised flirting and Sam's overly-helpful suggestions.

"Can I see ID?" Our usual server frowned when Knox asked for the ale Holden was raving about. Which Knox had, and totally wasn't a huge deal, other than the fact that it shoved home our age difference and reason nine hundred and forty-eight why I couldn't date Knox. Especially not in this town where it felt like dozens of eyeballs were already watching the three of us drink with the police chief's kid.

And with each question in the quiz round, I swore the eyeballs pointed in our direction increased, catching each high five and celebration. A few beers. Some appetizers. It wasn't like we were out to get Knox loaded, and indeed, he still had half of his first beer at the end of round one, but I still felt one wrong glance or touch away from the pervy old man label.

"Way to go." Holden had no such issues, slapping Knox on the back as we came in second for the first round.

"See, we've needed someone like you." Even Sam was laying it on super thick.

"Aw. You don't need me. Any warm body with a grasp

of basketball history would do." Knox laughed, and the rest of the table did too, but I did need him, specifically. I'd missed him the whole time I was in Florida, missed his scent and his questions and his cooking and his concern. I wasn't sure exactly when want had given way to full-fledged *need*, but here I was, absolutely certain that I'd needed someone like Knox for years and might never find another one like him.

"Now that we can rest on our well-earned laurels, tell me more about your interview with the suspect." Holden interrupted the biggest damn revelation of my life to redirect my attention to the case I was supposed to be focusing on rather than worrying how in the heck I'd survive without Knox.

"Frustrating." I took a sip of my beer to collect my thoughts. "Our suspect for the Stapleton disappearance was ruled competent to stand trial in Florida, where he was convicted in the other three murders, but good luck getting him to make sense. He thinks he's in some sort of thriller, speaking only in riddles and lines from obscure movies. I recorded everything he said, but it will take time to go through and unpack the quotes."

"Which movie?" Sam and Knox spoke at the same time.

"Does it—oh. Of course it matters." I slapped the table because if I hadn't been so distracted by thoughts of Knox, I would have thought of that myself. For a diabolical psychopath, every detail mattered. "Which movie might actually matter more than which line."

"Especially if it was filmed around here," Holden added, pulling out his phone, but Sam was already on it.

"Exactly. The iconic eighties coming-of-age drama *Treehouse* was filmed right in town here, but there have been plenty of others along the coast and in Portland."

"His choice of which he's quoting from could be a clue. But also, what part of the movie—first act, second, etc. Heck, even what season." Knox was also busy on his phone showing me memes of quotes from Oregon-set movies.

"You're brilliant." For a second, I almost forgot Sam and Holden were right there, and I very nearly kissed Knox. "I think a lot of what he said was actually opening lines to things. I'll show you back at our place." Before Holden and Sam could turn their speculative gazes my way, I turned toward Sam. "Oh, and Knox suggested talking to your mother. I pulled up the list, and she's not on the original interviews."

"They probably couldn't get an interpreter." Sam's mouth twisted. His mother was Deaf, and while Safe Harbor did have a fairly large Deaf community for a small town, it didn't surprise me that a low-budget investigation with a clear suspect had moved along without interviewing tangential friends. "But she knew both the husband and wife from church."

"And interviewing Rob's mom might have been seen as a conflict of interest because she's also not on the list. I'm going to want to talk to a number of people, show some pictures of the suspect, but both of those women should be included."

"Excellent point. Thanks for thinking of it, Knox." Holden beamed like Knox had single-handedly cracked the case. And perhaps he had. Or perhaps I was simply a jealous bastard who wanted Knox and his amazing brain and didn't want to share.

In the second round, we again came in a close second, miles better than our usual showing.

"Coming back next week?" Holden asked Knox as he rolled along to the exit with us. "We need your expertise."

"We'll see. Depends." Knox shot me a cryptic look.

"We need you." Sam gave him a brotherly hug on his way to the parking lot.

"That was fun." Knox's expression remained guarded. I dragged a hand through my hair to avoid the urge to grab Knox's arm and hold him close as we started our walk home. *Home.* When had it stopped being Aunt Henri's house? Huh. At some point in the last six weeks, I'd gone from dread over the house to something approaching affection. Ownership even.

"You fit right in." I tried to free the compliment from my jealousy because Knox truly had been a welcome addition to the evening. And he did. He fit right into this house, into my life, into that hole in my heart I hadn't been aware of. If only I could keep him. I pulled him tight against me the second the door shut behind us at the house.

"How tired are you, for real?" Knox asked without releasing me. Wallace delicately picked his feline way down the stairs to greet us, but Knox held my gaze. "If you need a shower and to go to sleep without fooling around, I'd understand."

"I wouldn't." I snorted and groped his ass, making us both laugh.

"Good. Because I was thinking..." He gave an unusual-for-him coy smile.

"I like it when you think. "

"Thinking I want to try to bottom. Been thinking all week about what you said in San Francisco. I want to see if it's different with you. You up for that?"

There was only one possible answer.

Chapter Twenty-One

Knox

"Absolutely." There was so much softness in Monroe's gaze I was surprised the air itself in the foyer wasn't filled with fluff. I wanted to tell him this wasn't a big deal, but we both knew it was. It had taken me most of the summer to get to this place where I truly wanted to try, and something about the solemn emotion in Monroe's expression made my chest tight and my eyes burn.

"That was easy," I mumbled, desperate for a laugh. "Didn't even have to twist your arm."

"All you ever have to do is ask." He held out a hand to lead me upstairs, but I paused at the second-floor landing to gather him close into another hug, this one from behind.

"You're pretty amazing." I buried my face in his short hair. "I missed you."

"Missed you too." He spun like he was about to kiss me but then stepped back, taking in the whole upstairs hall. Gone was the faded carpet runner, the chipped paint on the

160

built-ins, the dusty eaves, and the decades-old prints. "Whoa. You've been busy."

"You like?" I'd polished the hardwoods, which had been in good enough shape to not need full refinishing, then I'd painted the cabinetry and trim a bright true-white, setting off a light blue-green color that called to mind spring and Easter and little mint candies. I'd found a slightly damaged art book on the third floor and had salvaged the best abstract prints to swap out with the old drab Victorian pictures, refreshing the frames with some white spray paint.

"You truly are a magician." Monroe's tone held an amount of pride worthy of reaching a mountain summit or giving a valedictorian speech, his touch on my arm equally warm.

"I love how I can impress you with a little paint and some accessories."

"Maybe you impress me just by being you." He kissed my temple, brushing my hair out of the way.

"Hey, I'm already a sure thing tonight," I protested as I followed him into the bedroom.

"Even sure things deserve sweet talk." After shutting the door, he backed his words up with a kiss so gentle I couldn't help but shiver.

"You okay?" Monroe stepped back to peer at me. "I'd be fine if—"

"I want to try this." I pulled off my T-shirt with a flourish and shoved my shorts and briefs down to show him exactly how ready I was. "I do. I need you to trust that I'll say stop if I need you to change directions."

"I do trust you." The look Monroe gave me was so serious I stopped mid-naked flounce. My breath caught as I tried to decipher all the layers of meaning in his expression.

"I trust you too." I tried to match his nuance, and in

holding his gaze, each word felt like a vow. Emotions I didn't know how to confront threatened to overwhelm me, so I looked away, glancing at the bed. "I showered earlier, but I can go—"

"Only place you're going is right here." Smiling as if he also needed a break from the solemnness, Monroe tumbled me onto the bed.

"Only place I wanna be." I grinned up at him, way more comfortable being playful. As soon as he was naked, I was on him, both of us rolling around on the bed, covers and pillows going every which way. We kissed and touched and laughed and tickled because that was kind of our thing, getting turned on while also having fun. I loved goading Monroe into showing me some of his military moves, tickling his sides until he flipped me onto my stomach and nibbled at my neck and shoulders.

The light scrape of his teeth made my toes curl against the cotton sheets, and I lost interest in wrestling, stirring cock reminding me what I'd asked for. But Monroe didn't seem in any hurry, licking across my shoulder blades with the tip of his tongue like he was outlining an invisible tattoo.

"Monroe." I tried to roll, but he gently returned my head to the nearby pillow.

"Get comfy," he ordered as he dug his thumbs along my spine, a divine but way too damn slow massage. I made another impatient noise, which made him laugh. "I would think the king of slow could have a bit more patience."

"It's hard."

"I know." Monroe cackled and dragged his cock against the back of my thighs.

"Be serious." I'd meant that I was way more comfortable being the one setting the pace, as with dancing. Neither of us was the leader, precisely, but in both bed and on the dance floor, I usually set the tempo. Awaiting whatever dastardly bit of choreography Monroe had planned was a new form of torture. And then Monroe slithered backward, tongue following the track his thumb had made. *"Oh."*

He'd telegraphed his destination from that first bite on my neck, but knowing and experiencing were two entirely different things. I didn't always rim Monroe before we fucked, but I had enough of an oral fixation that there was usually some mouth action in the warm-up. So I wasn't surprised to feel Monroe's breath across my ass, but the way it made me shudder was new, this low knot of anticipation gathering deep inside me.

Unlike myself, who merely did a decent job of faking being able to wait, Monroe had actual patience, nibbling each of my ass cheeks while rubbing and massaging my glutes. He had his own style, too, different from my dive-in-and-get-to-it, which I probably also should have expected. Not knowing what he was about to do next made it easier to tolerate the delay in action.

But as it turned out, the delay *was* the action. Each touch and kiss relaxed me a little more until I stopped waiting for him to fuck me and started enjoying the unpredictability of his play. At some point, he'd added lube to the mix, and I barely registered the increased slipperiness of his fingers until he rubbed circles around my rim. The firm, steady pressure was familiar.

"Ah. I like this." This was similar enough to how I played on my own sometimes when edging that I further sank into the sensations.

"And this?" He took advantage of my relaxed state, easing a finger in then retreating, teasing with a mere hint of penetration, a little deeper each pass.

"More." The demand came from some guttural place in

my throat, the same place moans kept escaping from. And then he complied, finger curving, and I braced for the pressure on my prostate, the live wire feeling my body never seemed too sure whether it liked or not. But as soon as I tensed, Monroe backed off slightly, coaxing sensations rather than pushing, a distinction I'd never made. And instead of a live wire to avoid, he gave me a damn light show. "Oh wow."

"Relax into it." He added a second finger.

"I'm—*yeah.*" Whatever I'd been going to say was lost in the increased fullness. My body couldn't seem to decide whether the new deeper pressure was good or not. I moved my hips restlessly. Monroe shifted from thrusting to a different kind of play, rubbing and stretching, an amplified version of the one-finger action I was more used to. The stretch was good, each scissoring action of his fingers adding to that laser-light effect until I made a happy noise. "Oh, that's the part I like."

"Mm-hmm. You can have all of that you want." This was where his patience was the sexiest damn thing on the planet, the way he kept giving and giving, not seeming in a hurry to get to fucking. Inside me, that ball of anticipation grew and grew until my whole body was warm and wanting.

"Need...more." I existed in that marvelous limbo land where the build to climax was unmistakable yet still far enough off to be both frustrating and intoxicating.

"Here. Let's do this." Withdrawing his fingers, Monroe fumbled for the towel I'd left nearby after my shower. After wiping off his hand, he flopped onto his back.

I frowned. "But I want..."

"I know. This is where you trust me, okay?" Pushing on my shoulder, he encouraged me to sit up and straddle his waist. "I want you on top. That way, you control it completely. You're in charge. Whatever feels good, whether that's just the tip—"

"Just the tip." I snorted as he applied lube to his cock. We'd ditched condoms some weeks before, a casual decision born of an empty box and both of us coming off long dry spells where we each had negative test results and no intentions of taking on multiple summer partners.

"Whatever you want, Knox." He was back to that solemn stare, where I believed in my soul that he truly would offer me every damn thing I could want. And lord, how I wanted. He held his cock steady at the base, more of that bottomless patience of his. "This is your show."

Show. I liked that. I had always liked showing off, and all the attention on me felt far more comfortable framed as a show, something I could do for him. And I started that way, making an exaggerated display of rolling my hips, hovering above his cockhead, teasing us both. But then it started feeling better and better, little sparks racing up my spine as I mimicked what he'd done with his fingers, taking a little and then retreating.

"Wow." As it turned out, not trying to take the whole thing removed a lot of my anxiety. It let me focus on the parts I did like, the stretch and burn, gradually going deep enough for glancing contact on my prostate but raising again before it could get overwhelming.

"Yeah. That's it." Monroe was all encouragement, one hand on my thigh, eyes hooded, so much approval and desire my chest contracted.

"Want it good for you too." Showing off was all well and good, but guilt wormed its way past the pleasure.

"Trust me, remember?" He stroked my hip. "It's fabulous. Everything about you does it for me. Watching you is sexy as fuck."

"You like watching?" An idea flashed in my head, and I reached for my cock. Sure enough, Monroe smiled as I groaned. Felt decadent, teasing ass and cock at the same time.

"Hell, yes. You enjoying yourself is everything. Keep doing that."

"What if I...?" I panted, everything suddenly way more intense. "Come?"

The edge I'd flirted with while he played was suddenly a lot closer, my body loving the combo of my familiar hand and the new sensations in my ass.

"Come. Don't worry about me. Get yourself off on my dick." He sounded like that was the top item on his personal wish list, as close to begging as I was.

"You want that?"

"You know I do." He groaned as I started moving faster, little rocks and rolls of my hips, knees digging into the mattress. "Feels amazing. Come on, Knox." His gaze was riveted on my fist as I stroked myself faster and harder, breath coming in shaky huffs. "That's it. Let go."

Suddenly, I wanted more than the tease and reached down to bat away his hand, which had been keeping his dick steady. In one smooth motion, I sank farther down, all the air leaving my lungs in a single low groan.

"Oh." My thighs and abs trembled, everything slowing down and narrowing to the pressure in my ass and the pulsing tension at the tip of my cock. I needed to move, but it was almost too much, each new sensation more overwhelming than the last. "Monroe."

"That's it, sweetheart. I'm here." The quiet reassurance, the steadiness of his voice, my absolute belief that he wouldn't let me break was enough. More than enough. Another stroke. A little farther down. Back up. Again. And—

"Monroe. I'm coming." Like he could have missed the jets of come erupting all over my fist and his stomach. The orgasm felt less like an explosion than usual, more like a wave washing over me. A baptism of sorts, freeing me from long-held fears and beliefs, leaving room only for pleasure.

"Yes." Eyes fluttering shut, he groaned like he'd been punched, but he seemed more into my orgasm than the pursuit of his own. Indeed, when he helped me untangle myself, he was still fully hard.

"You didn't finish?" Accepting the towel he passed me, I stretched out next to him, running a hand down his torso. "I wanted to get you off too."

"Nah. That wasn't about me." He smiled and petted my hair which had come loose from my ponytail. "Keep lying here on my chest. You breathing hard and looking all blissed out is a huge turn-on."

"So you're saying all I have to do is look pretty?" I batted my eyes at him and danced my fingers across his abs.

"Yep." He nodded, then groaned as I reached his cock and took a firm hold of it, pushing aside his own hand. "But if you want to help..."

"Always."

"Kiss me," he demanded, our lips meeting in an urgent kiss, but it wasn't long before his head tipped back, eyes shutting.

"What are you thinking about?" I whispered.

"How damn hot you looked. How damn good you felt. How much I love—*fuck*." Monroe didn't finish the thought before he was coming, body curling tight around mine as he came and came, shudders so hard they were almost heaves.

And he didn't need to complete the sentiment for me to know exactly what he'd been saying. And what he'd likely say next.

"Oh my god." He sounded utterly stunned as he sagged back against the pillow. And yup, regret incoming in three, two, not sticking around for one. I scooted out of bed, dodging his attempts to keep me next to him.

"We're gonna need another towel." My voice was strange. Too fast. Too distant. And Monroe knew it, eyes going wide as he made a visible effort to calm his breathing.

"Knox." His tone was so reasonable as I dashed toward the bathroom, already at the door when he added, "We should talk."

Chapter Twenty-Two

Monroe

"Don't take it back. Please." Knox paused by the bathroom door, expression as stricken as I'd seen it. And there went my hope that maybe he hadn't heard and had simply been unusually focused on post-sex hygiene.

"I wasn't going to take it back. I couldn't." I was many things, but a liar wasn't one of them. Knox continued to have the wide-eyed look of a deer about to bolt for the tree line, so I tried again. "Sometimes things come out in sex..."

"Or explain it away," Knox interrupted with a huff, shaking his head like I'd failed to meet his already low expectations for this conversation.

"I'm not trying to wave it away," I said, even though I'd kind of hoped to do just that. But this was Knox, and if nothing else, he'd earned my trust and my truth. Especially tonight. God, he'd been so spectacularly brave and sexy, pushing his limits. The bigger surprise was that I hadn't said those three words a hundred times watching him during the sex. Taking a breath, I locked gazes with him. "I didn't mean to say that aloud, but not intending to say it isn't the same as not meaning it."

"You meant it?" He narrowed his eyes.

"Come here." I held out a hand, gratified when he left his death grip on the doorframe to come perch next to me on the bed. "I love you, Knox."

"Oh." He shut his eyes, inhaling deeply, hands clasped in his lap like he was receiving a benediction. "Say it again," he whispered.

"I love you." Try three, and the words came easier. Already, they felt so natural on my tongue. Loving Knox wasn't the hard part. In fact, it was simply an immutable truth of the universe, one I could no more influence than the ocean's tides.

"Thank you." It wasn't precisely the response a person hoped for, but I was the one who'd blurted the words during sex. And Knox's thank you seemed to come from somewhere deep inside him, husky and heartfelt. "No one's ever…"

"Fallen so hard for you that they aren't sure they'll ever get back up?" I had to go for a little humor but also more of the truth. There was no more hoping I wouldn't fall or knowing I was likely falling but trying to lessen the impact. I had fallen. Full stop.

"Really?" Knox bit his lip, a new vulnerability in his eyes. In his soft gaze, I saw Rebound, the cocky guy who was everyone's favorite hookup and no one's first call. I didn't regret telling him. The how, maybe. But not the words. He deserved to know. "Because I finished the hall while you were gone? That was just me keeping busy—"

"Now who's making excuses?" I pulled him to me, which was about as successful as moving a highway pylon. "No. Not because you work magic on the remodel. Because you've listened to me go round and round on the Stapleton case. Because you keep sneaking blue paint into this house. Because sometimes I see you looking at me and..." My voice cracked for the first time in twenty-odd years. "Because you're Knox. That's all."

"Wow." He sagged against me, losing the stiffness but keeping the trepidation in his tone. "I'm...scared."

"Me too. Terrified, really." I'd never said the words before, never expected them to feel so damn right, and hell if I knew what happened next.

"I know this is where I'm supposed to say it back—"

I stopped him with a hand on his shoulder. "There's no supposed to or should between us. You don't have to say anything. Or feel anything for that matter." That I loved him was a given. That he might return the sentiment was a whole different matter, and the last thing I wanted to do was put pressure on him.

"I feel...so damn much, Monroe." He sounded distraught, and I understood where he was coming from. Not all these new emotions were pleasant. I kissed the side of his head. "I don't have words, but..."

"It's okay." I pushed aside any disappointment to hold him closer, reveling in his warm skin and nearness. He hadn't pulled away yet. That had to count for something. "And this doesn't have to change anything."

"No?" Mouth twisting, he scooted back, taking all that warmth with him. "Are we going to pretend you didn't say that? Because from where I'm sitting, everything changes. You can't just detonate a feelings bomb in the middle of our nice, uncomplicated summer fling."

I gave a rough laugh at his choice of imagery. "I think you know nothing's been simple or uncomplicated from the start."

"Nope." His shoulders slumped, elbows resting on his knees. "This is gonna hurt like hell. And I hate that for you. For me. For us. I never wanted to hurt either of us, but you especially."

"Maybe I'd rather have the hurt than never have had you." And there was another sentence I'd never expected to say. I'd spent decades doing everything in my power to avoid entanglements and hurt. But never knowing Knox was unthinkable, and if hurt was the price to pay, so be it. He offered me a sad, sentimental smile, a ghost of his usual brightness, like the moon...

The moon. Knox in the moonlight was one of my favorite things, whether on the roof here or on that balcony in San Francisco, and a thought that had plagued me for a few weeks now crept back to the front of my mind.

"But what if it doesn't have to hurt?"

"What are you thinking?" he whispered like he both expected my idea to be outlandish but was also praying for it to be good.

"There are architecture programs in the Bay. Maybe not quite as highly ranked as the one you got into, but good ones. And you liked our trip to the city. You could be happy there. You've been debating between here and the East Coast all summer, but what if there's another option? You could come back to the Portland area often. It's a quick flight. You could see the kids as much as you'd like." The more I talked, the more I warmed to the idea, but the more Knox frowned.

"And maybe you don't know me at all."

"Knox." I made a pained noise. "I know. You're tempted by taking over the repair business. But isn't this other option worth thinking about? You could at least get the degree, decide what to do later as far as how you want to use it."

"Later." His voice sounded crackly like a radio coming in from a distance. "I need to think." Standing, he dodged my attempts to reach for him. "I'm gonna shower."

"Okay." My voice was small. *Buck up. It could be worse.* All my father's meaningless platitudes came filtering back. I wouldn't beg and wasn't going to burden him with how much his walking away hurt.

But somehow, like always, Knox seemed to know. Turning, he placed a hand on my shoulder, squeezed hard. "I'm not saying no."

Unable to speak, I nodded. The issue wasn't his words but rather everything he wasn't saying.

"Give me time?" He rubbed my shoulder when I nodded again, then kissed the top of my head. "Thank you."

"Jesus." I made a barky noise. "Don't thank me for making everything harder."

"You didn't." He said it like a promise, but I knew better.

Chapter Twenty-Three

Knox

I thought.

I thought about Monroe, about what he'd said, what I hadn't said, the major life change he'd proposed, and what in the heck I was supposed to do now.

I thought all Friday, leaving the house before Monroe was up. I thought at Blessed Bean for chai and a muffin, on the drive up the hills to the fancy house we were doing a kitchen refresh for, back down into town for a lunch break, and all damn afternoon.

"Looking good." Frank ambled through the side door, gait hampered by the four paint cans he attempted to tote. I rushed forward to take them from him.

"Here, let me help with those." I didn't wait for him to agree, taking all four cans and neatly stacking them against the wall.

"Day I can't carry a couple of cans of paint is the day I pack it in." Frank frowned, as reluctant to accept assistance as ever, even given his recent health issues. He'd had a heart scare in the spring, spurring a lot of Leon's retirement plans for the two of them. "Gotta stay useful."

"Better not let Leon hear you talking like that." I shook a finger at him. Frank liked to act like he was one foot from the grave, which drove the far more cheerful Leon up the wall.

"That man fusses too much." The fondness in Frank's eyes gave him away. With his Measure Twice cap hiding his bald head, his broad and tall stature made him look younger, more like the ox of a guy he'd been when I'd first started working summers for him and Leon. But he'd been retirement age then, which put him well past seventy now.

"Did I hear a grumpy old carpenter complaining about me?" Leon sauntered in, carrying a big box of paint rollers, tape, and drop cloths. Also well past when other men retired, especially in construction, Leon had a full head of bright-white hair and stooped shoulders that had seen more than their share of hard work.

"Hey, Leon." I took the box from him. Unlike Frank, he happily transferred his load. "I'll put the supplies over here with the paint."

"Good job with the demo." Leon motioned at the kitchen where I'd cleared out the old counters, removed the cabinet doors and hardware for painting, and ripped out all the chipped and worn flooring. "I swear you always do the work of a full crew."

"Demo is easy. Give me a crowbar and get out of my way."

"That's our boy." Frank clapped me on the shoulder, a rare moment of affection from the big guy, the sort of praise he'd been more generous with this summer than in years past. My throat tightened. I couldn't ask for two better bosses.

"Well, *your boy* says you need to let me do more of the heavy stuff." I gave him a pointed stare before turning back to Leon. "Frank tried to move the fridge on his own earlier."

Frank scoffed. "Telling tales on me again."

"You know the doctor would agree with Knox." Leon poked him in the chest, but Frank was uncowed.

"Doctor, schmocter."

"Let me work on the paint tomorrow." I spoke fast to defuse the argument. "You both need the weekend off. Go to the beach or something."

"Thought you had projects at Henri's house to get to." Leon turned a shrewd eye in my direction, seeming to see through my dusty T-shirt and ripped work pants to my bruised heart and troubled thoughts.

"The house stuff can wait." I waved a hand, continuing quickly before either could press me. "You need a break more. Heck, live it up. See if there's a B&B at the coast with an opening for tomorrow night."

"My." Leon took on an almost dreamy expression before he dabbed at his eyes.

"Did I say the wrong thing?" I reached for his arm, but predictably Frank got there first, pulling Leon close and glaring at me.

"I'm fine. And so is Knox." Leon shrugged off our attempts to comfort him. "I was just thinking about all the years when the pair of us couldn't dream of going to a B&B, especially not as easily as clicking around on some site. Or going to the doctor together, for that matter. It's a different world Knox lives in. He and all the baby queers coming up won't know the heart palpitations over something as simple as sleeping arrangements at a nice B&B."

"Roommates." Frank snorted, and Leon nodded.

"Exactly. We were roommates for so many years, hiding behind the business partnership, and sometimes I forget we can be anything else."

"But you've got the rings..." I gestured at their left hands.

"Courthouse wedding." Leon gave a wistful shrug. "Felt more like political rebellion or insurance policy for the health care stuff."

"Aren't you supposed to be the romantic one?" Frank nudged his bony shoulder.

"Sorry. You know I...care."

"It's Knox. You can tell him you love me." Frank rolled his eyes at Leon, and the weight of those words, the ones on my mind all damn day, smacked me in the chest. Not everyone got the luxury to say them aloud. Not everyone had someone to love, and not everyone who deserved it had someone to love them back. And here I was, terrified because Monroe had blurted out the words and refused to take them back.

To distract me from the ache under my ribs and to let Frank and Leon have a whole damn conversation with their eyes, I quickly clicked around on my phone.

"Here. I found the perfect thing. A honeymoon suite at a place near Seaside. Nice drive. Jacuzzi tub. Breakfast included and a complementary bottle of Oregon sparkling wine."

"Honeymoon suite?" Leon pursed his lips.

"We'll take it." Frank surprised the hell out of me with his sharp nod. "My old bones can use a soak. And I'll watch Leon enjoy that wine."

"You're an old fool." Leon laughed with a decades-worn tenderness, soft like jeans laundered hundreds of times.

"You're going to listen to the doctor about not drinking? And eating right?"

"If the doctor says not to mix my meds and alcohol, I'll do what she says. Gotta keep the ticker going to keep up with you. I plan to be here a good long while yet."

"You damn well better." Leon gave him a stern look that morphed into something so intimate I had to glance away.

"And, Leon, better check your email. Your reservation number is in there."

"Knox..." Leon made a warning noise, then trailed off with a shake of his head.

"What?" I faked innocence. "You guys are relationship goals. Celebrate that."

Later, after I'd organized the supplies for tomorrow's painting, helped Frank program the route to the B&B into his phone GPS, and listened to more protests from Leon and reminders from them both, I locked up the empty house and headed back to downtown Safe Harbor.

Each street, each landmark seemed brand new, like I was looking at the world through a different lens. I paused at the intersection at the base of the hillside neighborhood. *Right or left? Left or right?* Did it even matter? All roads led back to the same place eventually. In so many ways, the outcome of this summer seemed inevitable.

Left. I turned left, swung by Dairy Mart, picked up a pint of the cookies and cream flavor Monroe pretended he only mildly liked and a gold-lidded pint of the flavor of the month, a local peach crisp ice cream. The sample had tasted like honeyed sunshine and the end of summer: bittersweet perfection.

When I entered Monroe's house, the kitchen was empty. I paused at the doorway between the formal dining room and living room, drinking in the sight of Monroe working, notes on the Stapleton case spread out in front of him, earbuds in, reading glasses perched on his aristocratic nose, typing up a storm as he muttered to himself.

And then he looked up, concentration giving way to pleasure, bright and pure. Sure, he'd said those three little words in the middle of sex, but they were also engraved in his eyes, in the lift of his mouth, the arch of his eyebrows. I might be scared shitless, but I didn't doubt the truth of his feelings.

He loved me.

And hell if I was anywhere closer to knowing where we went next.

"You're back." A little caution crept into his tone, dimming the sparkle of pleasure in his expression. "How did work go?"

"Great. The kitchen refresh is coming along. The homeowners went along with my pitch for lemon-yellow walls." Not wanting to get overly sidetracked, I held up the paper sack with the Dairy Mart label. "I brought ice cream."

"The good stuff." He gave a tentative grin as he crossed the room. Rather than deal with whether to kiss him hello, I quickly led the way back to the kitchen and set the pints on the counter.

"Yep. Other towns can claim theirs is better, but this really is the best," I said firmly, daring him to disagree.

Which he didn't, merely nodding toward the bowls I placed on the counter. "Want backward dinner with ice cream now and ordering a pizza later? It's Friday night. Might as well live dangerously."

"Sure. Make it a feast of all our town favorites." I sounded so mournful it was a wonder violin music didn't start playing. Monroe opened his mouth like he might be about to ask what the hell was up with me, so I scooped fast and talked faster. "So I convinced Frank and Leon to take a spontaneous romantic weekend at a B&B."

"Good for you. And good for them." Monroe accepted his bowl of ice cream, leaning against the counter rather than heading to the nearby nook.

"Yeah. They were together for a lot of years when a same-sex couple couldn't do that. Even being roommates of a certain age was undoubtedly scandalous."

"Like Aunt Henri." Monroe's tone was thoughtful but guarded.

"Yeah. It's easy to forget how much of queer history is hidden, lost to secrecy." I took a bite of peach, let the sweet and tart mingle on my tongue. "And you lived part of that history. Don't Ask, Don't Tell left a scar on you."

"I wouldn't be quite that dramatic. But yes, serving with that hanging over my head certainly made it so I don't want to have to hide ever again."

"And that's why you want to be in San Francisco." I rubbed a non-existent spot on the tile with my foot.

"The huge queer community is definitely a plus."

"But what if you didn't have to be hidden here?" I set my ice cream aside before my stomach revolted. I couldn't give him San Francisco or New York, but I could give him Safe Harbor. "If we were openly dating—"

"Kinda hard for you to date my corpse." Monroe gave a bitter laugh. "I think you underestimate how much your dad will freak out. Hell, even my harebrained scheme for us to be together in the Bay—"

"Is that all it was? A crazy idea because you said you loved me and felt guilty you didn't have a forever and ever to back it up?"

"First, I do love you." He set his bowl next to mine with a loud *plink,* spoon clattering against the stoneware. "Second, I don't feel guilty for loving you or for telling you. And while my plan is pretty loose, it could work. However, the truth is that your dad is never going to be okay with us together, whether we're here or in San Francisco. Best I can probably hope is the distance softens any homicidal urges."

"I don't think it will be that bad. When I came out, the first thing he said was that he loved me and always would."

"And he will because you're his kid. But I'm his friend who broke a crucial tenet of the friend code. He's not going to forgive that." Monroe sounded resigned, and I was running out of ways to puncture his doubts. "You want to see a future for us here, one big happy family, and I wish I could share that optimism."

"You could." Giving up on logic, all I had left was a pouty tone. "You could at least *try* to love this town like I do."

"I don't hate it. And I understand you love it here."

"I don't think you do. This is *home.*" I'd truly raised my voice for the first time with him, so I took a long pause and tried for a more tempered tone. "This is where I found myself, where I came out, where I come back to, where my center lies. All roads point back to here, every star, every sign."

"I'm happy you have that certainty." He sounded anything but.

"You could too."

"You're going to take Frank and Leon's offer." He didn't offer it up as a question, and his mournful conviction pierced what was left of my hopes. His doubts versus my hopes. A battle for the ages, but I wasn't conceding quite yet.

"I am. And I'm also going to ask you to stay. You offered up your plan to keep us together. Well, here's my counter."

"This isn't a negotiation." Monroe held up his hands.

"It's not? Isn't that what love is? A give and take? Compromise." I stared him down, but Monroe held fast, mouth narrowing to a thin, hard line as he stayed silent. But I wasn't done. "You say you trust me. Then trust this. It could work out if you stayed here. You told me I'd be happy in the Bay. Well, I think you'd be happy here."

"Knox..." He sounded point-five seconds away from crumpling to the floor. No way could I keep waging war when every cell in my body longed to hold him up. So I did exactly that, wrapping myself around him, burying my face in his neck.

"You don't have to answer," I mumbled into his familiar, warm skin. "Just think about it? For me?"

"Not much I wouldn't do for you." He turned so he could hold me back, both of us clinging to each other. *Stay. Please stay.* I hugged him so tight that energy vibrated between us.

Oh wait. That was my phone.

"Crap." I fished it out of my pocket. "It's my dad."

Monroe closed his eyes while I answered the call. The guilt and sorrow creasing his face said everything those three little words I liked so much couldn't. I had to pace away to focus on my dad's news, only returning to Monroe after I ended the call.

"Jessica's in preterm labor." I relayed the news matter-of-factly because nothing about this evening would be served by my falling even more apart. "Dad and her sister are going with her into Portland. Jessica's mom is going to try to meet them there. They need my help with the girls. I told him I could stay tonight."

"I'll come too." Monroe didn't wait for a reply, gathering shoes, keys, and wallet by the back door. "You shouldn't be alone."

I nodded, wishing that was reason enough to keep him here forever.

Chapter Twenty-Four

Monroe

The late-setting Oregon summer sun was the enemy of early bedtimes and my sanity. I was not babysitter material by any stretch of the imagination, but I hadn't wanted to leave Knox to deal with the triplets by himself, especially given the emotional nature of our conversation back at my house.

So I'd accompanied him to Rob's place, much to the raised eyebrows of Jessica's sister, Angie, who gratefully handed over the triplet terrors. She was eager to go be with Rob and Jessica at the Portland hospital that the small local one had transferred her to in case the NICU was needed.

"Monroe was kind enough to offer to come help chase the girls." Knox had dismissed Angie's curiosity with a casual wave. Probably wouldn't have worked with Rob or Jessica, but Angie was already halfway out the door anyway, only too happy to leave us to the preschooler wrangling.

"Again." One of the triplets, the slightly taller and bossier one, Poppy, glowered at Knox until he pushed her on the playset swing. The other two, Lily and Iris, were hanging upside down off the monkey bar portion of the playset.

"Isn't it bedtime soon?" I asked, only to get three near-identical frowns.

"Noooo."

"They're already off their routine," Knox said reasonably as he pushed Poppy. "Might as well get them good and exhausted first."

"We don't go to sleep before it's dark." Poppy's arch tone would make me smile if I hadn't spent the last few hours listening to her explain all manner of rules and regulations. "We're not babies."

"Hey, Poppy, I bet you can't run a whole lap around the yard. Who do you think is faster, you, me, Lily, or Iris?" Knox set off at a slow trot.

"Me!" All three triplets raced after him until, breathing hard, they returned to where I stood.

"How about we go inside?" Knox asked after declaring a tie with no clear-cut winner to the race. "We can play a quick board game, then watch something on the TV before you get in bed."

"No bed." The girls hopped up and down like cranky frogs.

"How about after a princess movie?" Knox truly was the preschooler whisperer because they rushed ahead of us back into the house, debating which movie to pick.

"When will Daddy and Mommy come back?" Iris, the smallest and most emotional of the triplets, attached herself to Knox's leg like a baby koala. I sympathized with the impulse.

"We don't know. The doctors need to help Jessica—

Mommy—keep the baby inside a little longer so it can get bigger and stronger."

"She can't have the baby before the sprinkle." Lily's stubborn expression and blonde curls were near-identical to Poppy's.

"Shower," Poppy corrected.

"Sprinkle." Iris and Lily stared Poppy down, a battle seeming imminent, but then Knox swung both Iris and Lily up into his arms, resulting in much squealing.

"It's a shower, but also a sprinkle because it's her second pregnancy, and mainly it's a party for your mom and the new baby." Knox talked fast to stave off the battle of the sisters. "Now, let's see if we can beat Poppy to the TV room."

"Up." Poppy gave me a command worthy of a bejeweled empress, not a grubby four-year-old, and I was powerless to object, gingerly lifting her. Pursing her small lips, she glared at me as Knox and the other two girls dashed ahead. "Knox is better at piggyback rides."

"I'm sure," I readily agreed. Knox was better than me at most things, especially home repair, cooking, people skills, and anything involving small children. Poppy's light weight in my arms, her bony elbows and knees, made breathing strangely difficult. I'd carried heavier file boxes and walked far farther on way more difficult terrain, but the responsibility for the little human weighed on my shoulders, made me overthink each step toward the couch. I didn't know how parents hefted that kind of pressure around every day.

"We win." Next to us, Knox and his precious cargo celebrated as he dumped them onto the sofa, far more confident than me about tossing them around, apparently not concerned that they could break. He grinned widely, totally loving his role as the fun big brother. How could I even think of taking him away from this? To ask him to turn down Frank and Leon and more time with the triplets? The girls were little now, convinced Knox was their own personal superhero, but how many more years until they were bored teens? Did I want to cheat Knox out of that time?

Forget hard to breathe. It was hard to think, especially with the answers I didn't want so day-glow apparent.

"You okay?" Knox gave me a curious look.

"Fine." I quickly set Poppy next to her sisters. "How about I make some popcorn?"

"Great idea." Knox offered an encouraging smile, which made me feel worse about needing an escape.

In Rob and Jessica's kitchen, I took my time checking messages on my phone. First up was Holden, who said Sam's mom was out of town for a church conference but could answer our questions when she returned. More frustrating, though, none of my notes on the movie lines the suspect had quoted yielded a single good lead. We couldn't place him in town that summer, we didn't have a body, and my summer's worth of work was starting to feel particularly futile.

I wanted to solve this case. For Holden, because it would mean increased podcast exposure. For Worth, whose haunted eyes and damaged spirit demanded closure. For the memory of Worth's parents, who had deserved better. For Rob, who could use a departmental win. And for me. I'd been drifting for months, trying to figure out who I was away from NCIS. I needed this to validate my time in Safe Harbor—

"The prince is coming!" A shriek sounded from the other room, followed by Knox's easy laughter. Okay, that was a lie. I didn't need to crack the case for this to be a worthwhile summer, but I did need the victory to cling to while everything with Knox seemed destined to fall apart.

The next message on my phone was a revised bill from the termite service. I'd been back and forth with them ever since the San Francisco trip because the termite damage had been more extensive than Knox originally suspected, and while my savings account could take the hit, the bills on the house were starting to pile up.

And then I nearly dropped the phone.

Monroe. Ginny Davis here, realtor extraordinaire and friend of Rob and Jessica. Rob gave me your number because I have a buyer interested in helping you get out from under your aunt's house. Cash offer. As-is.

Huh. Well, there was an answer to the mounting bills and what to do with my churning emotions about Knox's decision to stay and my realization earlier that I couldn't fight or fault him. I could escape to the city that much faster, get a move onto the next phase of my life, move on from cases I couldn't solve and hearts I couldn't win.

"They're gonna kiss to turn him back into a prince! Hide your eyes!" One of the girls squealed, and Knox played up his own horror in response, and for a second, only a second, I wished I didn't know how magical and transformative his kisses could be.

"Everything okay?" he called out to me.

"Yep." I hustled out with the bowl of popcorn that had been ready ten minutes prior. Coward. I was afraid of three little girls, their intoxicating big brother, and my inevitable future without any of them.

Chapter Twenty-Five

Knox

Monroe wasn't going to win any acting awards. That much was certain. He'd been unhappy and frustrated back at the house with my counteroffer for our future, and his mood hadn't improved during childcare duty for the triplets. He said everything was fine, but the dude had seriously taken half an hour to make a five-minute bag of popcorn.

But it wasn't like we could have the giant state-of-the-relationship talk we needed with the overtired triplets present. I'd let Monroe sit too damn far away from me on the couch and have his pretending. For now.

"Any news from the hospital?" He glanced at my silent phone on the coffee table as the movie ended.

"Not yet. I'm sure no news is good news." My voice came out too bright, and Poppy immediately picked up on my fake cheer.

"I'm not going to sleep until Daddy comes home."

"How about we start with pajamas and a story?" I coaxed all three upstairs and into cartoon pajamas, but as soon as their teeth were brushed, they were running through the halls and doing everything other than getting in their beds.

"We're still not sleepy!" Poppy led the chant. "No bed!"

"Let's try something else." I herded them back into the TV room. "Do you remember when we played campout?"

"Yes!" The triplets started dancing around.

"I'll set up the tent in here, and you go get your sleeping bags and pillows while Monroe chooses a story."

"Brilliant idea." Monroe nodded as he helped me set up the indoor play tent the girls adored. "This should contain them."

"They're not hamsters." I laughed at how seriously he was taking this whole kid-wrangling thing. "But yes, this way, they can giggle and go to sleep, and we can watch something G-rated on low rather than escorting them back to their room a dozen times."

"Smart." His mouth twisted. "And you volunteered me for the story? What sort of book am I supposed to pick?"

I gestured at the overflowing kids' bookshelf in the corner. "Something short and funny with no scary parts."

"All right." Shoulders set like he was headed into battle, he considered several books while the girls piled into the tent. I knew he'd found a good one when his eyes went wide with quiet delight. He tried to hand it to me, but I shook my head.

"Your turn. You read."

"Okay." He took a deep breath as the girls crowded around us on the sofa. "This is the story of—"

"The two daddy bunnies," Lily crowed.

"And the baby bunnies! And their brand-new burrow!" Iris sighed happily as she snuggled into my side. The book was one of several in a series featuring diverse families.

Jessica had done an excellent job of ensuring their extensive picture book collection contained a lot of positive representation.

And Monroe, who had been a worried playtime supervisor, a reluctant piggyback giver, and a dour kid movie watcher, turned out to be the most amazing storyteller. Voices. Hand motions. Emotions. Pacing. All of it. He held the girls and me captive for the story of two gay rabbits in dapper bowties and their dozens of little adopted bunnies looking for a bigger home for their family.

"*And then Papa Bunny said, 'This is our forever home, and this is our forever family,' and all the little bunnies cheered because they knew he was right,*" Monroe read, voice thick, and my own throat tightened.

As he'd read the children's book, I'd heard an echo of some long-ago and undoubtedly long-buried want of Monroe's for a family and a home. And I wanted to give him that in the worst way. A forever home, a forever family, a forever life that we both needed and deserved. But for all that he said he loved me, I wasn't sure whether Monroe believed in forever or that he'd let himself reach for those things. He'd built a thick shell around all those old hurts and yearning, and he'd only allow himself to stick his neck out so far, an old tortoise who knew better.

I couldn't make him take the risk on us, nor could I fault his reluctance to make himself vulnerable. After all, I couldn't even let myself say those three words aloud. He at least had been that brave. Earlier, I'd wondered why in the hell he didn't want me enough to compromise, but the more he read to the girls, the more I saw the same fear I held in my own heart. We both wanted too much. Two scared rabbits, afraid to venture out of their safe spots.

As the book ended, he smiled softly at Iris, half-asleep on his knee, and put a finger to his lips.

"Shush." He scooped her up like she was made of gold-leaf tissue paper, delicately setting her inside the tent with her two sleepy sisters.

"Good night, Knox. Good night, Monroe," Poppy mumbled as he pulled up her covers, and my own protective shell cracked a little more in the face of such sweetness. A person's heart wasn't designed to hold this much all at once.

"Monroe—" I started, but he held up his finger again.

"Shush. They're finally asleep. You need to rest too." He arranged one of the fuzzy blue couch throw blankets over me, patting it into place with a gentleness I didn't deserve. No way could I get a single word out right then.

Nothing to do but drift off until a low murmur of voices pulled me out of a hazy dream world.

"Oh my gosh, look at that." Jessica's voice filtered into my waking consciousness first. Good. She was back, so that had to be a good sign. I was about to rouse myself to greet her and my dad when she added, "Looks like the girls wore Monroe and Knox out."

Oops. We were both asleep on the couch, holding hands under the blankets, and my head was half on his shoulder. Pretending to stay asleep was probably my best bet for the moment.

"They're cuties." Jessica's sister, Angie, laughed a little too loudly, but next to me, Monroe snoozed on.

"You don't think..." Jessica made a thoughtful noise.

"What?" Ah, my dad's voice from farther back, probably last in the house through the kitchen door. "You're supposed to be on bed rest. Why aren't you already upstairs?"

"Because we had to stop and see how cute the girls are

in their tent. And Monroe and Knox are cute too," Jessica explained, undoubtedly gesturing in our direction. "They do seem a bit...cuddly though."

"It's Knox." My dad groaned like he knew every bad habit I had. "He's always been a sleep cuddler. Swear that kid is part barnacle. But you've got a point. I'll say something to him later. Wouldn't want him to make Monroe uncomfortable."

"You never know. Monroe might like it." Damn Angie and her braying laugh and her way-too-accurate assessment.

"Hush." Dad sounded like he'd had about enough of her too. "If Monroe likes his skin, he better not ever let me catch him sniffing around Knox."

"What?" Jessica sounded legit surprised at Dad's harsh tone. "Monroe's a great guy. He's gay. Knox is gay. Would it be so terrible?"

"What the heck, Jessica?" Dad barked, then dropped his voice back to a low whisper. "We better get you up to bed. And Knox is a kid. A vulnerable kid who is still in college—"

"Graduate school." Bless Jessica for correcting him. And if anyone was vulnerable, it was Monroe and the gorgeous heart he'd exposed, knowing full well I might break it. "Knox is legally an adult now. Drinks. Dates. And he's going to be all the way across the country soon. You don't think he might date older guys out east?"

"Better not." Dad continued to sound ready to call Monroe out like some old western gunslinger. And I almost gave the whole sleep ruse away by cringing hard at the reminder they still thought I was going to graduate school. Hell, if I couldn't disappoint them about school, how in the hell was I going to tear apart a twenty-year friendship? "Knox needs to date people his own age. He's a kid. Monroe

193

is a grown adult who should know better. He's like...an honorary uncle or something. It would be *wrong*."

Wrong. Dad's certainty cut me to my core, but not how he intended. I was the one who'd taken advantage of Monroe. I'd set my sights on him from the club onward, never dialed back the flirting, and more or less talked him into the secret fling idea. I'd done a bad, bad thing, and worse, Monroe had tried to warn me. Dating me openly would mean the end of his friendship with Dad. Heck, probably others as well. Friends. Acquaintances. People, especially around here, would judge us and find Monroe the one at fault.

"Well, luckily for you, Rob, they're just roommates." Jessica gave a tired laugh, and I very nearly joined her. Roommates. *Uh-huh.*

"Who cuddle." Angie snort-laughed.

"Gah. I'm ready for Monroe to sell that damn house. Get Knox off to school. Monroe to the Bay. Everything back to normal." Dad sounded exhausted himself, but my chest still pinched. Was he that eager to be rid of me? The pain spread as he continued, "I saw Ginny Davis at Blessed Bean the other day. There's a developer looking to buy near downtown. She thinks they would pay Monroe cash and take it as-is since they'd likely do a teardown."

"Oh, that's sad. I hope he doesn't take the offer."

"Eh. It's life. The town needs to keep up. Those old houses are money pits. Monroe doesn't need that."

The voices drifted away as Dad likely steered Jessica upstairs to rest. What did Monroe need? That was the true question of the night? I'd been so damn sure it was me. And now...I had no clue, and my chest ached right along with my neck from holding this blasted position. Why hadn't Monroe told me he had an offer to buy the house? Was that why he'd been so sweet lately? Guilt? Knowing all my hard work was going to be bulldozed? And why was I so surprised? He'd always intended to leave. Loving me didn't change that.

He exhaled softly in his sleep, lips pursing. God, I loved him. I wished we were alone, back at his house, so I could show him. As soon as we returned there, I would make every one of our remaining seconds together count. I might not ever be able to tell him, but I couldn't keep lying to myself. I loved him, and he was leaving, two unchangeable truths in a sea of unknowns.

Chapter Twenty-Six

Monroe

"Naptime for everyone." As soon as we were back at my place after watching the triplets, Knox steered me to the back stairs. Apparently, Rob and Jessica had returned sometime around dawn. Now, it was a little before seven, warm summer sun making the kitchen glow. Wallace had greeted us at the kitchen door, and Knox had him stashed under one arm.

Meow. Wallace protested, undoubtedly trying to point out that it was an hour better suited for coffee and kibble, not naps.

"It feels decadent going back to bed with the sun up." I gave a halfhearted protest because I truly was still exhausted and wasn't going to turn down extra snuggle time with Knox, but years of diligent work ethic had me at least giving lip service to staying awake.

"Feels necessary." Knox clearly had no such conflict as he led the way to the bedroom. He gently set Wallace down by the third-floor stairs. "Later, I need to work on the painting like I told Frank and Leon I would, but right now, we both need some rest."

"True. I'm too old to be snoozing on couches all night."

"Yep." Knox gave me a long, speculative look that had me shifting my feet. The longer he looked, the more the skin on my lower back prickled.

"What?"

"Nothing." He shook his head, eyes far too full of emotion for nothing. "But you're not old."

Taking my hand, he pulled me the rest of the way into the bedroom and kicked the door shut.

"Poor Wallace." I chuckled, but the laugh caught in my throat as he skimmed his hands down my sides, touch heart-breakingly gentle, eyes serious. He removed my shirt, holding my gaze as he undid my fly next, his intensity unnerving. "Hey. I thought we were going to nap."

"Maybe I want to make sure you have sweet dreams." He palmed my cock through my boxers.

"Well, that's one way to do it." I'd showered after yesterday's run and before the babysitting gig, but nevertheless, I glanced toward the bathroom. "Maybe we should—"

"Nope. Not that patient." He pushed me to sit on the edge of the bed.

"Not gonna stop you." I tried for a lighter tone.

"Good." His expression stayed chapel solemn as he quickly removed his own clothes. I held out a hand for him to join me on the bed, but he shook his head, clearly operating with some unspoken agenda.

"You're in a bossy mood."

That at least got a laugh from him, a harsh bark. "When am I not?"

"True." Eager to get more of his usual good humor, I threw my arms wide. "Have at me."

"Oh, I will." Eyes dark and needy, he sank to his knees in front of me. I expected Mr. Oral Fixation to go right for my cock, which was certainly eager enough for him, jutting against my belly. However, Knox rested his face against my thigh, inhaling deeply for a few breaths, then pressed his head against my stomach, more shuddery breaths as he hugged me tight.

"Knox..." I didn't know what to say. Didn't know how to make this better. Didn't even entirely understand what was wrong, just that my guy was hurting, and I'd give a kidney to take on the pain myself, spare him whatever was troubling him.

"Shush," he said exactly as I had last night. I hadn't been entirely sure what he'd been about to say at the time, but emotions had been running high. My chest had felt like crystal, thin and fragile, one sharp note from shattering. So I'd tried to will him to sleep, and now he was the one who looked two breaths from breaking. His mouth was a thin line, prominent cheekbones even more defined than usual, and his eyes begged me to not make him talk.

"Okay," I whispered. "Okay."

"Thank you." He inhaled so deeply that his ribs lifted against my leg. I adjusted my posture so he was kneeling between my thighs, and he held me that much tighter, ear pressed to my torso. God, I hoped he heard whatever it was he was searching for. I'd move Mount Hood myself if he asked, and since all he'd asked for was quiet, I tried to will him peace. Pulling loose his messy ponytail, I stroked his silky hair, wound the curls around my fingers, and rubbed the back of his tense neck. Not talking wasn't easy, especially when he started nuzzling my belly with his soft lips. His stubbly jaw dragged against my skin, and I moaned softly.

"Mmm. Yes. That's the only sound I wanna hear. You moaning for my mouth." He was a dirty-talking sex god staring at me, and I would have given up talking entirely to get his lips around my cock. As it was, his warm breath had me shuddering long before he traced my cockhead with his tongue. Moisture had already gathered at the tip, and he lapped it up eagerly. Jacking my shaft with one hand, he sighed like my cock in his mouth was the answer to all his worries, and lord, I wished it was that easy.

He took me deep, immediately finding my favorite rhythm, long, slow swallows where I could feel every inch of his tongue working the underside of my cock, and each time his nose rubbed against my trimmed patch of hair, I moaned shamelessly. And not because he'd ordered it, but because it felt so damn amazing.

Didn't take long at all before I was fighting for control, trying not to come in record time. "Why are you so good at this?"

"You complaining?" Eyes twinkling, he grinned up at me, and damn, I'd missed that smile.

"Never." Meeting his gaze, I stroked his jaw, but before he could resume his oral symphony, I tugged at his shoulder. "Come up here. Don't wanna come this way."

"Maybe I want you to." His chin took on a stubborn jut.

"And maybe I want something for both of us."

"Now who's bossy?" He laughed, likely because we both knew how unlikely I was to stop him if he resumed sucking. What Knox wanted, Knox generally got, but I truly was craving his warm weight on me, and when he rose up to straddle my thighs, I groaned low, hands immediately going to his round ass.

"If bossy gets me a lapful of you, I'll give all the orders."

"No, you won't. Lie back," he commanded, proving his point as I obediently scooted back and stretched out as he'd urged. He settled himself fully on me, ass resting on my thighs as he lined up our cocks.

"That works," I said gamely like I had any illusion of control over this encounter. I reached to fist us both, but he batted my hand away.

"Let me be the one." He wrapped his strong hand around our cocks.

"You are." He was the one. The only one. The one I needed and wanted and couldn't live without. As he stroked us together, emotion more than pleasure kept threatening to overwhelm me.

His cock fit perfectly against mine, the curve of his crown matching my own, sensitive shafts aligned. But it was his strength I loved the most, the flex of his biceps, the tension in his thighs, the quiver in his abs as he held himself above me. His mouth hovered maddeningly just out of reach.

"Kiss me," I demanded, adding, "Please, please, please."

"That's a lot of please." He chuckled warmly. "I love it."

Love me. Love me, my brain demanded as he met my mouth with his, a deep, searching kiss. He kissed me like he owned me, and still, I wanted more. *Love me.* I wouldn't ask that aloud, not ever. It wouldn't be fair even if we weren't in the middle of the most emotional sex I'd ever had. My feelings for him weren't dependent on him returning the sentiment, no matter how much I wanted it.

"Oh. That's..." I moaned as he again found the most

perfect rhythm, ideal pressure, showy twist at the top, firm grip at the bottom.

"Monroe." His breath hitched, the first sign he might be as affected as me. His eyes bored into mine, oceans' worth of churning intensity.

"I'm here."

"Tell me," he ordered, and I didn't bother playing dumb.

"I love you," I said firmly. Simply. Truthfully. His eyes shut and his breathing sped up. "Are you getting off on those words?"

I'd meant it as a tease, but he groaned like he'd taken a fist to the stomach. "Yes. God, yes."

"I love you, I love you, I love you," I chanted, waiting for the moment when his eyes fluttered open, wide and plea-sured, face going slack as the rest of his body tensed. He came with a broken noise, cock erupting over his fist, making the slide against mine that much slicker and hotter. Only took a few more slippery strokes of his hand before I was coming too, moaning along with him. The climax hit, not like a peak or a wave, but like a grenade, clearing out any last resistance to Knox's hold over me.

I was his. That certainty was every bit as intense as the pleasure, and hell, the certainty of my feelings was the plea-sure, and the pleasure was the certainty, an endless loop. He worked us both through the last shudders, finally releasing my cock right as it reached too-sensitive levels of post-orgasmic bliss.

"Lord, I do love you bossy." I sagged against the mattress as he fetched his T-shirt to clean his hand and my stomach.

"You love me." Knox gave a little shake of his head, voice mournful. "You really do."

"I do. I love you, Knox." I paused, not really expecting a

reply but trying to read the kaleidoscope of emotions on his face. Jaw set, he studied me with the saddest eyes I'd ever seen. And even though I didn't want to ask, didn't want to know, didn't want to make him say aloud what we both knew, I couldn't keep quiet a second longer. "Why did that feel like goodbye?"

Chapter Twenty-Seven

Knox

"Maybe—never mind." Sitting next to Monroe on the bed, I twisted a handful of the comforter. "You should sleep."

"Sleep?" Monroe joined me in sitting up. "I'm supposed to sleep right now?"

"You could try." My tone came out pouty like Monroe was the problem here. Taking a breath, I stroked a hand down his chest, trying to coax him to lie back down. "I didn't mean to ruin our nap by getting all emotional."

"You didn't ruin anything. You couldn't." Monroe was so much nicer than I deserved, voice low and soothing. "But talk to me. Please."

The please got to me. He was always so much more ready than me to confront the hard questions. I looked at him for another long moment, teeth digging into my lower lip. "You were right."

He nodded, then, when I didn't add anything else, he gave a nervous chuckle. "I generally am. Sorry. Not the time for humor. Can you be more specific?"

"You were right that my dad would flip out if we were dating." I addressed the lines on the comforter rather than meet Monroe's concerned gaze. "Like he went seriously worrisome levels of aggro at the tiniest joke. And Jessica might suspect something already."

"Oh." Monroe went still, a chill wind creeping between our bodies, summer heat be damned. His voice lowered, a wounded tone I hadn't heard from him before. "You figured out you don't want your dad knowing. I get it."

"Not for me. For *you*." The frosty air between us, a gulf that wasn't there five minutes prior, had me reluctant to reach for him, but hell, how I wanted to. "You've been friends twenty years. And that means something."

"And so do you." Braver than me, he took my hand, squeezing tightly.

"Thank you." I studied our linked hands, trying to memorize how perfectly they aligned. "But does it really matter when you're leaving anyway?"

"What happened to you asking me to stay?" His tone was resigned like he already knew the answer.

"That was before I heard my dad and Jessica talking. And before you put the house on the market for teardown developers." Now I was the one with the wounded tone, small and soft.

"On the market?" Mouth twisting, Monroe sounded legit confused. "I haven't listed the house yet. I got a random text yesterday that I've yet to respond to."

"But you're tempted." Of that, I was certain, and the way he exhaled didn't contradict me.

"Knox. You knew all along I was planning to sell."

"And nothing's changed," I said flatly, removing my hand from his grip.

"Everything has. Every last thing." Monroe took my

hand right back. "And I'm trying to catch up over here, figure out what the hell I'm doing with my life."

"Sorry to be a complication." If there was an Oscar for pouting, I was surely in the running to win it. I couldn't seem to dial back my hurt, and pushing it all on Monroe wasn't fair, but it seemed like the only way out of the jumbled maze of conflicting thoughts and emotions in my brain.

"The last thing I want is for you to be sorry. But I'm not going to beg you to give us a shot either. That's not fair to either of us. If you don't want your dad to know, then it has to end." Monroe was so damn reasonable. A scream gathered in my throat, and I swallowed it as he continued, all measured and adult. "Your relationship with him is too important for me to ask you to risk it."

"It's not my relationship I'm worried about. Like I said, he'd be livid, but not at me, despite it being my fault—"

"Hey now." Giving up on trying to hold my hand, Monroe gently rubbed my shoulder. "No fault. Neither of us is to blame."

"But that's what I'm trying to say. Everyone *will* place blame, and they'll try to pin it on you because you're the older one. Which shouldn't matter, but apparently, it does."

"It does." Monroe gave me a level look. "What am I supposed to say? Of course, it matters. It's always mattered, and if anything, it matters more now that real feelings and futures are involved. I'm eighteen years older than you. I can't wish that away, no matter how much I love you. When you're thirty-two, I'll be fifty. You'll be in the prime of your life."

"And so will you." I groaned dramatically, flopping back on the bed. "I don't care about the math. I fucking hate that everyone else will have opinions though. Probably more so here than in the Bay, which I hate even more because that means you were right there too."

"Mixed-age couples are more common there, yeah." Shaking his head, Monroe looked like he was debating joining my sprawl. His voice turned wearier. "But I'm not going to ask you to leave, Knox."

"But—"

"I know I asked that. But I saw you with the girls last night. I hear you when you talk about Frank and Leon's business. I feel it when you wax poetic about the town." Pain mingled with certainty in his tone and eyes both. The lines around those gorgeous, expressive eyes I treasured were deeper and his mouth sagged. "You do. This is your home. It's where you belong."

"And you don't." I had to work to keep my voice from cracking.

"No."

"Damn it, Monroe." There it was, the break in my control. "Disagree with me."

"How am I supposed to?" Monroe threw up his hands. "Knox, you don't even want to tell your dad about the career you truly want. Your reluctance is not only about his reaction to me. You don't want to let him down, and I'm not going to come between the two of you."

I made a low, pained noise because I couldn't argue, and that made me even more upset and confused, mainly at myself, not him.

"You want me to fight for us, but you've already decided not to. I can't do this on my own. You want me to stay and keep our relationship hidden? I can't do that either."

"I know." I had to whisper past the burning in my throat. Tears were perilously close. I couldn't ask him to hide indefinitely. "Fuck. I hate this."

I launched myself off the bed, searching for clothes, most of which were already living in this room. Like me. I lived here too. It wasn't Monroe's room. It was ours, and I couldn't be in it a second longer.

"Where are you going?" Monroe asked as I yanked on pants and a shirt suitable for painting.

"Work. Not like I can sleep. And those cabinets won't paint themselves."

"Okay." Monroe nodded, which cut far deeper than if he'd tried to force me to stay and talk. He was right. Again. I was desperate for him to fight for us, to show commitment to a future, yet I couldn't do the same. I wanted him to cling to me at the same time that I was trying to do the right thing and cast him free. Fuck. What a mess.

Chapter Twenty-Eight

Monroe

I was a firm believer in the power of routine. Thus, when Monday dawned, clear and sunny and no Knox in my bed, I leaned hard on what little routine I'd developed here in Safe Harbor. My years in the navy had shown me that any manner of hard things could be overcome through a routine. Need to pass a fitness test? Make exercise as routine as teeth brushing. Need to handle a complicated court-martial case? Work through all the steps in the investigation, each detail part of a routine. Need to deal with the loss of a buddy? Routine, routine, routine.

Even before the navy, routine had saved me. When my mother died, my dad kept us on a strict schedule of school, work, exercise, dinner. Years later, I was able to see things I'd hated at the time, like up early on Saturdays to clean, as light buoys illuminating an endless ocean of grief. When I came to stay with Aunt Henri, routine had been my friend then too. Wake up. Make bed. School. Watch a mystery with her. Parts of her habits had become mine, providing soothing normalcy at another time when I could have gone adrift.

Out of the navy and back in Safe Harbor, I'd struggled with sticking to the rigid routine the navy had required. Finding what worked for me in this strange new landscape of post-service life had been a challenge. And then Knox had barged into my life, so far outside my carefully crafted rules for myself. But somehow, over the weeks together, I'd finally found my footing, little rituals and schedules that served me.

But the too-quiet house and start of a new week, one with little hope of a resolution with Knox, had me off my game. My feet had seemed to drag uphill through wet cement my whole run. Same route as usual, different me. He'd changed me, and I wasn't sure a change back was possible or if I wanted such a thing.

And now I was in the grocery store, list in hand, unsure why I'd come other than routine. But sticking to a schedule wasn't doing a damn thing to make me miss Knox less. We remained in the same house, but forty-eight hours of tapdancing around each other, no talking or touching, had worn me down. I'd sniffed his shampoo in the shower. Used his almond hemp creamer in my coffee. Taken a swipe of the thick hand lotion he kept by the kitchen sink. No use. Missed Knox that much more.

I saw reminders of him in every aisle of the grocery store, every box and can I examined, to the point where I was tempted to abandon the whole damn cart. And it didn't help that my phone had buzzed three times since eight a.m. The realtor friend of Rob and Jessica's was eager to pitch me her proposal for the house, and I should have been similarly eager to hear it, move on, and get out of town.

But I wasn't.

And that had me even grumpier when I heard my name at the end of the cereal aisle. "Monroe!"

Frank and Leon, owners of Measure Twice and Knox's bosses, were apparently also doing a Monday-morning stock-up. The taller Frank was pushing a full cart with Leon beside him toting a long baguette in one hand and a list in the other.

"Frank. Leon." Forcing a smile, I greeted them each in turn. "How are you?"

"Damn good." Frank nodded. He'd always had that military bearing and authoritative voice, but as far as I knew, he'd lived his whole life in Safe Harbor and always worked construction. Measure Twice had already been a successful small business when I was in high school, and like back then, I reflexively stood a little taller when Frank spoke. "The weekend away was exactly what the doctor ordered."

"Well, maybe not exactly..." Leon's tone was mischievous, and Frank's blush further gave his meaning away.

"Hush."

"I'm glad the trip went well." I leaned on my cart, wanting out of the small talk but also knowing an empty house awaited me. "Knox mentioned you went to a B&B he found."

"Yep. There was a time when that sort of spontaneous weekend away wouldn't have been possible for us." Frank gave me a level stare, the sort that had intimidated me as a teen, but now I saw a kinship there, an acknowledgment of our similarities.

"Then came all the years of word-of-mouth and travel guides for the confirmed bachelor," Leon added with a laugh.

"Yeah, the world sure has come a long way," I agreed, thinking of their link, both to queer history but also to this area. Back in high school, they'd been one of the first same-sex couples I'd known, and even then, it had been one of those open secret things, not the wedding rings and shared property of the present. "You've always lived here, right? Never tempted to go somewhere...easier?"

"Easier." Frank snorted like I was a silly new recruit. "Easy is what you make it."

"It never felt...lonely here?" I pressed. They had to have been the only openly queer couple in the area for years and years.

"It's home. Always been." Leon peered at me, undoubtedly seeing far more than I wanted. "Henri sure wanted it to be a home for you too, you know. I remember you. Seventeen and skinny with big joints and more than a little lost. The sleepless nights you gave Henri."

"I did?" I never thought she'd cared enough to deviate from her careful routine.

"Of course. She thought the world of you." Leon frowned like I should have known.

"Bragged on you every chance she got." Frank also glowered, making me feel about three inches high for not appreciating Aunt Henri more.

"I never realized you were friends."

"Birds of a feather and all that." Leon's expression changed from censure to smug. "She might not have gotten out much, but she did love a good neighborly gossip."

"Which you were only too happy to give her." Frank rolled his eyes at Leon, but there was also a fair bit of affection in his tone. "Honorary town scribe, this one."

"Huh." Despite my preoccupation with all things Knox, a small light started blinking in my brain. "Leon, do you remember the summer Worth Stapleton's mother disappeared?"

"Of course. Frank was out every night for weeks with the search parties."

"Nasty business, but better that than the other type of parties that summer." Frank groaned, stretching a little.

"What parties?" My scalp tingled.

"Oh, nothing you'd remember." Chuckling, Leon waved a hand. "More housewife gossip. Who could sell the most pie pans and pizza stones."

"Some of our regular clients kept inviting Leon." Frank huffed like he was growing weary of the conversation, but Leon kept his affable smile firmly in place.

"I do make a nice spinach dip."

"Leon, could I stop by later?" I asked, already mentally composing a message to Holden. "I'd like to show you some pictures."

"Sure thing. I probably have a few more Henri stories for you too."

"I'd like that." My mouth went dry and chalky. "I didn't guess..."

"That you were the apple of her eye?" Frank laughed, but he was already turning the cart slightly away from mine.

"More like the marionberry of her pie." Leon chortled, even as the bottom threatened to fall out of my stomach. She'd *picked* me for the house. Not because there was no one else, but because, apparently, she'd *loved* me. And I'd never known. Or appreciated. My insides kept churning as Leon continued, "But those first few months until you found your people...?" He whistled low, then sobered. "But isn't that life? Doesn't matter who or where. Find your people. Find yourself."

"Yup. You asked about lonely. Our people were always here." Frank gave me a hard stare. "And where else were we going to get to work together every day? Sure, Portland had the bars—"

"And the boys." Leon's chuckle shifted to an adorable giggle coming from someone well past seventy. "But we had each other, and the town had us. Silently, then quietly, and now Knox is talking about a public retirement party at the community center."

"Pillars of Safe Harbor, that's us." Frank shrugged. "Better get on with our shopping list."

"Take care, Monroe." Leon patted my arm as they both walked past me. "Take care of our boy too."

Ouch. I nodded even though my heart was breaking because I had no clue how to take care of Knox. I wanted to. I needed to. But I wasn't sure if I'd get the chance, especially with him not wanting to tell Rob.

After the encounter with Frank and Leon, I was strangely sentimental. *Find your people. Find yourself.* Knox was absolutely my people, but he wasn't the only one. I might not have a huge social circle, but I did have a few friends and a sudden need to see them. Since I didn't have any frozen items, I didn't feel guilty swinging by Blessed Bean for a refill.

"Two cups in one day?" Sam greeted me as soon as I opened the door. "To what do we owe the pleasure?"

"An unwillingness to brew a pot at home for only me," I answered a little too truthfully.

"Ah." Sam narrowed his eyes, seeing all as usual. "Another cold brew? Or could I interest you in the special?" He gestured at the young person next to him behind the counter. "Weaver here is our newest trainee. We were just going over blended drinks."

Weaver was gangly, almost alarmingly thin, with faded shaggy rainbow hair, a thick stack of plastic bracelets, and an assortment of buttons on old-fashioned leather suspenders. They had the air of a spooked rabbit looking for a hole in the fence, so Sam definitely had his work cut out.

"Sure. I'll try one." I tried to give Weaver an encouraging smile before turning back to Sam. Like Frank and Leon, Sam had always lived here, never left, and had carved out a nice little life for himself. "How did you get started in the coffee shop business anyway?"

"I'm not in the coffee shop business." Sam's eyes sparkled as he moved out of Weaver's way so Weaver could access the row of blenders.

"He's out here saving souls," Holden added with a chuckle as he rolled through the door of the coffee shop.

"Wouldn't say that either." Sam shook his head. "But to answer your question, I saw a need. A lot of struggling kids and not-quite adults around here. The shelter was already up and running, but it didn't seem to be making enough of a difference. Our clientele needed a purpose."

"Funny. I always thought shelters were more of a big-city thing."

"Says who?" Sam quirked his mouth, as close to irritated as I'd seen him. "We get more homeless every year. It's an everywhere and everyone problem."

"Sorry." I winced because I wasn't usually such a lumbering dumbass.

"You won't find a place anywhere that doesn't have problems. This is just my little scrap of earth where I get to make a difference."

"Saint Sam, throwing truth bombs." Holden mock saluted Sam. "Doesn't even drink coffee."

"You don't like coffee?"

"Shush. That's a secret." A sly smile teased the edges of

his mouth. "I like what coffee does for people. Brings people together. Don't have to drink it to appreciate a good brew."

Oh. Like how I could appreciate this town, what it gave people, what it was to Knox, and people like Frank and Leon. All day I'd felt like I was circling around some bigger truth, getting closer and closer, like unraveling a case.

Case. Oh yeah. "Sent you a message," I said to Holden. "Call me later?"

"Will do. Your message was like three pages of text long. I've been telling you to write up this case." Holden had been on me ever since I'd first been on his podcast, reminding me how much I'd enjoyed journalism and English classes in high school. But for the first time, his suggestion wormed past my initial resistance.

"Maybe." If Knox could follow his heart, his deepest desires, could I unlock dreams I'd long ago put in deep freeze?

"Good." Holden's smile slid into alarm as Weaver brought my drink. "Is that the special?"

"Yup. Looks great." I gave Weaver another encouraging smile before taking a sip. It tasted like coffee and cough syrup, and I had to work to swallow the vile brew down.

"Sam thought black cherry mocha might be an ideal flavor combo to try Weaver out on the blender with." Holden chuckled. "Weaver, it's not your fault the non-coffee drinker put himself in charge of the specials board."

"Cold brew to go?" Sam suggested a little too brightly.

"Please." As soon as I said the word, I heard Knox's laugh inside my head, the way he loved when I begged in bed, and how his eyes had pleaded with me the last time we talked. *Please.* How was I supposed to help when I wasn't sure where to start?

New drink in hand, I made my way back to my car. Sam

loved it here. Frank and Leon too, and Holden sure seemed happy enough. This was Knox's home, yet without him willing to tell Rob about us, did I have enough of a reason to even think about staying, let alone do it? But at the same time, how could I walk away?

Words from Knox, Sam, Frank, and Leon all bounced around in my brain, but I didn't feel any closer to—

There. As I pulled into the driveway, there was a perfect rainbow over the house. Had it rained while I was in the coffee shop? It must have sprinkled at some point because there it was, as bright as any I'd ever seen. It made the house look like a postcard or the cover of a book, a rainbow version of one of Safe Harbor's historic homes.

And in that instant, I finally understood why Aunt Henri left me the house. This wasn't some investment. An asset to put toward my future. No, this was a part of the community. She'd left it to me, specifically because she'd loved me. She'd loved and trusted me, and maybe I hadn't known, but I could do right by her now. It was on me to find a purpose for the house and maybe for myself. Aunt Henri had seen so much more than I'd ever given her credit for and had believed in me. Now it was time to pay her back and pay myself forward.

As I stood there staring at the house, my day, my summer, my whole damn life made sense. Forget routine. Fuck schedules and plans. I finally, finally knew what I was supposed to do.

Chapter Twenty-Nine

Knox

I didn't want to go home. And perhaps more depressing, I was no longer sure where home was. The house Monroe was bound to sell sooner or later? The Portland apartment that new tenants already occupied? My mom's empty condo in Seattle? Even Dad's house here in Safe Harbor no longer felt like home, but here I was, avoiding Monroe and the house and the mountain of unsaid words and unresolved problems.

"A little to the left. No, right. Perfect." Jessica was installed in the rocker in the soon-to-be nursery, feet up on an ottoman, pillows behind her, giant mugs of ice water and herbal tea next to her, crochet project in her lap. She'd messaged because her sister had taken the girls to the zoo in Portland for the day, and Jessica wanted out of her bed and to put the finishing touches on the nursery. "Thank you, Knox. You're the best."

"I try." I stepped away from the wall of nursery rhyme

prints. I'd happily agreed to stop by after working on the kitchen remodel for Frank and Leon, both to keep Jessica off her feet and as an excuse to stay away from Monroe and the house that much longer. The sun was starting to fade, and my dad would be home soon, but I kept finding more reasons to linger.

"Are you okay?" Jessica tilted her head, studying me in the way all school counselors had, peering deep into my eyes, seeing every transgression and making me squirm.

"I'm fine." My tone was too sharp to be believable.

Predictably, Jessica sighed like my lack of honesty was a personal disappointment. "I know I'm not your mom, but you *can* talk to me."

"What do you mean?" Frowning, I crossed the room to crouch by her rocker. "Of course you're my mom. My second mom, and then Candace is mom three. I'm blessed with all the moms."

"Yes, yes, you are." Jessica's eyes got misty. "And thank you for saying that. But I mean it. You could tell me anything. Even confidential stuff."

"I know. You're a great listener. It's why your students and the rest of us love you so much." I patted her arm. "And you're an even better mom."

"Aww. Now you're gonna make me cry." She waved her other hand in front of her face, yarn flapping from her crochet hook.

"You're nine hundred months pregnant." Chuckling, I rescued the crochet project before it could go flying. "Everything makes you cry."

"True." She laughed along with me.

"And you *are* a good mom. I saw you with Poppy yesterday, letting her wear your heels and that fancy wig." When

I'd stopped by the day before, Poppy had greeted me in a platinum wig, tiara, magic wand, nightgown, and two of Jessica's favorite designer heels. She'd declared herself Empress Poppy of Poppy Land and needed me to say the magic word before escorting her to her royal throne in the backyard.

"We just have to let Poppy be Poppy." Jessica gave a fond shrug. "I don't even try to control it anymore. Parent the kid you are given, not the kid you might wish they were."

"Wow." I sank down from my crouch to sit on the floor. That was it. For years, I'd tried to live up to the kid my dad seemed to wish I was, but Jessica was right. I was simply Knox, exactly how Poppy was Poppy, and we all loved her for it, and not one of us was disappointed and wanted Poppy to be more like Iris or Lily or some other kid. We loved Poppy, not the idea of who she *should* be. And it was long past time I gave myself the same grace.

"What?" Jessica looked mildly alarmed, enough to shift in the rocker, round belly moving, a reminder that this next kid would also be loved by all of us for whomever they were.

"I'm okay." I patted Jessica's knee, which was covered by her long blue maternity dress. "I mean it. I'm really, really okay. I'm not a disappointment."

And, of course, my dad chose that moment to come in, uniform on, hearty grin in place, with absolutely zero ability to read the room.

"Of course you're not a disappointment. You're a star student."

"Rob..." Jessica made a warning noise, one that emphasized her Australian accent. As usual, she'd heard far more than my words.

"What? I'm only saying the truth. He graduated top of his art class and got into—"

"I'm not going," I interrupted before he could rattle off my whole list of accomplishments.

"What? Don't be silly. You're going. We'll be fine here. The baby will be here any time now. You'll have a chance to meet it before you leave."

"It's not about waiting for the baby. I'm going to take over Frank and Leon's business. That's what I really truly want to do with my life." I tried to channel the passion and conviction I'd had when I talked to Monroe or my other friends, along with the certainty Jessica had shown a few minutes ago. This would be okay. It had to be. I'd waited too damn long to be honest with my dad. And myself too. "I want to stay here, run the business, make a difference in the community, maybe sponsor a tee ball team when the girls are older."

"That's wonderful," Jessica enthused, not surprisingly the first to respond. "I'm sure Frank and Leon will be delighted by that news. I'm proud of you." She gave my dad as pointed of a look as I'd ever seen between them. "Aren't we?"

"Knox." Ignoring Jessica, Dad groaned. "This is a once-in-a-lifetime opportunity. A chance to go to an Ivy, to have your future set, to never have to worry about money or making ends meet."

I opened my mouth to curse. Closed it. Opened my lips again on an angry huff of air. "I'm so sorry I ruined your life by being born."

"What? You didn't ruin my life. You're the best"—he glanced at Jessica—"one of the best things to ever happen to me."

"You're always going on about how because you had a kid at eighteen, you had to go to community college, struggle with bills, and eat cheap food."

"Well, we did." He threw up his hands. "And we—all of us, me, your mom, Jessica, Candace—sacrificed where we could so you'd have a better future."

"I get that, and I'm not unappreciative, but do you hate being a cop that much?"

"I have no idea what this has to do with you and graduate school, but I don't." Dad's whole face wrinkled like I was taxing his every last brain cell. "Law enforcement is in my blood like art and drawing has always been in yours. I love being a cop. I can't imagine doing anything else."

Well, that was at least moderately reassuring. He wasn't doing work he hated on my behalf. And he saw the creativity in my soul. I tried to force my facial muscles to relax, maybe even smile.

"See, the way you feel about law enforcement, that's me and home remodeling. I love it. I love helping people refresh their spaces, like working with budgets, and love being able to set my own schedule." I'd come to see over the course of the summer how much that mattered to me. I simply wasn't a big corporate firm sort of guy, and the image of Worth Stapleton, all burned out in his fancy suit in downtown San Francisco, loomed large in my head. I didn't want to become an empty hull in some big-city high-rise. I knew who I was and where I belonged. "I don't need a ton of money, and I want time for other projects like fine art too."

"You're good at it. But you can always be an architect specializing in remodels." Dad waved a hand like he remotely understood what I'd been saying. "If you pass on graduate school now, you might not have a second chance.

Life has a funny way of getting complicated fast. You'll see when you're older."

"I'm an adult *now*." Pushing myself up off the floor, I stood in front of him. Deliberately. I was taller now, and he knew it. I wore bigger shoes, drank better beer than him, and probably knew more about wine and current politics for this year's election.

"Not exactly—" The man was going to make me burst a vessel in my tense neck right there. I cut him off with a loud harrumph.

"I'm twenty-three, not ten. I'm not drawing skyscrapers and superheroes in your basement, and I haven't in forever. I'm an *adult*, and I have an amazing opportunity to run and eventually own a successful, established business."

"You don't know what you're giving up." Dad's face was bright red, and I couldn't tell whether he was closer to tears or rage.

"And you don't know me."

"You—" Dad raised a hand, fingers tightening. Anger. He was definitely angry, but Jessica made a sharp noise before he could continue.

"Rob. Think. Don't say something you can't take back later."

"Sorry." He dropped his hand. "We shouldn't be fighting in front of Jessica. And you shouldn't get Jessica all worked up with this impulsive decision."

"Trust me that Knox isn't the one getting me worked up," Jessica said dryly.

"You're supposed to be resting." Dad glared at us both.

"And I am. Knox made sure I had a delightful afternoon." She gestured at the nest I'd made for her in the rocker. "The nursery is all finished now, and I can't wait to meet our new baby. Whom we will love unconditionally.

222

College or not, circus juggler or future cop. Come on, Rob. Tell Knox you love him."

Dad clamped his lips together and shook his head sorrowfully. And that was all the answer I needed to head for the door.

"I'm out of here. Love you, Jessica."

"Knox!" Dad called after me, but it was too little, too late for whatever he wanted to say.

My pulse didn't slow down until I pulled back into the driveway at Monroe's.

Home. I'd driven here on autopilot, trusting the car to take me where I needed to be. Here. This was home, or at least it could be if Monroe would let it. *Let.* I was allowing that word to do far too much work, waiting passively for Monroe to wake up.

No. I was who I was, and I was stronger now for having stood up to my dad. The worst had happened, and I hadn't crumpled. If anything, my shoulders lifted higher, footsteps echoing louder on the porch. No *let*. *Let* was barely better than giving up entirely. No, I was going to *fight*. Demand. Me. Not Monroe. No waiting around.

He liked when I took charge, so take charge I would.

And his car was in the driveway, so there was no time like the present.

"Monroe?" I called out as I entered the house. Silence. "Monroe?"

But no Monroe downstairs at all, only a pissed-off Wallace who wanted to express his extreme displeasure with the world in a series of loud yowls and meows. Letting Wallace lead the way, I checked the second floor, finding only a perfectly made bed in the primary bedroom.

The third floor, though, yielded an alarming assortment of tools, most of them mine, and a cracked window with

Monroe out on the balcony. The last of the summer sun glazed the house and yard in warm tones while Monroe had strung little fairy lights all along the railings. The lights welcomed the coming darkness with an aggressive optimism that seemed at odds with the gulf between us. The whimsy was also most unlike Monroe.

"What's this?" I asked, careful to pitch my voice low so I didn't startle him as I opened the window wider. Turning, he straightened with a boyish grin, innocent but vulnerable in a way that made my heart twist.

"I decided to shore up the old balcony." He held up an electric screwdriver. "Tightened all the screws, checked for any additional wood damage, replaced a few of the worst planks."

"Good work." I hefted myself out the window, sitting down next to where he stood. "And the lights?"

"I wanted to give you the stars. But it's supposed to be overcast and hazy tonight. These will have to do." He slumped to the narrow deck floor, wrapping his arms around his legs and hugging them close.

"They'll do. They're pretty." I ran a finger down the nearest strand. And there we sat in silence, breathing in, breathing out, thighs brushing, fingers resting millimeters apart, night falling, daytime sounds like lawnmowers and sprinklers giving way to distant music and the soft rustling of foliage. The lights were totally out of character for Monroe, but this gift of space was all him, the part of him I loved the most, how he never forced things.

I'd come into the house with a full head of steam, but this gesture had disarmed me. I'd needed the time to collect my thoughts, and he'd offered me exactly that, sitting patiently.

"You want to give me stars?" I asked at last.

"I want to give you everything." His voice came out a whisper, quietly certain and more forceful than any yell.

"Oh." My fight, along with the anger and confusion and hurt I'd carried for days, gave way like an old brittle board. Maybe I wasn't going to have to battle him after all. Perhaps we could *build*.

Chapter Thirty

Monroe

"I want to stay." I kept my voice firm and clear. Despite my sure tone, Knox's eyes narrowed like he was ready to pounce on the slightest hint of doubt.

"You can't say that."

"Of course I can." I'd expected skepticism, but not this irritation. I risked reaching for his hand, grateful when he allowed me to take it. "And it won't be easy. But I want to stay. I want to try, Knox."

"No, I mean, you can't say that *yet*." He groaned like I was supposed to follow his convoluted logic. "I had this whole speech planned about how you need to give us a real shot, not just wait for us to fail in some all-white condo in the Bay because you're scared to commit to a place. To me."

"You're right. Part of what was holding me back from staying was the fear of succeeding. You're everything I ever wanted, the dream I buried deeply, and I was afraid to unearth anything else. Letting myself love the town and want the whole happily-ever-after package with you felt like a step too close to the sun. So yeah, I was terrified of going all in."

I briefly closed my eyes, heart hammering from the effort each honest word took, heavy swings of a sledgehammer to open that box of dreams I'd hidden so well. Under my thumb, the pulse in Knox's wrist fluttered. I wasn't the only one with buried wants. "But you've also been running scared."

"Yep. I haven't made it easy on you." He agreed far faster than I'd anticipated. "But I'm done sprinting away from the things I really want, done holding back from getting everything I want, and I'm ready to take responsibility for my future. All of that. I started by telling my dad I'm taking Frank and Leon's offer."

"Oh." I had no idea what the correct response was supposed to be, so I kept a wary tone. "How did that go?"

"About how you might expect. Jessica loves me and is proud of me. Dad? Well, I guess he loves me, but he sure didn't say it when he had the chance. And now we're not exactly talking."

"Oh." I inhaled sharply before forcing a more moderate tone. "I would understand if you don't want to make things worse by openly being with me."

"And I wouldn't." Knox snapped before gripping my hand tightly and softening his voice. "You can derail that train of thought right there. I no longer care about making things better or worse with him. I care about making things right with *you*. My dad is my dad, and things will either work out there or not."

"Yeah." I hated this for him and hated that I couldn't fix it even more.

"I'm in love with you, not him. I want a future with you. And if you want one with me, if you love me as much as you say you do, then who cares what my dad or anyone else thinks?"

"You love me?" I made a small startled noise. The night sky blanketed us, but bright light flashed behind my eyes.

"Of course I love you, Monroe." Knox tugged me closer, putting an arm around my shoulders. "How could I not love you? You gave me a room, but it's really about *space*. You give me space. Space to be me. Space to fly. Space to fail."

"But I don't want you to fail." My lips gave an involuntary quirk. "Or us."

"That's not what I mean. You let me make my own mistakes." He kissed me right above the top of my ear. "You trust me."

"I do."

"You're so damn strong, but somehow you love me bossy."

"Color me surprised too." I laughed and let my head fall against his shoulder. "I love you."

"You do." He made a happy noise before gesturing at the twinkling lights on the balcony. "You give me stars. And I love you."

"I'd give you a lot more than stars."

"Thank you." His shoulders stiffened along with his jaw and arm. "And because I love you and me and *us*, I'm not gonna offer to go to the Bay. I know that might seem like the right thing to say next, but I'd rather fight for us *here*, for the future I know we can have."

"I want that." I leaned into him. My throat tightened. My Bay Area plan had been a little selfish and certainly didn't reflect the Knox I knew and loved. "I don't want to put you in a box, Knox." That made him laugh so hard that both of our sides shook. "Okay, okay, laugh at my bad rhymes. But I want to put you in a home, not a box." And then we were both giggling like twelve-year-olds. "Damn it. I'm usually better with words."

"You are." Knox nuzzled my jaw. "You want to give me a home?"

"Not give. You *are* home." I paused, drunk on his scent and nearness, trying to wrangle my fuzzy thoughts. "This town—what it means to you. That's you for me. You're the place I want to return to, over and over. My north star. The thing that makes everything else all right."

"Aww. There's the poetry I'm used to."

"I mean it. You are *home*. And you already gave me a home. One I hope can be for us both. This home. This house. You made it into a real home, one blue shade after another, art and linens and all your repurposed finds. You made a home, and I'm so sorry it took me way too long to see it."

"Guess I did make a home." Knox nodded, giving me his small pleased smile that I loved so much. "And you're going to keep it?"

"I'm going to keep *you*." Wiggling around, I freed an arm so I could cling to his torso. "And the house. And...I'm going to turn it into a low-key queer B&B."

"You're gonna what?" Knox made a show of examining my face and patting me all over. "Where's your robot switch? Can the real Monroe come out, please?"

"I'm serious. It's too big for just the two of us. I've been waiting my whole life to have community, to finally feel like I fit in. I thought I'd need a city if I wanted to live among my people, but what if my people have been right here all along? And what if I could help create that community I want instead of racing toward something premade?"

And that was it exactly. In the Castro in San Francisco, the Village in New York City, or Boystown in Chicago, I could be around plenty of queer people, sure, but they wouldn't be *mine*, and I'd still have to work to feel included, to not be an outsider. And that was really it, the realization that I couldn't simply wait to feel like an insider somewhere. I had to do the work, put myself out there.

"You want a custom solution." Knox seemed to smile with his whole body, voice included. "But a B&B? You? No offense, because I really do love you, but you don't cook. Much."

"I said low-key. I'll figure out the food part." I waved away the comment on my cooking. Surely some B&Bs served bagels and toppings or a cereal bar. Whatever. Those details could be worked out. "Coming back here today, I saw a rainbow over the house, and I saw a home. A *feeling* I want to share. A potential community. Like rooms to stay for couples like Frank and Leon and younger people too. This is what Aunt Henri would want. I feel it in my bones. And maybe I'd have help with the cooking part?"

I tried to do my best impression of the triplets, big eyes, soft mouth, silent pleading.

"Oh. Don't turn those eyes on me. Those eyes get you everything you want and then some." He groaned, then laughed. "Okay, *fine*. I know how you like playing sous chef more. I can help you make hash browns and decent eggs and probably come up with some other recipes for us."

"Good." I beamed at him. "I was hoping you'd want in. And I know it would have to be a side hustle for you, but I am going to need an exclusive repair contract with Measure Twice."

"Personal service with a smile?" He grinned right back at me before standing and holding out a hand. "Dance with me, Monroe."

"There's no music." I let him pull me up anyway, using

the excuse to press myself tight against him on the little scrap of balcony.

"You need an orchestra?" He chuckled warmly.

"Nope. Just need you." I obediently wrapped my arms around his neck and swayed to whatever internal beat always drove Knox. Tonight's rhythm was a slow, sultry waltz, and I wanted to stay forever on that third-floor balcony, lights twinkling, dancing with my guy, who said he loved me. "Say it again."

"I love you, Monroe." He tilted my chin for a quick kiss before peering deeply into my eyes. "Sure you won't be bored as a B&B owner?"

"You're the one who's always telling me how poetic I am. I'm going to solve the Stapleton case. And then I'm going to write a true-crime book about it, the kind Aunt Henri would have loved." I'd been thinking about that option ever since leaving the coffeehouse. I sure did love typing up my notes on the various cases. And if Holden believed it was worth a book and Knox believed in me, no matter how wacky the idea of me as a writer seemed, I could give it a go. "And maybe I'll cobble together some other cold cases to work on, do some consulting. I don't have to be in a city to be involved in investigations."

"What if my dad decides to be a dick and doesn't want you working his cold cases?" Knox wrinkled his nose.

"So be it. This is hardly the only small town with secrets around here." I wasn't going to add to Knox's worries. I had my military retirement along with the equity in the house. I'd get by even if my B&B idea took some time to get up and running.

"That is true. And so you're gonna be an investigator with his own B&B..." Knox grinned slyly as he pulled me snuggly against him. "Dude. I'm officially living with a gay

Annabeth Albert

cozy mystery romance hero. No tripping over bodies in the flower bed or cozying up to the local baker."

"Eh. Cozies don't have enough sexy parts." If he was going to grope me, I could at least return the favor, so I squeezed his ass.

"We can make our own sexy parts." He waggled his eyebrows at me before sobering. "You really think you can be happy here?"

"Yes." I held his gaze. "And I'd stay even if you weren't ready to go public. I want to stay for *me*. Find my purpose for the first time in my life. Maybe it's the Stapleton case. Maybe it's the B&B idea. Maybe it's something else. But I'm not going to find it by running away. You're the bonus and the inspiration."

"I like that." He continued his exploration of my butt through my jeans, squeezing and rubbing. "Sweet talk gets you everywhere and everything."

"I want it all." I leaned into his touch.

"Good. Gonna let me give it to you?"

Trying to invite more kissing, more touching, more everything, I arched my neck. "Please."

Chapter Thirty-One

Knox

Dancing with Monroe on the balcony under the dark night sky was sublime, but as soon as he said *please,* I hissed out a hot breath.

"I do love that word from your lips." Reluctantly removing my hands from his body, I stepped closer to the window. "Please, what?"

"Please fuck me." Monroe pushed open the window, almost making me fall through it with his sexy words. "And please, could it be in the shower?"

"Oh my, a please and a location request. I feel special." I groped him again as he climbed back into the house.

"You are." He turned once I was through the window, wrapping himself back around me. "So special."

"So special I can nail you through the shower tiles?" Dipping my head, I kissed my way up his neck until I hovered right above his lips. "Gonna beg for me, Monroe?"

"Yeah." His voice was little more than a husky breath as I claimed his mouth, kissing him thoroughly, tongue-fucking my way into his mouth until we were groaning and his cheeks were flushed.

"Oh, now you blush," I teased as I grabbed his hand to lead him back down the stairs to the second floor.

"Still not used to being able to ask for it so easily."

"Always. You can always ask." I paused by our bedroom door to give him another kiss. "And I'll always do my best to give you whatever you need."

Backing up my words, I nabbed the lube from the bedside table and pranced into the bathroom, leaving him to follow with a bemused smile.

"Same. I want to give you what you need too." He pulled off his shirt. "That's why I think we'll make it."

"Because we're both givers?" Chuckling, I pulled him to me by one of his belt loops.

"I meant because we listen to each other. But yeah, that too." He ended with a moan when I unzipped his fly and palmed his already hard cock. "Lord, yes, you're a giver."

"Gonna make you all clean. And then dirty you back up." Winking, I backed away to flip on the shower, placing the bottle of lube next to the soap dish. I'd replaced the old showerhead with a newer, wider high-pressure one. However, quarters remained a little cramped. Whoever had done the original remodel had not planned for two full-size adults to share the shower, but I didn't mind pressing up against Monroe. I stripped quickly, then dragged him into the shower ahead of me, letting him have the majority of the spray while I draped myself over his back.

"Mmmm." He made a series of happy noises as I grabbed the soap and started lathering him. I loved his strong chest and lean arms, long runner's back, and flat stomach with the perfect amount of fuzz on it. I continued to his apple-shaped ass and marathon-worthy thighs, loving how he trembled when I soaped his cheeks and crack. "Fuck. Yes."

"You're easy." I nipped the back of his neck as I continued my thorough washing of all my favorite places on him.

"And you love it."

"Love you," I corrected with a laugh, spinning him so he could rinse and also so I could kiss his mouth again. We made out slowly under the steamy water. He took a turn washing me, delicately shampooing my hair. "And I do love your thing for my hair."

"It's gorgeous."

"Even wet and stringy?" I stretched into his scalp massage.

"Nothing stringy about you." He fisted my cock, a firm grip that had me moaning and pulling him tightly against my body, our slippery cocks sliding past each other.

"Damn." He moaned low. "I love how perfectly we fit together."

"We do." Raising my eyebrows, I held his gaze as I slowly sank to my knees in front of him. "And you fit perfectly in my mouth too."

With that, I sucked him deep, immediately going for the Monroe Special—deep, slow, lots of tongue action and suction. I knew what he liked, and I loved that we had such familiarity now. Just one summer, and I already knew his body so well. I couldn't wait to see how much I learned with more time together. And we'd have the chance now. Thinking about him staying here in Safe Harbor had me sucking that much harder until he moaned and pushed at my shoulder.

"Don't make me come yet."

"I wouldn't mind." I grinned because I already knew his reply.

"I would." He reached for the bottle of lube and handed it to me. "Fuck me, Knox."

"Mmmm. You know I want to." Using my hands, I urged him to spin again, taking the opportunity to rim his squeaky-clean hole, licking and teasing until he was chanting my name and begging.

"Knox. Come on. Please. Now."

"This?" I worked two slick fingers into his tight hole, scissoring them and stretching him with the confidence born of numerous encounters together. His head fell forward on his bent arms by the shower wall.

"Not enough. More." He stuck his ass out to meet my thrusting fingers, and that hint of demanding submission was all it took to make my control fray. I slicked my cock and moved in behind him, but our small height difference worked to my disadvantage when it came to wall fucking. He spread his legs, and I bent my knees, but it was still an awkward fit. We both chuckled as I tried to get purchase with my feet.

"Fuck. Too slippery in here." I tried putting a hand on his shoulder but still couldn't get the leverage I needed.

"Aye-eeee," he yelped as the water went from hot to pleasantly warm to frigid within ten seconds.

"Add new tankless water heaters to the B&B plans." Shutting off the water, I yanked him, me, and the lube out of the shower. As I toweled us off, I caught sight of us in the mirror. "Here, I've got an idea."

"Bed?"

"Bed is boring. And too damn far away." I guided him to the vanity in front of the mirror, urging him to bend forward. Releasing him, I quickly wiped the steam off the mirror with the towel. "Right here. Watch us."

"I am." He sounded breathless as he arranged himself so his head was propped on his arms and turned toward the large mirror. I'd redone the bathroom lighting myself to ensure a soft, romantic glow, and the globe fixtures made Monroe's skin golden and the droplets of water clinging to both of us sparkle. "Do it."

"So demanding," I chided as I added fresh lube to my shaft and his rim. "Watch me push in."

"That's it." He thrust his ass up to meet me, and with the added traction of the fluffy rug, I easily found the best angle to press in. Slowly. Like always, but smoother now because I trusted Monroe that much more these days, knew he wanted it.

"God. Your face." I stroked his back, marveling at how his eyes went wide like he was trying not to blink, pupils blown with pleasure, jaw falling open on a moan, muscles in his neck and shoulders flexing with each thrust. His body was hot and tight, and *mine*. I made a possessive noise, wanting more moans, more closeness, more Monroe. "Come here."

Adjusting my hips, I pulled his torso up and back, holding him to me with one hand right below his throat and the other on his abs, using the grip to go deeper and harder against that spot he loved so much.

"Damn." He moaned, head falling back against mine. "You look like an immortal vampire lover, about to turn me to the dark side."

"The fact you can still spout poetry says I've got work to do." I thrust again, harder, faster, watching us in the mirror. My hair hung around my shoulders in damp strands, but it was likely my intense expression that inspired Monroe's remark. Like my grip on his body, my eyes were deadly serious, yet the emotions churning in me were anything but grim. Every time he moaned, I loved him that much more, loved that he so willingly gave himself, loved that he let me take him to this place of pure need.

"Do it." He stretched his neck against my hand until I got the idea and more securely dug my thumb into his collarbone, splaying my fingers over his throat. "Bite me. Mark me. Come in me."

"Fuck. You keep talking like that, and this is gonna be quick." I couldn't reach his mouth for a kiss, but I could nip at his shoulders, watching the way each graze of my teeth made his eyes flare.

"Good. I want that." He clenched his internal muscles hard and then released, sucking my cock deeper, working my cock with a precision I hadn't known was possible.

"Hey, now. None of those naughty tricks." I groaned because it felt so fucking spectacular. I was going to have to read up on this ass wizardry so I could pay Monroe back the next time I bottomed. And hell, simply the thought of him in me, flipping the fuck, had me pushing that much harder into him. "Want you to come too. Want you to watch your-self in the mirror."

"I am." He locked gazes with me in the glass as he wrapped a hand around his cock. He didn't have much room to work but didn't seem to need it, breath quickening and body tensing from the first stroke.

"See how gorgeous you look with me in you."

He made a low, desperate noise. "Please. Please."

"That's it." I licked what I could reach of his ear. "I said you were gonna beg me for it."

"Fuck. We're so hot together." Monroe stopped mid-stroke to admire us in the mirror, and that wouldn't do, so I yanked him more firmly against me, the deepest thrust yet. He clenched and rippled, involuntary now, shudders racing through him.

And then I slowed the fuck down, little shallow thrusts as I ate up each of his whines and moans. "Come on, now. Ask me."

"Please. Please. Harder. You know what I need."

"Always. Always. Always gonna give it to you." All I'd needed was that first *please,* and I was hammering deep and fast. "Whenever you ask. And sometimes, even when you don't. Because I know you. I know what you need. Don't need words."

I wasn't sure if I was even making sense anymore, but from the way Monroe moaned, he understood me just fine. "You do. You give me so much."

"Everything. I want to give you everything."

"You do." Monroe tensed, every muscle underneath me vibrating, hand slowing on his cock. "Come on, Knox. Please. Please."

I knew exactly what he was waiting for, but I was waiting too. And I was exactly greedy enough to demand what I wanted most. "Tell me. Tell me, and I'll come."

"I love you. I love you. I love—" Monroe came on a strangled shout, come splashing all over the vanity. Some wild spurts even managed to hit my clutching hands and his chest. The picture he made was that damn hot, and I gasped as the last of my control shattered. Monroe made a satisfied noise. "Yeah, come inside me."

"Fuck. Love you too." My orgasm often seemed to pull me away from the earth, making me all floaty and dreamy, but this one slammed into me, gluing us together, atoms to atoms, skin to skin, heart to heart. Instead of distance, it gave me presence, making me more aware of my body than I'd ever been, more connected, more everything. "Fuck. *Monroe*."

"I know. Damn." Laughing, he slumped against me. "I'm old, and you killed me dead. You'll have to carry me to bed."

"Ha. After another shower." Joining his laughter, I shook my head at the mess of white streaks on the marble vanity. "And we've got some cleaning to do."

"Worth it." He sighed happily.

"So worth it." Withdrawing carefully, I turned him so I could look into his eyes for real, not just in the mirror. "We gonna be okay?"

"I think so." He licked his lips as if searching for the conviction we both needed. "We can do this. Together. It'll be worth it."

Throat thick, I nodded before giving him a soft kiss. "It better be."

Chapter Thirty-Two

Monroe

Mornings after some big event always brought weird energy. And I'd had a variety of mornings after—after a loss, after some investigation gone wrong, after victory, walks of shame and triumph. But never after the guy I loved said he loved me back, our agreement to make things work long-term simultaneously ramping me up and settling me back down. I watched Knox stir a pan of hash browns, a giddy smile refusing to leave my face.

"I feel far lazier than an average Tuesday." Knox glanced over at me, the same dopey expression on his face. Nominally, he was teaching me how to ensure crispy potatoes, but in reality, he was cooking, and I was sipping coffee and appreciating Knox shirtless in the morning. "Speaking of lazy..."

"Hey, I made coffee," I protested with a laugh, sliding his mug closer to the stove. "Not my fault you wore me out last night."

"Round two was your idea." He waggled his eyebrows at me, gesturing with the spatula.

"But the early morning round was definitely all you." I gave him a pointed look, more than a little tempted to grope his ass in the thin shorts he'd pulled on to cook.

"Uh-huh. That wasn't you enthusiastically participating." Removing the potatoes from the heat, he stepped over to the sink, and I took the opportunity to drape myself over his bare back, my chest hair prickling at the contact. Like him, I hadn't yet dressed for the day and was in shorts and nothing else.

"Nope." I huffed against his neck. His gorgeous curls were down for a change, and I drank in their sweet scent and silky softness. "I was sleeping."

"Rather loud sleeper." He snorted.

"It's not my fault you make me scream."

"I think it—"

A loud rap at the kitchen door cut him off, Rob opening the door before I could fully spring away from the embrace. "Knox?"

"Dad." Knox sounded as wary as I felt. Hell, I wasn't sure exactly what Rob had seen, but it wasn't good.

Eyes narrowed, Rob's gaze flitted between Knox and me and the too-little space between us. "I was on my way into the station, and I kept thinking about how we left things last night."

"Oh." So much longing in Knox's voice. His need for Rob's apology was written all over his face, but unfortunately, Rob continued his suspicious glower.

"But what's this?" He gestured at us. "What's going on here?"

"Could we start with your apology for last night?" Body and tone stiffening, Knox drew himself up taller.

"I was coming by to say you were right about me not wanting to see you as an adult." Rob waved a hand like that no longer mattered when I knew full well it was all Knox wanted. "But what the hell is this? Laundry day?" Face wrinkling, he pointed at our bare chests. Not waiting for a reply, he asked, "Is something going on between the two of you?"

I forced my breath to stay even. The choice, and the reply, had to be all Knox, not me. If he wanted to deny us, I'd cope. We'd cope. Maybe there would be a better time. But Knox seemed similarly conflicted, no rush to speak. By now, I'd learned that meant he was thinking, but Rob had no patience.

"Monroe? Dude?" He gave me a hard, cop-special stare. "Nothing to say here?"

Knox stepped slightly in front of me, protective in a way that made my chest ache. "We're seeing each other."

"No shit. You're roommates. You see each other all the time." Rob's tone went from snappish to a sharp, angry inhale. "Wait. You mean *sex*? You guys are sleeping together?"

"It's more than that." Knox kept his voice firm and steady, and I was so damn proud of him that I had to work to not smile.

"No, it's not," Rob shot back.

"How would you know?" So much for steady, Knox was full-on angry now.

"Knox." I made a warning noise, but not surprisingly, he entirely ignored me.

"Seriously. How would you know?" Knox demanded of Rob. "You just got done admitting you're having a hard time seeing me as an adult, and now you want to tell me you know better than me what my relationship is?"

"It's not a relationship." Rob groaned like Knox was hopelessly naive, and I didn't need to glance over at Knox to know he was spitting mad.

"The hell it's not."

"I love him." I spoke up finally, playing my trump card like all those old late-night card games my senior year with Rob, Holden, and Worth.

"What. The. Absolute. Fuck?" Rob was unimpressed by my admission, if anything getting more pissed, hands fisting. "I get it. I watch enough of those dramas Jessica is addicted to. Old dudes love...what do they call kids...twinks? Yeah. That. But this is *my* kid. You can't go screwing *my* kid and then deluding him into thinking it's something real."

"I'm not deluded." Knox's glare was fiery. It was a wonder Rob wasn't already smoldering.

"Knox, I'm talking to Monroe here." Rob's tone was just this side of patronizing. "Monroe, who should have known the hell better than to screw his best friend's kid. Knox is barely legal, and you're over forty. You don't think that's taking advantage?"

"He's twenty-three. Not eighteen," I said through gritted teeth. "And it's not just sex. I love him, and I want to build something here with him."

"You're staying?" Rob's eyes went wide. Hell, maybe I'd revealed too much too soon, but it was too late, and he was already whirling on Knox. "That. That's why you turned down graduate school? Because Monroe made you think you could have a future together? Knox, he's twice your age."

"Not exactly." Knox's surly response didn't do a damn thing to dial back the tension in the room. "And you're talking like I was some innocent virgin who needed protecting. I was the one who talked Monroe into—"

I cut him off with a sharp noise before he could give Rob a rundown of our history. "You didn't talk me into anything."

"That's right. He didn't have to." Rob scoffed. "Hot twink under your roof? Jesus, why didn't I see this coming?"

"All right now." I stepped out from behind Knox, truly mad at Rob for the first time. "You're upset, and you're feeling protective of Knox. But watch your mouth. You don't get to talk to me like that, and you for sure don't get to talk to your kid like that. Knox is so much more than his age."

"Of course you'd say that." Rob's eyes went interrogation-room hard, twin daggers. "Have you always been into younger guys?"

"Stop." Knox threw up a hand. "You're acting like Monroe is a predator."

"And he's not? Taking advantage of someone younger and more vulnerable?"

I had no appropriate response to that, the accusation hitting me in the softest of spots, the place I kept my last few doubts and guilt. Mouth slamming shut, I tensed, but Knox wrapped both arms around me, holding me tight.

"You didn't. I promise." He kissed my neck before turning his attention back to Rob. "He didn't. We fell in love."

"Love? What do you two even have in common?"

"Club music. Potato dishes. Weird pizza combinations. Long talks. A love of small balconies and hot showers." Continuing to hold me close, Knox rattled off a quick list, and if I hadn't already been head over heels for the guy, his fast-talking would have done it. "I don't know how to describe it. We just click."

"I give it six weeks, tops." Rob didn't sound at all

impressed, and my fingers flexed. Shaking sense into him wasn't an option, but hell, I was tempted, especially as he added, "Knox, you're throwing your life away for this?"

"That's not fair. I'd throw a hell of a lot more than stupid graduate school away for Monroe. He's a good person. And just so we're one hundred percent clear, I was always going to stay. Monroe gave me the space to figure that out, though, unlike you."

Rob made a singular, pained noise right as his phone started jangling, a high, urgent tone, and he ripped it from his pocket to bark into it.

"What?" He listened intently, frown deepening with each passing second. "I'm on the way."

"Is it Jessica?" Knox demanded as soon as Rob ended the call.

"Yeah. Went in with her sister for a routine appointment this morning, but now the doctors are saying the baby has to come today and to get to Portland for delivery, so we're back with the better NICU just in case."

"Damn." Releasing me, Knox crossed to the hooks by the back door, grabbing one of his hoodies and pulling it on. "I'll get the girls. Jessica will want her sister at the hospital, especially with the baby coming early."

"I'll help," I added, grabbing my own sweatshirt, something I likely should have done five minutes ago rather than have this argument with Rob half-dressed.

"Haven't you done enough?" Rob shook his head at me.

"Dad. Go. Be with Jessica." Knox stomped back to stand right in front of Rob, toe-to-toe. "But don't you dare take it out on Monroe."

"You can trust me, Rob." I tried for a more conciliatory tone. We needed a cease-fire, at the very least.

Rob only glowered as his phone buzzed. "Fine. Guess I have no choice."

None of us did, honestly. We needed to get through this emergency, but as to whether Rob would ever truly trust or respect me again, I had only the barest of hopes.

Chapter Thirty-Three

Knox

Monroe sat on the rug in the TV room, surrounded by the triplets, and I'd never been more in love. His usual carefully combed hair was a mess, dirt smudged his aristocratic nose and cheekbones, one side of his lip was puffy from where Poppy had hit him with a ball, and his sweatshirt had bitten the dust several hours prior, along with my hoodie, when Iris and Lily had "accidentally" turned on the garden hose. Luckily, I'd found two of my old T-shirts in the laundry room, but Monroe was stuck in my I Do Crew T-shirt from the night we met.

Maybe someday...

Nah. I couldn't think that far ahead right then, even if my heart wanted with a fierceness that couldn't be denied.

"And then we fold the bottom up." Monroe was demonstrating the art of making origami frogs, and I had to stifle an inappropriate laugh. Apparently, Monroe's love of little scraps of paper like fortunes had extended to learning a few origami shapes, and the girls were riveted by this new magic.

Monroe had set each of them up with a colorful piece of construction paper, and he patiently helped the girls follow his directions.

"A frog!" Poppy squealed as she finished the creature and made it hop around the floor. "Now, I kiss it, like in the movie. And it'll turn into my prince."

My prince was right there, smiling indulgently at her, carefully helping Iris finish her frog, and my heart was so full I could hardly stand it.

"Any news?" Monroe asked me in a whisper as the girls raced their frogs all over the carpets.

"Not for a bit now." I pulled out my phone like that might make news from the hospital come faster. Jessica had had a c-section with the triplets, but she had been eager to try for a vaginal birth this time. The medical team had started an induction as soon as she'd arrived in Portland, but that had been hours ago. We were fast approaching the dinner hour.

"What shall we feed these beasties?" I asked Monroe. Lunch had been PB&J for all of us. Easy. But I should probably make more of an effort for dinner.

"Not sure. What do you girls want for dinner?"

"Rookie mistake." I groaned as we got three different answers.

"Spaghetti!"

"Nuggets!"

"Spaghetti, nuggets, and burgers," Poppy went for broke after Iris and Lily chimed in.

"Spaghetti sounds easy enough." Monroe had clearly never seen the carnage preschoolers could do with tomato sauce, but he was greeted by cheers, so to the kitchen we went. In a stroke of genius, he set the girls up with more drawing paper and crayons at the breakfast bar to make pretend menus for dinner, like we were at a diner, then joined me at the stove.

"Here. Made you something," he said in a low voice as he slid me a small origami shape.

"You made me a paper fortune cookie?" If I hadn't been in charge of a skillet of browning ground beef, I would have swooned. Right down to the tile floor. Keeping one eye on the beef, I opened the red paper cookie to reveal the fortune inside.

If you can dream it, we can do it.

"Monroe." I waved the spatula. "No fair being all sweet when I can't kiss you."

"Like the frog?" Poppy asked, listening in far more intently than I'd suspected.

"Uh-huh." I hoped she'd forget the exchange because the last thing I needed was my dad thinking we'd been kissing in the kitchen when we were supposed to be babysitting.

Buzz. A phone buzzed, but it was Monroe's cell, not mine, darn it.

Monroe glanced down at the incoming message. "Holden spoke to your dad yesterday and to the state task force today, who gave the go-ahead to get a statement from Leon on Friday."

Monroe had filled me on his hopes that Leon would remember something relevant to the case.

"Cool. I hope this is the break you've been looking for."

"We. You're part of the team now too. Couldn't do this without you."

"Thanks." I couldn't exactly kiss or hug him right there,

but I tried to tell him with my eyes how much it meant to me to be included.

Buzz went the phone again, and I groaned. "More from Holden?"

"No, it's your phone this time."

"Oh!" I scrambled for where I'd set it on the counter.

Baby here. It's a boy. Few scary moments, but he's a fighter, as is his mama. Off to the NICU for some extra help. You can tell the girls. We're still working on the name.

"I have a brother." Dazed, I stared down at the phone.

"Baby?" Poppy was the first to look up. No surprise there.

"Yeah, the baby's here. It's a boy! He's going to need some time in the hospital to get big and strong because he's still a little early, but hopefully, you can meet him soon."

"What's his name?" Lily demanded, little forehead furrowing under her blonde curls.

"They haven't picked yet," I admitted, immediately regretting it as they started yelling a flurry of suggestions.

"Kermit!"

"Bluey!"

"Prince Charming." The last was Poppy, of course. I calmed them down long enough to eat the spaghetti, laying waste to the counter, their clothing, and a good chunk of the floor in the process. As soon as I finished cleanup, they were back on the topic of the baby.

"The baby needs a birthday cake!"

"I'm not sure—"

"Cake! Cake! Cake!" All three marched around the kitchen, chanting.

"That's not a terrible idea." Monroe, who had relaxed into the worst kind of enabler, opened the pantry to pull out a boxed mix and tub of frosting. "Let them have their fun."

Fun meant more cleanup and sugar-high kids who refused to settle until we did the camping game again. It was late when I pulled a cover over Monroe, who'd fallen asleep with a storybook on his chest. He'd read from a chapter book until they'd each fallen asleep, Monroe included.

I settled myself next to him, but I was too wired to sleep, heart so full from listening to Monroe read, all his voices and careful glossing over of the scary parts. He was absolutely everything I'd ever wanted, and I needed the other important people in my life to see that.

And right on cue, as I was just about to shut my eyes, I heard a car, then a key in the lock. I trotted into the kitchen to meet my dad so he wouldn't wake the girls or Monroe.

"You're back?" My voice came out wary for a multitude of reasons.

"Yeah. Jessica insisted I sleep here so Angie could stay with her at the hospital." Dad scrubbed at his short hair. "Baby's still in the NICU, so it's mainly about getting Jess some rest. And she wanted me to be here when the girls wake up, so I can show them pictures of the baby and let them know..." He swallowed hard, looking down at his battered sneakers. He'd been in uniform earlier in the day but had changed at some point into what seemed like a random assortment of items from his gym bag. "I'm supposed to let them know how loved they still are. Don't want them feeling left out."

"That's important," I said evenly.

"It is." His tone was strained, and he still wasn't meeting my gaze. "I love you, Knox. I will always love you, but I can't support this decision of yours."

"Which one?" My voice came out surly, my inner teenager roaring to life as soon as he got all parental.

"Take your pick," he shot back, then slumped against the nearest counter. He looked utterly wrung out, and despite the argument, my chest pinched for him. "Sorry. It's been a long day. And Jessica says I need to let you make your own choices and mistakes. She might have a point, but I can't seem to stand by and let you ruin your life."

"Jessica's right. And how can you think Monroe is the type of mistake that will ruin my life?" Crossing to the fridge, I pulled out the remnants of the cake.

"He's twice your age."

"Ignore that for a second. You've been friends for a long time. And he's a damn good person." After cutting Dad a generous piece of the lumpy-but-tasty cake, I handed him the plate and a fork. "You're friends with everyone, but Monroe's special. He's more than another acquaintance."

"He's not a bad guy." Dad saluted me with his fork before taking a bite. "Thanks for the cake. And Monroe should know better."

"And so should you. You want to push me away?" I gave him a hard stare. "You want to drive us apart while I'm right here in the same town? This is how."

"Knox..."

"I'm serious." I handed him a glass of milk to accompany the cake because I knew him that well. And it was because I knew him that I could be firm here. "I was happy to help out with the girls today, but unless you can welcome Monroe here along with me, I'm done with the favors and gatherings and pretending like you respect me when clearly you don't."

"I love you."

"Yes, but do you respect me?" I went to the opening from the kitchen to the TV room, lowering my voice as I gestured at the couch. "Look at Monroe, Dad. Really look at him." On the couch, Monroe snoozed on, one hand holding tight to the book, the other on the blanket I'd laid over him. "He's exhausted from chasing the girls. He went so far outside his comfort zone today. Baked that birthday cake with the girls. Scrubbed your counter after. Read to the girls until he was hoarse. That's the guy I love. The one who does the right thing, the best thing, even when it's hard."

"I understand—"

"No, you don't. This is *Monroe*." Even in a whisper, my voice still wavered. "He put twenty years into serving his country. Maybe he would have rather been an English major somewhere, but he put his all into NCIS, and he's a hell of an investigator. He's determined to do right by Worth and the Stapletons."

"He is." Dad nodded, so I plowed ahead, not nearly done yet.

"He's been hurt before, and he's scared to reach for the connections he craves, but he's here doing it. He says I make him brave, but he makes me *whole*. He inspires the hell out of me, the way he pushes past fear to love me anyway." I had to pause to swallow hard, try not to swipe at my burning eyes. "This town is damn lucky to have him decide to stay, honestly. I wish you could see that. And I know you'll say they're lucky to have me too and how I could do better, but I'm lucky to have the town."

"I know you love it here." Dad sighed, not exactly resigned but definitely more deflated than a few moments ago.

"I don't think you've ever quite grasped why though. Growing up, I bounced between two houses, had rooms at both places but never really belonged at either. The years you and Jessica were focused on dating, then the wedding, then IVF—"

"I'm sorry." His face creased with emotion.

"I'm not blaming you. My point is that I still loved coming here, no matter what was going on with you or Mom or anyone else. People like Frank and Leon, Sam and his family, others always made sure I felt like I belonged."

"You did belong. You do belong." Dad's voice came out all thick.

"I do. And I belong with Monroe." As I said the words, I truly *felt* them. We belonged together. We did. And nothing my dad could say would convince me otherwise. "Monroe says I give him a home, but he's that for me too. He's where I truly belong, at last. No more bouncing around. I'm happy, so happy."

"I'm glad," Dad whispered, but I wasn't quite done pushing.

"Are you? Are you really? Because if you were happy for me, truly happy, you'd stop treating Monroe like some kind of criminal and me like a child. I plan to keep him around a good long while, so you better get used to us being together."

"I'll try." His jaw hardened along with his eyes, and I wasn't sure how convinced I was.

"What is that you're always telling me? Saying you'll try without actually putting effort and action in is meaningless. Something like that?"

"God, you're definitely your grandparents' kid. I can hear your grandpa in every damn word. I'll..." He moved his jaw side-to-side. "I'll try to make an effort."

"Without looking like I'm asking you to eat gravel instead of cereal?"

"Knox..." Dad groaned, then gave me something approaching a smile. "I love you. And your stubbornness.

And I can't wait to watch you be amazing with the new baby. Your brother."

"Who needs a name."

"He's got one. You're Knox Robert because you get a part of me. And he's Keller Glenn. Grandpa's middle name and the same first initial as you. Wanted my boys to have that bond."

"Oh." All the fight left me in a single breath.

"Give me time? Please?" Setting his cake aside, he touched my upper arm. "I'm not gonna be able to move at the speed you want, but I mean it. I'll try to see things from your perspective."

"And Monroe's. You owe him an apology."

"Yeah. Give me time on that too."

Time. I wasn't at all patient. I wanted everything solved *now*. The case, the tension, the worry over the new baby in the NICU, but I could try for patience. Try.

Chapter Thirty-Four

Monroe

The end of summer was also a beginning, one filled with anticipation. In the week since Rob and Jessica's new baby had arrived, I'd been in a blissful bubble with Knox, making plans for my B&B, daydreaming about a future together, and working on the Stapleton case. Leon had been forced to move our initial interview time because of a doctor appointment for Frank. Now it was Wednesday again, late afternoon, and Leon and I were in Holden's cheery front room. Stacks of syllabi on the dining table foretold the coming of the Fall semester, as did Holden's dress shirt and askew tie. He'd come from a faculty meeting, less coffee shop time as the semester drew closer. He'd set up a recorder for Leon's statement, and luckily, Leon didn't disappoint.

"Yep. That's him all right." Leon pointed at a picture we had of the suspect from roughly the right time frame, between college and when he later turned up in Florida. "Slick fella. Came into town with a door-to-door knife sales pitch but got caught up in the kitchen doodad craze."

"How long was he around?" Holden glanced at me as I shuffled papers to reveal our working timeline.

"He was here for the summer and fall that year. I'd have to ask Frank, but he might have gone out with the search parties a time or two." Leon narrowed his eyes and adjusted his glasses. "Had a rental outside of town, nearer to the coast, up by the lake and quarry."

"The lake." I set the timeline aside and pulled up the report of the cursory search they'd done around the lake area. Diving and sonar equipment had improved over the twenty years since the last lake search. "If we went for a drive, think you could show us?"

"I reckon." Leon made a sucking noise through his teeth. "We gonna take Holden's hot rod?"

"If you ask nicely." Holden smiled at him. He had a custom sports car that accommodated his larger frame, wheelchair, and other necessities, and the bright-red color stood out around town.

"I always do." Leon smirked. We continued asking him questions and making arrangements to drive up to the lake later in the week. The more Leon talked, the more my excitement grew that we might be able to tie the suspect to the area if nothing else. As we wrapped the interview, I made notes for pulling rental records, fishing licenses, and other document searches. I was deep in my head when Leon tapped my arm.

"I hear you might have need of some breakfast recipes."

"Has Knox been spilling all my plans?" Smiling, I looked up from my laptop and piles of papers.

"Yup." Leon gave a toothy grin. "And making some of his own."

"Should I be afraid?" I snapped the laptop shut.

"Probably. Way we see it, Knox is about to be busy, while Frank and I are about to be at loose ends all retired."

"What are you three thinking?" Holden asked before I could.

"This B&B is going to need some help. Knox thinks Frank and I are the guys for the job."

I blinked. "I wasn't aware I had job openings."

"You do now," Leon cackled, and Holden joined in before Leon continued, "You'll let Frank putter around, be your resident handy person, but leave the heavy lifting to the rest of us. And me, I'll ply you with recipes, do a little baking for you till you get your sea legs, so to speak. And cleaning. I'm good at that. Ship-shape, Lieutenant." He gave me a jaunty salute.

"What's the catch?"

"No catch. The whole damn town, or most of it minus the realtor lady, wants to see you succeed."

"They do," Holden heartily agreed. "And I want that book on the Stapleton case. We're going to crack it. I can feel it."

"We're closer now, thanks to you." I nodded at Leon, who waved off the praise.

"Nah. Thanks to you two and your detective work. And thanks to Monroe, our boy came in all smiling this morning to the work site. Brought donuts even."

"On time," I coughed because it had been a close thing, frantic frot, rushed showers, and gulped coffee.

"Close enough." Leon shrugged, then hardened his eyes to deadly diamonds. "You hurt Knox, and Frank'll bury the body so deep even Holden's sleuthing skills won't find it."

"Duly noted." I matched his solemn tone. Knox having people looking out for him was a good thing, even if I was chafing at all the protectiveness. Leon. Frank. Rob. Hell, even Holden had murmured a "hope you know what you're doing" before Leon arrived at the interview.

"Rushing home?" Holden gestured at how I'd packed up the laptop and my papers, almost unconsciously, brain, body, and heart ready to see Knox.

"Smart man." Leon clapped me on the shoulder, and it was only a short walk back to my house. *My home.* My future business and community hub. I took a long moment on the sidewalk, drinking in the house and all the dreams contained therein. And then Knox came bursting out the front door, the embodiment of every last hope I had.

"There you are! I've been waiting." He swept me into a sweet-smelling hug. Unusual for Knox, he wore a dress shirt tucked into pressed khakis and even had on a belt and nice shoes. "Jessica called. They brought Keller home a few hours ago. Turns out he didn't need the NICU as long as everyone feared. A week, and he's out! Passed the carseat test with flying colors. He's teeny but mighty. Jessica said for me—for *us*—to come meet him when you got back from Holden's."

"Ah. Invite come from her or your dad?" My tone was both weary and wary, a week of dancing around the arctic freeze that was Rob's reaction to us together as a couple.

"Jessica. But I said I wasn't coming without you. I meant what I told Dad. We're a package deal. And Jessica said he understands and to hurry up and come meet the baby so she can get a pic of me meeting him for the wall."

In the NICU, baby Keller had been limited to visits from parents and support persons like Angie, leaving Knox and everyone else back in Safe Harbor desperate to meet the little guy.

"And you're nervous about the baby or your dad?"

"Who says I'm nervous?" Knox smoothed a hand down his crisp white shirt, and I gave him a pointed look.

"Shirt with buttons? Hair all neat? The baby's gonna love you, Knox. And your dad already loves you. Promise."

"Hope so." He sounded so uneasy that I gave him another tight hug before he retrieved a bag with a present for the baby from the house. I drove to Rob and Jessica's house while Knox played with the ribbon on the gift bag. If Rob said one single thing to make Knox unhappy, he'd have me to deal with.

At the house, Angie let us in amid shrieks coming from the TV room.

"Jessica and the baby are upstairs in the nursery." She gestured at the stairs. "I'm keeping the girls quiet—ish—down here."

"We better sneak up before the triplets spy Knox." Chuckling, I followed Knox upstairs and down the hall.

"Knox!" Holding the smallest bundle, Jessica stood from the glider in the corner of the green-and-yellow room. "You made it! Meet Keller!"

Standing in the doorway, I gave Knox a little shove so he met Jessica in the middle of the room, gazing down at the swaddled baby in her arms with nothing short of wonder.

"Oh wow." His face creased as he sniffed deeply. He looked a breath away from either crying or crumpling, and before I could step in, Jessica had deftly steered him to the rocking chair.

"Sit right here. Keller's been waiting all day to meet you." She promptly deposited her armload in Knox's lap, exchanging the baby for the gift bag. Eyes going wide, he inhaled sharply. Jessica patted his shoulder. "Honey, he's bigger than the girls were when we brought them home. He's not gonna break."

261

"Okay." Knox had a better grip on the baby than his voice, which wavered. "Hello, Keller. I'm your brother. And I brought you a bear."

Jessica made the same *aw* noise aloud as the one in my brain as she removed the little stuffed bear from the bag. It was a very Knox-like gift, a tie-dyed bear with the softest fur, wearing a shirt that proclaimed, *Property of Safe Harbor*.

"So he'll always remember where he's from." Knox tucked the bear next to the baby in his arms, resettling both to a more comfortable, less stiff position.

"This deserves my better camera," Jessica announced brightly. "And I deserve a brownie from the fridge. You sit right here and get to know each other."

"Be quick." Knox continued to sound rather dazed.

"Thanks for coming," Jessica whispered as she passed me, taking a moment to pat my arm.

Rather than enter the room, I took the chance to stand in the doorway, watching Knox and Keller. He cuddled the baby close, and a wee hand crept out of the blanket to grab Knox's finger. Humming softly, Knox rocked him, patting and singing a song I didn't recognize, part of his endless internal playlist. In the distant hallways of my brain, a memory pinged, and for the first time in years, I heard my mother's voice, high and sweet. A lullaby. A promise.

My heart was so full that my chest clenched around its weight, and I had to lean on the doorframe heavily. When footsteps sounded behind me, I held up a hand so Jessica wouldn't break the moment. But as I whirled my head, I discovered Rob, not Jessica.

He was in uniform, looking more imposing than usual, but his entire expression softened as he gazed into the dimly lit room.

"Look at that." His voice sounded like a rusty faucet. "My boys."

"You did good." A few weeks prior, I wouldn't have hesitated to pat his arm, but now I kept my hand glued to my side. "Congrats on bringing Keller home."

"Thanks." Mouth twisting, he stepped away from the door and lowered his voice. "Knox says I need to apologize to you."

"It's okay." I also stepped back from the door so as not to disturb Knox's time with the baby. "You should focus on the baby today. And I understand your reaction to Knox and me being a couple. You're unhappy. You want better for Knox."

"No, I don't. Or rather, I thought I did. But then Knox..." Trailing off, he shook his head, fondness softening his expression further. "Man, that kid is so in love with you. He made me remember you're a pretty decent guy. Listed off all your good qualities."

"Oh, I've got bad ones too."

"Yep. I know. Lousy card player. Broody. Horrible taste in baseball teams. Bad swimmer. It's a wonder the navy took you." He whistled low, then chortled. "You're all right, Monroe. You're a decent guy. Good person. I'm not gonna pretend the age gap is nothing. But Knox could do a hell of a lot worse."

"Thank you." I barely got the words out past the knot in my throat. It wasn't a full apology or complete acceptance, but it was something. A start. "I'm not going to let you down. Or him."

"You take good care of him." Rob wagged a thick finger at me.

"Or you'll hide the body. Already got that lecture from Leon today." I laughed quietly. "But, really, Knox takes care of me. We take care of each other. I know you don't always see it, but Knox is an amazing man. Not a kid."

"He did grow up." Rob glanced back into the nursery, lines around his eyes and mouth deepening, sentiment clouding his tack-sharp eyes. "He says you make him feel like he belongs."

"He does belong. I belong with him too. I'm not sure what it is between us. Fate. Souls recognizing each other. Something. And I look at him, sitting there, singing to his brother, and I think I'm the luckiest guy on the planet. I'd jump in front of a bus for him, Rob."

"You love him," he whispered like he was testing out the words.

"I do. I love him. I love how he gives me no quarter. You and Leon don't have to worry. Knox won't accept anything less than my best."

"Good."

"Rob!" Jessica came bustling up the stairs, camera in one hand, brownie in the other, looking ready to mediate a cease-fire. "Angie said you came in. Everything okay?"

"Yep." Rob jerked his head in my direction. "Monroe and I had a chance to catch up."

"Good." Jessica's mouth tightened like she was hoping that was the right answer.

"Knox?" Rob called out. "Be sure and let Monroe have a turn with the baby."

"Oh, I don't think..." If Knox had looked scared about holding the baby, I probably looked downright terrified.

"Get in here, you," Knox demanded, freeing a hand to usher me closer. The baby's teeny face scrunched up. He was fair like Jessica and bald, but in the purse of his mouth and stubborn set of his little jaw, I saw a glimmer of Knox. He passed me the baby like we were transferring a crystal vase. Something sparked between us, the electricity that always lurked when we touched but amplified now by emotion. "Isn't he perfect?"

"He is." I agreed, but my eyes were more on Knox than the precious bundle in my hands. "And so are you."

"Thanks." He put his hand on mine, holding the baby and me both. "You and my dad okay?"

In the doorway, Jessica was hugging Rob, both their eyes sparkling.

"I think we will be." And for the first time, I actually believed there might be a future for Rob's and my friendship, right alongside the future I wanted with Knox.

Family. Knox would always belong to me, but he belonged here too, and together we were carving out a space for ourselves within this loud, welcoming family. Our own little family. I saw that now. Not just home. *A family.* The two of us. And I couldn't wait to watch the seasons change and little Keller grow up together.

Chapter Thirty-Five

Knox

"You made it!" Holden was first to greet me as I entered the bar for the last trivia night before Labor Day weekend. Monroe and Sam also waved as I plodded my way toward our usual table.

Summer was officially coming to a close, and I was bushed between work projects with deadlines, helping out with Keller, dreaming with Monroe on the B&B details, and planning the Labor Day retirement party for Frank and Leon.

"I did. Barely." I yawned as I sank down into the chair next to Monroe.

"You look exhausted." Next to Holden, Sam leaned forward, concern creasing his forehead.

"He is," Monroe answered, putting an easy arm around my shoulders. A few weeks into officially being a couple, PDA was already coming naturally to both of us. We'd spent all summer struggling to keep our hands off each other. It was no wonder that now that we didn't have to hide, we were the touchy, cuddly couple who drove others nuts. And Monroe's proud voice was as good as another caress. "He's been working so hard on the retirement party for Monday and everything else." Pausing, Monroe signaled the passing waitress before I could. "Water, please. And another ale and order of the fried pickles."

"You take good care of me." I let my head fall against his shoulder.

Monroe lowered his voice to whisper in my ear. "And I'm going to take good care of you later too."

"Counting on it." I forgot to moderate my volume, which earned us a groan from Holden.

"Awww. You guys are so cute."

"Leave them be." Sam sounded as snappish as I'd ever heard him.

"Sam? In a bad mood?" Holden frowned right along with Monroe and me. "Never say. What's up with you?"

"Nothing." Sam huffed. "Or at least it's silly. I was out for a run this morning. Saw the Stapleton place is up for sale. Again. And it just makes me sad how into disrepair it's fallen. And that the case still isn't solved."

"But we're closer than ever before." Monroe drummed his fingers against the table, excess energy a sure sign he'd had a good day. "In fact, I got a break this afternoon. Finally got in touch with the old landlord of the place Leon remembered by the lake. She's pulling rental records, but the first name sounded familiar. I'm waiting on those, then I may fly back to Florida for another interview with the suspect with the new evidence."

"That's awesome. Well done." I smiled at him. I'd miss him if he did another business trip, but like everyone else at the table, I wanted him to solve the case in the worst way.

Annabeth Albert

We all wanted that for Worth and for the town too. For the community—

"*Oh.*" My eyes went wide, and I grinned at Sam. "You should buy it."

"Buy what?" Monroe frowned.

"Not you. Sam. Sam should buy the Stapleton place."

"And do what?" Sam pursed his lips and dropped his chin.

"Stop living over your parents' garage?" Shaking his head, Holden used a joking tone. "You're over thirty."

"I live simply." Sam rolled his eyes at Holden. "I don't need a huge house."

"Yeah, but you want it."

"It's too much house for one person." Even as he protested, the longing was clear in Sam's voice.

"One person who keeps rescuing others could use a few spare bedrooms," Monroe said pragmatically.

"True." Sam's face softened.

Seizing his agreement, I added, "You should think about it."

"After we get the work on Monroe's place done, I could help you with the Stapleton house," I offered, even though I could see the lecture already starting in Monroe's eyes about overextending myself.

"Our place," Monroe corrected, eyes so full of love I couldn't help but sigh.

"Ours."

Holden groaned. "Your domestic bliss is as saccharine as one of Sam's coffee specials."

"Sorry." I moved a few millimeters away from Monroe, who yanked me right back. Sam and Holden seemed more on edge lately, not only about the Stapleton case. I didn't think either was jealous, precisely, but I'd been on the

268

outside looking in often enough to know that happy couples could grate on a friend group.

"Don't apologize. I'm the one who keeps screwing up the coffee specials." Sam laughed good-naturedly. "But I try."

"You're spread so thin." Holden clapped him on the back. "Get a manager who knows coffee."

"The three of you are determined to rearrange my life." Sam stretched backward as our appetizer order arrived.

"It's all out of love," I assured him as we divided up the food.

"I know." Sam paused to eat a fried pickle, nodding in my direction. "I'm glad you're staying, Monroe."

"Me too." Monroe's emphatic tone made me look up from the wing I was munching on. Our eyes met, and the rest of the bar faded away. Nothing, not our friends, not trivia night, not even the Stapleton case, was more important than what we had together.

Of course, however, it was still nice when we came in a respectable second place again for both rounds of trivia night.

"We're an old movie buff and history expert away from cleaning up," Holden joked on our way out of the bar.

"I'll be on the lookout." I laughed, but expanding the friend group was an awesome idea. And I was still chuckling when Monroe let us into the house a short while later. "That was fun."

"It was." Monroe steered me toward the stairs as Wallace came out to greet us. "And now you need rest."

Scooping up Wallace, I made a comically rude noise to make Monroe laugh. Wallace jumped right back out of my arms, fleeing toward the third floor.

"Seriously, I'm too wired to sleep."

"I can help with that." Pushing me into the bedroom, Monroe pulled at my T-shirt until I got the idea and helped him undress me. And him. I might be tired, but I was entirely on board with the sex-before-sleep plan. As soon as we were both naked, I attempted to drop to my knees, my mouth already watering, but Monroe gently shoved me back onto our bed.

"None of that." He straddled me, effectively trapping me. I had to smile at his unusually bossy mood. Knowing I could easily reverse our positions had me more willing to go along with whatever agenda Monroe had. After giving me a sound kiss on the mouth, he stroked a hand down my chest. "I'm going to take care of you tonight like I promised.
"

"But I like taking care of you." I made a pouty face that would ordinarily work on him, yet when I reached for his cock, he batted my hand away.

"I know. But it's my turn now."

"I—ah." I started to protest, then had to moan as he leaned forward and captured my nipple in his mouth, worrying my nipple ring with his tongue. I let out a shaky laugh instead. "Okay. That'll get you whatever you want."

"Good." He gave me a fierce look. "Lie back and let me love you."

"When you put it like that..." I made a happy noise as Monroe repeated the attention on the other nipple. He seemed singularly focused on maximizing the full value of my piercing, a slim silver ring, as he alternated licking both nipples and flicking them with his fingertips, making the ring dance and sparks sizzle up my spine.

Abandoning my sensitized nipples, he kissed his way down my stomach, leaving a love bite on my ribs, making me that much more desperate for him.

"More." I rolled my torso, trying to get his kisses lower to where my hard cock was bouncing on my abs.

"That's it. Tell me what you want." Sliding backward, he stroked my stomach with his palm, tracing all around my aching cock. "This is for you. Whatever you want tonight."

"Don't want to be greedy." Mumbling, I turned my head toward the pillow, but Monroe turned it back, peering deeply into my eyes.

"Be greedy. Please," he demanded, and as always, that *please* did it for me. Like him, I wasn't used to asking for things solely for myself, especially in bed. We were both givers, but if Monroe wanted specific direction, I could try.

"Suck me?"

"Gladly." He slithered between my legs with a wink. "Thought you'd never ask."

As much as I loved sucking cock, getting oral was always a little uncomfortable, all the attention on me, worrying about whether my partner's jaw was getting tired, whether I was taking too long or too short a time to come, whether they were truly into the act or merely hoping for a trade. All that. It ordinarily kept me locked inside my brain, unable to fully let go.

But Monroe had spent all summer proving he was different. He gave me pleasure because he wanted to, not out of any quid pro quo obligation, and when he took my cock in his mouth, he moaned right along with me. The sounds he made when he sucked my cock were my favorite part, happy hums, sexy groans, and wet, overtly sexual noises.

I loved how my neat-and-clean guy had no problem getting messy with sex, his saliva coating my cock and his lips, some smearing across his smooth jaw. I reached down for the sole purpose of rumpling his perfect hair, but he nodded, moaning around my cock, grabbing my hand and holding it tighter to his head.

"Monroe." My voice came out more anxious than I'd intended, and he glanced up.

"It's okay, baby. I want it. Fuck my face."

"I haven't..." I trailed off, but he'd get my meaning. I'd never fully let go with another person like that, always felt a little guilty about going too hard or too fast.

"Trust me." He held my gaze. "Use my mouth, Knox. Please."

"Well, since you said please." I let out a shaky laugh that turned into a moan as soon as he resumed sucking, deep and hard, faster and faster until I clutched his head.

"That's it." His face was damp, lips swollen, and he looked as happy as I'd ever seen him. He wasn't lying. He wanted this, and knowing that, I gave in to the impulse to direct his mouth. Gently at first, guiding him up and down to the rhythm that would get me there.

Monroe moaned around my cock, arching his back so he could work a hand under his torso. That was usually my trick, not his, and I groaned at how damn into this he was tonight.

"Fuck yes. Show me. Wanna see you stroke yourself."

"Sucking you gets me so hot." He wiggled around, positioning himself more perpendicular to my body so I had a good view of his hand working his cock.

"Yeah. Like that. Fuck. I'm close."

"Good. Come for me." He growled and sank back down on my cock, letting me direct him, moaning louder as my hand tightened and my motions became more frantic. I lost control over my hips, thrusting into his tight, warm, willing mouth.

"There. There. There," I chanted, then gave it all up to

him with a single long groan. I trusted him. I'd trusted him long before that moment, but I trusted him on a deeper level, trusted that it was okay to want and need. I wasn't too much for him, wasn't ever going to be too much for him, and he gladly welcomed all I wanted to give him.

"Monroe." I managed to put a whole novel's worth of meaning into his name. I came and came, so much that it dribbled back out of Monroe's full lips and onto his sharp jaw. He gazed up at me with glassy eyes. My gorgeous lieutenant, come-drunk and all messed up. The sight was enough to coax one final spurt out of my cock before he released me.

"Damn. So beautiful." He groaned like he wasn't the sexiest thing I'd ever seen himself. Pulling back slightly, he stroked himself hard and fast. "Gonna get me off too."

"Do it. Come on me." I pointed at my nipples which were still pink from his earlier attentions.

"Oh, I love that idea." He pushed onto his knees, jacking his cock right over my torso.

"Love you." I grinned at him, knowing how much he got off on those words. "I love you, and I want you to come all over me."

"Yes." His voice broke, and he painted my chest with creamy white ropes all over both nipples. Panting hard, he laughed as I reached down and smeared the come into a heart shape, right over my actual heart. "Leave it to you to make a beautiful mess."

"You love it," I said smugly.

"Love you. So much." His voice was slightly hoarse, which oddly turned me on, knowing he'd loved me that well, loved me using his mouth, loved me taking over.

He hopped from the bed long enough to retrieve a warm washcloth, washing more than the come off my skin, taking time to wipe me down all over. I stretched languidly under the cooling breeze of the ceiling fan I'd installed in the room.

"You take such good care of me."

"We take care of each other." His expression was so tender that I had to pull him close for a kiss. And, of course, Wallace chose exactly that moment to burst through the cracked bedroom door, sending it smacking into the frame.

"Cat, we were having a moment!" I complained as he planted his feline ass right between us and started grooming himself.

"Hey, he's part of the family." Chuckling, Monroe stretched out, facing me on his side, reaching around Wallace to stroke my damp belly.

"He is." My throat felt fuzzier than Wallace's furry belly. "We're a family."

And we were. I might be home to Monroe, but he was family to me, a place all my own to belong and be loved. A place to grow and plant roots. A place to return to, over and over, with my person at its heart. *My person.* More than a boyfriend. More than a partner even. Way more than roommates. We were family.

Chapter Thirty-Six

Monroe

I had been many things. Cadet. Ensign. Lieutenant. Investigator. I'd been a son and friend as well. But until that summer in Safe Harbor, I'd never been a partner. Knox liked to call me his person because the word boyfriend didn't seem to fit, and I'd never been happier to be human in my life. And at Frank and Leon's Labor Day retirement party, I'd never been prouder either, watching Knox work the large meeting room at the Safe Harbor Community center.

Knox shook hands, passed out slices of sheet cake, and directed people to sign the giant toolbox-shaped retirement card for Frank and Leon. A table at the front of the room featured photos of them over the years, alongside notable Measure Twice remodels and many charitable and community contributions. Leon stood proudly by the front table, greeting guests and accepting hugs.

"All this fuss." Leaving the front table, Frank lumbered over to where I stood at the rear of the large open room, back by the dusty trophy case filled with youth rec league winners over the years. I spied at least one picture of a younger Holden and Worth among other town residents I recognized. "We're retiring, not dead."

"Hey, I'm not sure about you, but I want my flowers while I'm here." Knox trailed after Frank, carrying two cups of punch and steering Frank into a nearby chair.

"Amen. Sing my praises while I can hear." Holden rolled over to the space next to Frank's chair as Knox drifted away to retrieve more cups from the food table.

"That's assuming we have praise for you." My tease got a laugh from everyone in earshot, including Holden himself.

"Hey, now. That's no way to tease the guy who got a call Friday from his contact at ODFW."

"What did Fish and Wildlife have to say?" Pulling out my phone, I opened my note-taking app, immediately sliding from joking to all business.

"Fishing license from that year was registered to someone living at the rental Leon pointed out. Same first name. Mother's maiden name as the last name. We're gonna get him. I can feel it." Holden waved as Rob came striding over to our group, a diaper bag over one shoulder and a large gift bag in his hand.

"Hope so." Rob clapped Holden on the shoulder with his free hand. "I've got a meeting with the feds. Think we're going to be able to officially reopen the case on what you've both found so far."

"Nasty bit of business, but a long time coming." Frank gave a sharp nod before Rob walked away to open the door for Jessica, Angie, and the triplets. At the same time, Sam came over, carrying a stack of folding chairs.

"Yes. Justice for the Stapletons." Sam arranged the

chairs around Frank, then turned toward me. "Have you heard from Worth lately?"

"Nope. I've left messages. I should give you the number. Maybe you'd have better luck."

"Me?" Sam sank into the empty chair closest to me. "I've got no connection to Worth."

"Just a two-decades-old crush and an unwavering conviction that Worth's dad was innocent." Holden's tone was joking and not at all unkind, but Sam's bleak mood from trivia night hadn't improved any over the weekend. He didn't even crack a smile at Holden.

"Holden." I gave him a warning look. "I meant more you have a way with people, Sam. Maybe you can get through to him since the rest of us can't."

"Send him pics of the specials board. Make him laugh." Returning with more cups of punch, Knox handed Sam one.

"I could do that." Sam took a long swallow. "Sorry. I'm down because that realtor lady is sniffing around the Stapleton place. If someone doesn't make an offer soon, the developer who wanted Monroe's house will snatch it up, raze it to the ground, and that doesn't seem right."

Frank harrumphed. "It's a piece of Safe Harbor History. There's none of them around now, but the Stapleton family dates back to the town's founding. Seems like someone needs to step up."

"Yup." Speaking in unison, we all stared at Sam.

"Fine." He threw up his hands. "I'll talk to a banker this week, see if I've got a prayer of getting a mortgage."

"If anyone's got a prayer, it's you." I smiled encouragingly at Sam, then turned as Rob returned with Jessica and family in tow, fussy baby now in his arms.

"Knox!" Jessica greeted him with a big hug. "It's the man of the hour."

"I am not." Blushing, he gave her a fast kiss on the cheek. "This is Frank and Leon's party."

"And your show. You did all this." I gestured at the community center filled with people, many of whom were there as much for Knox as Frank and Leon.

"Look at you." Shifting the baby to one arm, Rob duffed Knox's shoulder. "You brought the whole damn town together."

"Keller is unimpressed." Knox extricated the baby from Rob's grasp and put him on one shoulder, rubbing his little back.

"Keller is unimpressed with anything not milk-flavored right now." Jessica sounded painfully exhausted.

"After we clean up here, Monroe and I are gonna come help at the house so you get a nap, poor tired mama." Knox was quick as ever to volunteer, and I immediately started planning his own rest later, even as I nodded.

"We'll do some cleaning and take turns in the rocking chair." I ushered Jessica to the nearest open chair in our circle.

"You're the best. Both of you." Jessica's eyes were misty, undoubtedly with exhaustion as much as emotion, the way she always got choked up when Knox referred to her as his mom.

"You're pretty awesome." Rob retrieved the gift bag he'd had earlier, holding it up to Knox as the girls dashed to the cake table. "Here, give Jessica the baby. We have a present for you."

"A present?" Knox's eyes went wide and delighted. "It's not my party!"

"We brought Frank and Leon a gorgeous potted Dahlia

to celebrate their retirement." Jessica patted Knox's hand as he passed over the baby. "But this gift is for you. It was your dad's idea."

Lips pursed, Rob nodded at Knox. "Man's gonna run his own business, he needs to outfit his office."

"Office? Oh yeah, guess I'm gonna have one of those now." Chuckling, Knox opened the bag to reveal a heavy gold desk sign, the kind used by bankers and executives everywhere. *Knox Robert Heinrich, CEO Measure Twice, LLC.*

"We approved of the title," Frank cackled. "Pretty spiffy, eh?"

"It's amazing." Knox's voice came out all breathless.

"You're the amazing one. And we're so proud of you." Rob pointed at the bag. "And there's something in there from all of us too. For your office wall."

Reaching back in the bag, Knox pulled out a large framed picture collage. The center was carved wood that read *Family* and surrounding it were all different pictures with Knox in them. Not off to the side, but centered, surrounded by the triplets at different ages, holding baby Keller last Wednesday, with Rob and Jessica at his graduation, with his mother and her wife, and with the grandparents. And one in the corner with me holding Keller while Knox crouched next to us, looking protectively at the baby and me.

"You chose one with Monroe in it." Knox beamed, which was good because I was struggling not to cry. I pinched the bridge of my nose.

"He's one of us now." Rob slapped me on the back. "And if he doesn't—"

Frank cut him off with a rude noise. "Take a number."

"Quiet, you rowdy boys." Free from greeting guests,

Leon joined us, pointing at Knox and me. "These two are the real deal."

"You'd know." Frank snorted affectionately.

"I would," Leon said archly. "And Rob's right. Monroe is one of us now."

"He is." Setting aside his gifts, Knox came around to wrap his arms around me. "He's one of us."

And with that, I added another new label for myself: *resident*. I belonged here in Safe Harbor with Knox and my friends, and the community I wanted to create, the community that was already here, and the past which touched us all. And as Knox held me close, all my senses tingled, the sort of certainty reserved for unraveling a big investigation or discovering some fundamental truth. I was finally home. And that, along with my unwavering love for Knox, was my truth. This was *home*.

Epilogue

Holden

A single party. Couple of hours. I could get through one party for two of my best friends, even if I had to give myself a hell of a pep talk to get out of my car. Knox had texted that they'd left the driveway open for me to park. If I didn't hurry up and get out, one of them would inevitably come out to see if I needed help with my chair.

"Did you bring a present for Monroe and Knox?" I asked Sam as I freed my chair from the special holder behind the driver's side, setting it up before Sam could make it around from the passenger's seat. Not unusual for December in Oregon, the weather was cold and rainy, a bitter wind matching my mood. I'd insisted on picking up Sam after he closed the coffee house for the evening rather than let him walk. I might be reluctant, but I wasn't going to leave a friend to freeze.

"Of course." Sam retrieved a small bag from his back-pack in the car. Naturally, the guy who was in the middle of running a charity, a coffee shop, and closing on the

Stapleton house had managed to come with what was undoubtedly the perfect gift. "It's an ornament for their tree. One of the kids at the shelter is making them for sale, so I had one custom done for Monroe and Knox with their names and the year since it's their first Christmas together."

"Crap. I don't have anything." If I'd been thinking with anything other than end-of-term fuzzy brain, I would have brought a bottle of wine at least. Yesterday had been a bad pain day as well, with the cold weather rolling in, and I'd been more concerned with showing up, period. "I thought this was more of an open house for the B&B than a holiday party."

"It's both." Sam's smile looked as tight as mine felt. "It's a chance for them to show off all their hard work here. When they do a tour of the upper floors, I'll take lots of pictures for you."

"Thanks." A jaunty new sign on the front lawn proudly proclaimed *Lucky Penny B&B* with a large coin with a rainbow in the center off to one side. We'd all helped brainstorm names at trivia night a few weeks back, but in the end, Knox's original suggestion had won. As I stared at the sign, my brain pinged with an incoming idea. "Hey. What about a coin machine?"

"A what?"

"They need one of those machines that flattens coins for the front hall. Like with the B&B logo or the town crest or something. I'm going to make some calls, see if I can find one used at a decent price."

"Leave it to you to go from no present to blowing the rest of us out of the water." Chuckling, Sam followed me up the path to the wide, covered front porch. "The new ramp looks great with the original porch design."

"It does," I said evenly. I knew they'd added the ramp

mainly for me. Oh, Knox had touted their accessible guest suite on the first floor, and Monroe had talked about the growing number of elderly and disabled tourists, but their words felt too careful, the ramp too big a priority to be merely a business tool. "Rides smooth."

I wheeled myself up the ramp easily, Sam trailing next to me, but he paused before I could knock on the door.

"You okay?"

"Fine. Just a lot on my mind." No way was I confessing the bad pain day, crappy sleep, or conflicted feelings about this party. Instead, I waved a hand. "Stapleton case. End of semester. Finals. Podcast."

"Understandable. We all want the case solved." Sounding distracted, Sam pulled out his phone, idly clicking the screen on.

"What about you?" I pointed to the phone. Four months ago, I never would have seen Sam with his phone. He was polite to a fault, not the type to scroll while friends were talking, but lately, he was every bit as distractible as me. "You're way more married to your phone these days."

"Me?" Sam played dumb, then huffed a breath. "Nah. But you mentioned the Stapleton case, and I wanted to see if I had a new message from Worth."

"New? As in, there have been multiple?" I tilted my head, considering him more closely. Monroe had given Sam Worth's phone number a few months earlier, but I hadn't been aware of that leading anywhere. None of us had heard from Worth since Monroe and Knox's San Francisco trip during the summer.

"Nothing related to your case." Sam's tone was dismissive, but I wasn't buying it. "I send him funny memes. About every tenth meme, he texts back something other than LOL. Very occasionally, I get more than three words."

"So you're friends." I laughed because Sam's puppy crush on Worth back when he'd been in eighth grade while the rest of us were seniors was practically town legend by now. Sam had managed to turn up all sorts of places that last year before everything changed. Before Rob and Petra had Knox. Before Monroe left for the navy and I'd headed to the police academy. Before Worth's mother disappeared the following summer. Back then, Sam had been an annoying pest, but now he was a decent friend, and I honestly hoped he got through to Worth. "Good for you."

"Wouldn't go that far."

"Keep trying. I'm sure reopening his mom's case has been hard on him, even if he's not saying."

"Yeah." Sam's mouth moved like he might be about to say more, but the front door burst open to reveal Monroe.

"You guys made it!" Monroe greeted us by throwing his arms wide. Thank God he was not in a Christmas sweater, but he still radiated domestic bliss in his usual button-down, khakis, and fuzzy slippers. It was the slippers that did it, both because they loudly announced this was his home and because I'd put money on them being a gift from Knox. "Come in, come in."

"Brought you and Knox a little something for your first Christmas." Sam held out the small gift bag as Monroe ushered us in.

"Thank you, Sam. You're the best." Monroe was all jolly host energy, completely unlike his formerly broody self. I peered around him and Sam to the living room where Knox stood near the Christmas tree, talking to Frank and Leon. He wore his baby brother, who was all chubby and drooly now, in some flowered sling thing.

"Dude. Your boyfriend has a baby strapped to his front," I joked to distract from my own lack of gift.

"He's helping out while Jessica and Rob show the girls the upstairs. Knox had the idea to do one of the new guest suites with a family theme. Built-in double bunk beds plus a nook for the parents too."

"Fun." I forced a smile. I'd compliment the idea again when Sam showed me pictures later.

"And, of course, we can't wait to show you the accessible suite behind the kitchen."

"Of course." I kept my face neutral. They were trying. I could too.

"Did you tell them?" Knox strode over, bouncing the baby as he walked, a huge grin on his face.

"Tell us what?" I asked. *Please don't be engaged. Please don't be engaged.* I wasn't jealous. Never had much of an attraction to either dude, so it wasn't that, but there was only so much domestic happiness a dude could take.

"A new development in the Stapleton case." Monroe smiled, and so did I. Thank God. This I didn't have to fake enthusiasm for. "A few weeks ago, when the case stalled again, I reached out to an old military contact who put me in touch with Saving Grace Diving. It's a nonprofit run by a former SEAL rescue diver. They specialize in recovery efforts, especially on cold cases."

"They're willing to come search the lake?" I leaned forward, hands on my thighs. This was huge. Monroe and I had long suspected valuable evidence in the Stapleton case might be in the nearby lake.

"Yep. And I offered to let the lead dude stay here. We're getting our first guests and a chance to crack the case both." Monroe beamed, as happy as I'd ever seen the guy.

"That's awesome. Let me know how I can help." It wasn't like I could dive into the lake, but I was sure there was something I could do. Make myself useful. "Maybe I can interview him for the podcast."

"That's a great idea." Knox shuffled from side to side while patting the sleeping baby. "Your podcast gets so many listeners. It could be great publicity for the organization and the case both."

"Yeah, I'll tell my contact." Monroe nodded. "The head guy I spoke with is rather...dry, but I bet you can get him to open up."

"That's me. The icebreaker," I joked even as I internally groaned. Great, a dry, inevitably egotistical former SEAL who probably only talked in diving math. We'd be lucky to get ten listeners, but if Monroe and Knox were this enthusiastic about the diver's arrival, I couldn't steal their oxygen tanks, so to speak.

"Heck, you're likely to get his whole life story in under ten minutes." Knox laughed. "You're always the best at getting the good gossip."

"Uh-huh." Actually, it was more that I was super observant: once a cop, always a cop. I wasn't any more social than the rest of them, but at this point, everyone expected it of me. The jokes, the smart remarks, the town news. Being the life of the friend group was exhausting, but it beat the alternative.

"Oh, babe, Sam brought us a present." Monroe held up the gift bag from Sam. *Babe.* That was new. Supposed it was better than some pet names, but not much. Monroe opened the bag to reveal a round, wooden ornament. The rustic piece featured a little painting of the B&B, complete with their overgrown fuzzy cat in the window.

"I might cry," Knox threatened.

"Please don't." Even Sam looked alarmed.

"Let's put it on the tree." Hand on his back, Monroe led

Knox over to the Christmas tree in the front window. They might as well have been the picture on a gay greeting card: two super attractive men, utterly in love with each other, standing in front of their perfect tree, ornaments glimmering next to the sparkly strands of white lights. All that was missing was some Christmas music—

Wait. I heard some faint strains from farther in the house. Of course. Knox leaned in to kiss Monroe's cheek, sharing some special secret in his ear. My chest tightened. *Not jealous. Not jealous.* Their type of domestic bliss simply wasn't in the cards for me, and that was the icy truth, sharp and unmistakable.

* * *

Want to see Holden get his own happy ever after? You can read it now in Make Me Stay! Turn the page for a sneak peek of Make Me Stay.

Sneak Peek of Make Me Stay

Holden

"Come on, come on. I have a case to solve." Fingers drumming on the steering wheel, I glared at the ancient, plodding RV in front of me. This country road led into the state park that surrounded the nearby lake. Tourists were a given, even in early spring, but I had no patience that morning. The sun was out after a long, long winter, and it was exactly warm enough to crack the windows and blast one of my favorite classic rock songs. My zippy Mustang was itching to take these curves at something other than tortoise pace. The curves, however, meant I had to wait for a passing lane to open up. *Torture.*

"Move. Faster. At least go forty," I bargained with the RV, which predictably went slower, not faster. I shook my head, mentally cursing the driver to a damp campsite and poor hookups. "Tourists."

Finally, a passing lane opened, and the second it was safe to do so, I zoomed around the RV. However, as I prepared to slide in front of the RV, a squirrel darted out from the dense green foliage, and I had to swerve far sharper than I'd intended. As a result, I nearly cut the RV off and undoubtedly looked like an asshole trying to make a point rather than a dude who preferred not to flatten a squirrel.

The RV honked twice as if to show how doubly perturbed the senior citizen driver was. At least, I presumed it was someone older, out on a scenic drive. It was hard to tell from a fast glance at the driver's side. A dusty and battered ball cap pulled low was the main thing I'd noted.

"Whatever." Eager to leave the irritating RV behind, I sped to the lake. The dense foliage continued as the road narrowed past tiny clapboard cabins ringing the eastern shore of the lake and huge hills of evergreen trees behind the row of little houses. The skinny, barely maintained road led past the public swimming area and several docks that would see far more use in the summer months. The eastern side of the lake—complete with cabins, a community center, Adirondack chairs, and volleyball courts—was a popular family retreat despite being in Middle of Nowhere, Oregon. The nearest town, Safe Harbor, was over a half-hour away, and we were hardly a metropolis.

Past a grove of haphazardly laid out picnic tables, warning signs started cropping up about deep water and steep drop-offs. The way more dangerous western side of the lake had an irresistible pull over local daredevil teens drawn to legends about the old timber railroad and wrecked train engine under this portion of the lake. Safety concerns about the dam that had created the lake in the fifties further added to the intrigue. And even the limited parking along the western shoreline wasn't enough to discourage thrill seekers.

But I was forty, not sixteen, and despite my need for

speed, I wasn't out to catch an adrenaline rush. I was here in pursuit of answers for a twenty-year-old cold case surrounding the disappearance of the mother of one of my high school friends. My friend Monroe and I had traced a serial killer to one of these very idyllic lake cabins that fateful summer, long before his first known victim. Both of us were professional investigators, but our personal interest in this case had driven us to spend long hours analyzing interviews with the killer, who spoke almost exclusively in movie quotes.

All signs pointed to the possibility of answers being under the lake, so here I was, impatient and ready to find out if our hunches were correct. I found the most level place to park near the designated meeting spot, but getting my chair set was tricky. The mix of gravel, dirt, and old asphalt was hell on my tires and made me glad I'd packed my wheelchair gloves for better grip.

"Sorry." Monroe hurried over, looking flawless as ever in a polo and pressed khakis. "I should have thought more about accessibility issues here at the lake. Maybe—"

"I'm fine." I waved his concern off with a flick of my wrist. "And I love the smell of potential evidence in the morning. Wouldn't miss this."

"Ha." Monroe shook his head at me. "Don't you ever run out of bad jokes?"

All the damn time. "Nope."

And if it kept Monroe and others from dwelling on accessibility issues and limitations, well, I'd keep right on rolling with the same class-clown routine that had served me well for over thirty years now. I'd discovered laughter hurt less if you laughed first yourself.

But this time, I must not have smiled widely enough or

something because Monroe narrowed his eyes, gaze going sharp, exposing all his years as an NCIS investigator.

"Maybe Knox is right." His tone was thoughtful. Too thoughtful.

"He generally is." I kept my tone jovial, complimentary even, about Monroe's boyfriend. No sense letting on how my neck prickled under his careful concern.

"There's an...edge of sorts to you lately. Knox thinks you're lonely."

"I'm not," I shot back, then softened my voice. "I'm an extrovert. We're always lonely unless there's a party of two hundred of our besties."

"Exactly." Monroe smiled like I'd rolled right into the center of a trap he'd laid. Damn it. "Knox thinks you should get a roommate. You said it yourself. You're an extrovert. Maybe you simply need more people around."

"I don't need a roommate." What I needed was fewer meddling friends and a solution to this case. Neither thing seemed forthcoming. Pity. We were the first on the scene, with no rescue from Monroe's good intentions. "No roommate means no one to care when I leave my grading on the dining table or when I want to record an emergency podcast episode."

"Don't be so quick to dismiss the idea. Knox said you likely miss having your sister living with you."

"And my brother before that, but I launched the kids." I grinned, hopefully wide enough this time. "I'm okay with extra rooms at my place. Still debating whether to turn Marley's old room into a home theater or sex gym. I'm coping fine."

"No one said anything about coping. You always cope." Monroe said this like it was a bad thing. "But if you're lonely, you could try putting an ad up on the bulletin board at Blessed Bean."

"And get a ton of responses from college kids I've had in criminal justice classes? Pass. I'm too old for a roommate."

"Or too stubborn." Monroe exhaled as an engine rumbled behind us. "Oh look. Here's Phillips now."

I carefully swiveled in time to see the same ancient, rusty, and battle-scarred RV I'd pissed off pull up behind Monroe's compact.

"Seriously? This is the famous SEAL rescue diver you recruited?"

"Yep. I offered him a ride this morning, but he said his gear was all in the RV. He got in late yesterday and was super grateful for the dinner Knox saved him and the chance to get a better shower than the one in his old RV. Real polite guy. You'll like him."

Doubt that. But I made myself nod as a slim man exited the RV. No more a senior citizen than I was. Maybe late thirties. Hard to tell with the hat and unshaven jaw disguising one of those timeless faces, like an old western sheriff. He carried himself like one too. The classic military bearing made it so I could always spot a fellow first responder. He walked toward us with long strides, though he wasn't particularly tall. He did have surprisingly broad shoulders, given his narrow waist and hips.

Well, at least he looked the part of a legendary diver.

"You made it." Monroe waved him over.

"Yeah, a few minutes behind my ETA, thanks to this idiot who tried to run me off the road." The guy had a small hint of country to his voice, southern perhaps, but not Deep South.

"It's me." I held up a hand. He'd spot my car soon

enough. Might as well own up to it with a smile. "I'm the idiot who was trying to save a squirrel."

"More like the idiot who couldn't deal with going under forty-five." This Phillips guy didn't even crack a hint of a grin.

"Holden." Monroe and I were roughly the same age, which made his tendency to act all paternal to me frustrating as fuck. "You should try slowing down sometimes. Might do you good."

"Hey, I'm a safe driver." My declaration earned pointed looks from both men. "I am. Trust me, I spent enough customizing my Mustang. I'm not going to take stupid risks."

"You're a good guy." Monroe's tone was the verbal equivalent of a head pat. Good thing I loved my friends. He gestured at Phillips. "Holden, this is Chief Callum Phillips."

"Just Cal is fine." The guy continued his flat delivery, no smile as he shook the hand I offered.

"When does the rest of your team arrive?" I asked.

"I am the team." Chiseled jaw firm, Cal pursed his lips as if his dry tone hurt his full mouth. "Director, assistant director, employee of the year, and intern, that's me."

"Seriously?" As usual, I hadn't thought before I spoke, so I quickly backpedaled. "I mean, I was under the impression from Monroe that multiple people were coming."

"Whenever I do a recovery dive, I find local volunteers from the dive and veteran communities to help with logistics. They should be along any time now. But I dive solo."

"Is that smart?" All I could picture was Cal struggling on the dive and me helpless on the shore. I didn't even know the guy, so the vision shouldn't have hit me on such a visceral level. Yet, my chest ached and my breath caught. I knew diving, knew how indispensable dive buddies were, knew procedure, and damn well knew the value of a good team. "I'm not sure we should allow—"

Cal made a disgusted noise. "You need to see my stack of certifications? Discharge papers? Medals and commendations? My last five years of solo recovery dives?"

"No. Sorry. I'm sure you know what you're doing." I offered a smile but wasn't surprised when he didn't return it.

"I do."

"Cal comes highly recommended." Ever the peacemaker, Monroe had a too-bright tone. "We've been discussing the case and evidence for months, waiting for the right timing to do the dive. I'm excited to see what we find."

"Me too. And I'm here to help." I kept smiling even as Cal raised his eyebrows. "Put me to work."

"Good to know." He nodded sharply, but the brush-off couldn't have been clearer. "I better start assembling my gear. Back in a few."

With that, he strode back to the RV, leaving Monroe to glare at me. "Well, that could have gone better."

"Hey, it's not my fault the guy has the personality of a weathered fence post. Probably doesn't know how to smile." An uninvited urge to see Cal smile took hold. I wanted to know how a grin transformed his grim features, and moreover, I wanted to be who put it there.

"Not everyone is the life of the party." Monroe put a hand on my shoulder. "And I know you're trying. But give Cal a chance to impress you. He doesn't need a sparkling personality to crack this case for us."

Oh, he'd impressed me all right, not that I'd confess that to Monroe. Instead, I nodded. "Let's see what he can do."

Also By Annabeth Albert

Amazon Author Page

Many titles also in audio and available from other retailers!

Mount Hope Series

- Up All Night
- Off the Clock
- On the Edge

Safe Harbor Series

- Bring Me Home
- Make Me Stay
- Find Me Worthy

A-List Security Series

- Tough Luck
- Hard Job
- Bad Deal

- Hard Job

Rainbow Cove Series

- Trust with a Chaser
- Tender with a Twist
- Lumber Jacked
- Hope on the Rocks

#Gaymers Series

- Status Update
- Beta Test
- Connection Error

Out of Uniform Series

- Off Base
- At Attention
- On Point
- Wheels Up
- Squared Away
- Tight Quarters
- Rough Terrain

Frozen Hearts Series

- Arctic Sun
- Arctic Wild
- Arctic Heat

Hotshots Series

- Burn Zone
- High Heat
- Feel the Fire
- Up in Smoke

Shore Leave Series

- Sailor Proof
- Sink or Swim

Perfect Harmony Series

- Treble Maker
- Love Me Tenor
- All Note Long

Portland Heat Series

- Served Hot
- Baked Fresh
- Delivered Fast
- Knit Tight
- Wrapped Together
- Danced Close

True Colors Series

- Conventionally Yours
- Out of Character

Other Stand-Alone Titles

- Resilient Heart

- Winning Bracket
- Save the Date
- Level Up
- Sergeant Delicious
- Cup of Joe
- Featherbed

Stand-Alone Holiday Titles

- Better Not Pout
- Mr. Right Now
- The Geek Who Saved Christmas
- Catered All the Way

About Annabeth Albert

Annabeth Albert grew up sneaking romance novels under the bed covers. Now, she devours all subgenres of romance out in the open—no flashlights required! When she's not adding to her keeper shelf, she's a multi-published Pacific Northwest romance writer.

Emotionally complex, sexy, and funny stories are her favorites both to read and to write. Fans of quirky, Oregon-set books as well as those who enjoy heroes in uniform will want to check out her many fan-favorite and critically acclaimed series. Many titles are also in audio! Her fan group Annabeth Albert's Angels on Facebook or Patreon are the best places for bonus content and more!

Website: www.annabethalbert.com

Contact & Media Info:

patreon.com/AnnabethAlbert

facebook.com/annabethalbert

x.com/AnnabethAlbert

instagram.com/annabeth_albert

amazon.com/Annabeth/e/B00LYFFAZK

bookbub.com/authors/annabeth-albert

Acknowledgments

All my literary roads lead through Abbie Nicole, and this new series is no exception. I told her last fall that I wanted to write a series centered around unexpected roommate situations, and she was as supportive as ever. Her cheerleading, plot sounding board, editing, and promo savvy are the motor that keeps my business humming.

I couldn't have finished this book without my writing sprint buddies, my author friends, my beloved readers, and the cheering squad pushing me on.

A huge thank you as well to Lori at Jan's Paperbacks. She makes providing signed copies to my readers so painless, and she's an amazing beacon in the romance community to boot! Her tireless advocacy for romance, queer fiction, and small businesses inspires me.

Deidre Knight, Elaine Spencer, and Tantor came together to make audio for this series possible. I so appreciate everyone at the Knight Agency, which handles my foreign rights as well. And this series was inspired in part by Wander Aguiar's Black Friday photo sale, but it's Reese Dante's cover magic that took the incredible photo to new heights with the cover of my dreams. Thank you to Reese for always going above and beyond.

Reviews, ratings, likes, mentions, comments, and shares are the lifeblood of the modern author. Thank you to every reader who makes what I do possible. If you loved this book, please tell a friend! And thank you simply for reading my work. You make it all worth it.

Last, this series is about change. Coming home. Finding home. Discovering one's self and sense of place. Found family. Thank you to everyone who makes up my family of choice, the family of my heart. To my kids, I'd choose you a million times over. To my friends, I wouldn't be here without you in my circle. And I mean that on so many levels. Thank you to everyone who enriches my life.

Made in the USA
Las Vegas, NV
10 December 2024

13718056R10184